RICK PARTLOW
DROP TROOPER BOOK ELEVEN
TANGO DOWN

www.aethonbooks.com

TANGO DOWN
©2023 RICK PARTLOW

This book is protected under the copyright laws of the United States of America. No part of this publication may be reproduced, stored in a retrieval system, or transmitted, in any form or by any means, without the prior permission in writing of the publisher, nor be otherwise circulated in any form of binding or cover other than that in which it is published and without a similar condition including this condition being imposed on the subsequent purchaser. Any reproduction or unauthorized use of the material or artwork contained herein is prohibited without the express written permission of the authors.

Aethon Books supports the right to free expression and the value of copyright. The purpose of copyright is to encourage writers and artists to produce the creative works that enrich our culture.

The scanning, uploading, and distribution of this book without permission is a theft of the author's intellectual property. If you would like to use material from the book (other than for review purposes), please contact editor@aethonbooks.com. Thank you for your support of the author's rights.

Aethon Books
www.aethonbooks.com

Print and eBook formatting by Steve Beaulieu.

Published by Aethon Books LLC.

Aethon Books is not responsible for websites (or their content) that are not owned by the publisher.

This book is a work of fiction. Names, characters, places, and incidents are the product of the author's imagination or are used fictitiously. Any resemblance to actual events, locales, or persons, living or dead is coincidental.

All rights reserved.

ALSO IN THE SERIES

CONTACT FRONT
KINETIC STRIKE
DANGER CLOSE
DIRECT FIRE
HOME FRONT
FIRE BASE
SHOCK ACTION
RELEASE POINT
KILL BOX
DROP ZONE
TANGO DOWN
BLUE FORCE

[1]

"That's the worst smell in the history of bad smells," Kyler Dunstan declared, not trying to keep his voice down but muffling the words nonetheless because of a protective hand shielding his nose and mouth. "Holy shit!"

"Stow it, Dunstan," Vicky warned him, and from the way Dunstan yelped, I figured she'd kicked him under the mess hall table. She nodded toward the Tahni flight crews shuffling into the compartment and heading for the food processors. "They're going to hear you... and some of them understand English now."

"Yeah," I agreed between bites of my sandwich. "It's taken us months just to get us all to the point where we can eat in the same compartment without anyone starting a knock-down, drag-out fight. Besides, those are their corvette crews, and they've been stuck in those little pieces of shit for a couple weeks now without a bath." I frowned. "Do Tahni *take* baths?"

"Not enough," Dunstan said with conviction, and I couldn't hold back a sharp laugh.

It hadn't been that long ago that I'd found Dunstan annoying and vapid, back when we'd first met him flying a cutter as a mercenary for the Corporate Security Force. He'd saved our lives when we were working undercover for Fleet Intelligence, infiltrating the CSF at the behest of Top and Colonel Hachette. But he'd pulled our asses out of so many tough situations now, I'd even come to appreciate his sense of humor.

Had it been that long? It surely didn't feel like it. It could have been yesterday that Vicky and I were back on Hausos, trying our hand at farming, giving up our lives of war and violence for a chance at a new start. That had worked for a year or so, until a gun-running bandit had decided to use our colony as a depot for his cargo... including a Skrela seed pod. That was all it had taken to draw us both back into this nightmare. Wade Cunningham and Ellen Campbell playing on our old semper-fi, oo-rah Marine sensibilities.

They were both dead now. So many people were dead, friends and fellow Marines and innocent civilians, that I had trouble naming them all. Dave Clines, Wade, Ruthie Amendola, Karen Fargo, Captain Solano, and now Top—Command Sgt-Major Ellen Campbell, perhaps the finest Marine I'd ever known. All gone. Dropping off one by one, until I wondered why it hadn't been me.

"What?" Vicky asked, her dark stare discerning. She'd recognized the funk I was falling into. We'd been married three years and two of them had been spent killing and trying not to get killed, but she knew me better than anyone. Knew me better than I'd *let* anyone.

"I ever tell you," I asked her, "about that guy I knew back in Alpha Company who thought he was immortal?"

"Probably," she guessed, leaning on the table with her chin propped on a fist. "But tell me again anyway."

I laughed at the combination of dry humor, strained patience and, beneath them, the ever-present compassion she tried so hard to conceal, as if showing it was a sign of weakness.

"Okay. This guy Svenson in First Platoon used to talk all the time about alternate realities and Quantum theory. According to him, there are infinite worlds out there, realities where I got killed in the desert and my dad and brother lived, where I got killed and Tommy Kurita lived in that first combat we saw. And since I'm the one who's experiencing this particular reality, it only makes sense that I'm the one who survives it. If someone else is experiencing their own reality, *they'd* be the one who lived and I'd have gotten killed already. That's what Svenson used to say, except about himself." I shrugged morosely. "He got killed on Brigantia. Burned in after his shuttle got hit."

"Well, that only makes sense," Vicky said, snorting a humorless laugh. "After all, you're seeing it from *your* version of reality, so *you* can't die."

I tried to chuckle but couldn't muster one.

"Y'see, Svenson, he thought the whole idea was comforting, that it meant he couldn't die, that he'd live through everything. It was his own perfect world." I sighed, tossing down the last couple centimeters of processed soy and spirulina disguising itself as a chicken sandwich. "But I think it's more like Hell. If it's true, we all get to see our friends and relatives and loved ones die around us, picked off by blind chance while we stay behind, maybe hurt, maybe scarred, maybe in pain, alone and, even worse, knowing that any new friends we make, any new love, is going to end with their death. And maybe if you and I were still farmers, or running a fabricator service shop on Eden, with everyone living a safe, staid life and an auto-doc available within minutes if anything bad *did* happen, it wouldn't be so bad."

"But we're Marines," Vicky finished for me.

"And we're out here on our own," Dunstan added, jumping into the conversation whether I'd intended to include him in it or not. "No one to help. And it feels like every time we turn around, someone else gets skragged." He sucked down a gulp of his drink, then shook his head. "I'm gonna miss you guys when I'm the last survivor of this whole shitshow."

"And we'll miss you too," Vicky said, toasting him with her juice bulb. "Be sure to teach us how to fly a starship before you die, okay?"

"Oh man, I don't know." He shook his head, trying to look grim and serious but unable to pull it off. "Just because you guys have the 'face jacks doesn't mean you can handle an Intercept. I mean, you're like... *Marines*, you know?"

And that was more than any of us could handle, even me in the current mood I was in. We descended into soft laughter... and caught the side-eye from people at the other tables. Fleet crew, not Marines. Marines would understand. We'd mourned Top in our own way, the way she would have wanted us to. Not everyone mourned like we did though.

Colonel Marcus Hachette shuffled into the mess hall like a drunk fresh off a four-day bender. And he might have been. I didn't know how much alcohol the man had brought on board with him or whether he'd finagled a food processor to manufacture more for him, but it seemed as if every time I visited his cabin, it smelled of cheap gin. Not that I'd made that many visits. Hachette had struck me as a ramrod-up-his-ass STRAC Jack recruiting poster the first time I'd met him, and all the times we'd butted heads since then, it had been because he was still thinking of this whole mess from the point of view of a Fleet Intelligence colonel while I had regressed into my civilian days.

The Marcus Hachette that walked through the mess hall entrance bore little resemblance to that man. He hadn't bothered with his typical, sharp-cornered dress uniform, instead pulling on wrinkled, unwashed utility fatigues, their gig line so far out of regs that any self-respecting sergeant-major would have dropped him for fifty pushups out of sheer principle. His haircut had always been at the edge of regs, probably because he knew full well how much better the short-but-not-buzzed look went with the square-jawed, straight-nosed face his parents' money had bought him in the womb. Now it was ragged, unkempt, strands hanging in his face, his stubble at least two days old, and I would have had a tough time deciding who smelled worse, him or the Tahni corvette crews.

Hachette mumbled responses to the few crewmembers who greeted him, barely acknowledging their presence, and God alone knew how the man would have reacted if any of them had dared to offer their condolences for Top. The fact that the two of them had been involved was perhaps the worst-kept secret on a ship full of Fleet Intelligence spies, but the fiction that it had been their own business and no one else had known about it was perhaps the only thing keeping Hachette on this side of sanity.

The colonel stepped ahead of three others in line and grabbed a cup of coffee and a pair of glazed donuts, not offering an apology or so much as a look in the eyes before he shambled to a vacant table and swiveled the seat outward, falling into it heavily.

"Jesus," Dunstan murmured, and I could see in the eyes of the crew at a dozen other tables people whispering similar sentiments. "Someone's gotta have a talk with the dude."

"We already tried," I reminded him. "Two weeks ago. We were lucky he snapped out of it enough to give Captain Nance the order to set course."

"We Transition in a few hours," Vicky said, nudging my shoulder. "You should go ask him what his orders are for security."

I'm not sure whether my face reflected the annoyance behind it, but I knew my voice did.

"Are you kidding?" I motioned toward the man. "This is the first time he's come out of his quarters in three days." I was about to say it was a good thing he had a shower in there, but it was obvious he hadn't been using it. "You think he's in any mood to hear me talk about security deployments? We don't need him for that anyway. We know how to get our Marines ready for a Transition."

"Of course we do," she agreed. "But Hachette needs to feel engaged if he's ever going to pull his head out of his ass. Go make him believe we need him, that he's letting us down if he doesn't do something... that he's letting *her* down."

I squeezed my eyes shut, rubbing at the sudden ache in my temples.

"Oh, good. Why don't I just go slap him in the face while I'm at it?"

"Hey, dude," Dunstan said, shrugging, "whatever works."

I sighed, biting down on a curse. Didn't want to attract any more attention than I had already. Hachette didn't look up at my approach, staring intently at his coffee as if the mysteries of the universe were floating in shifting patterns on the pale brown liquid. I waited a second for acknowledgment, then figured the hell with it and just sat down across from him.

"Evening, sir," I said with fake geniality.

"Is it?" he mumbled in a wash of bad breath.

"Yeah." I let the word out slowly, with more syllables than it deserved, using the time to control my temper and come up with the best way to broach the next subject. "We have like six hours until we make our first Transition in this sector... in this Cauldron of Creation place." I rolled my eyes. "Who came up with that damn name anyway?"

"Records indicate that, although we learned of the existence of the star cluster from the Khitan, the name is likely Resscharr in origin."

I looked around instinctively before I could stop myself. It wasn't some crewmember listening over my shoulder, it was Dwight buzzing in my earpiece, as usual. The Predecessor artificial intelligence usually stayed silent in the background, but any direct question that he considered in his purview would bring an answer, wanted or not. We'd discovered that the quickest way to let him know a conversation was private was to simply ignore him. I wasn't sure if the answer had been for my ears only or if Hachette had been a recipient as well, but he didn't seem to take notice, not looking up as he took another drink.

"Anyway," I went on, "I just wondered if you had any thoughts as the disposition of my Marines and the Intercepts for security when we arrive. Do you want us suited up and in the drop-ships, or should we stay strapped in for possible high-g maneuvering?"

Hachette finally met my gaze, but only to roll his eyes.

"Seriously?" His laugh was harsh and cutting. "Don't give me that shit, Alvarez. You need advice from me on how to deploy a Drop Trooper company like I need your opinion on how to cultivate HUMINT assets in a hostile zone." Hachette scowled over at the table with Dunstan and Vicky, and Dunstan offered an awkward wave. "Did Sandoval send you over here to try to drag me out of the sewer?"

"More or less," I admitted, which was easier since I didn't want to be there in the first place. I rubbed again at my eyes. "Look, sir, if anyone understands what you're going through, it's me."

"Is that so?" He tilted his head, regarding me from a new angle, eyebrow cocked upward. "Is this where you tell me about your tragic childhood and how it allows you to empathize with everyone who ever had a loved one killed?"

Once upon a time that would have really pissed me off, enough to risk striking a superior officer. But there'd been a lot of water under that bridge and now, I felt more annoyance than fury.

"You wanna know what I think, sir?" I replied, settling back in my chair and returning his stare. "I think you've had a pretty cushy life. Your father is a Commonwealth colonial administrator, your mom is a physics professor at Capital City University, you got into the Academy on your first try after being accepted to every school you applied to, got your first choice of branch and assignment, and got promoted to colonel faster than anyone in the last ten years, even during the war." His mouth opened soundlessly, consternation in his knitted brows. "Yeah, I can read a personnel jacket just as well as you can. You got a chestload of medals in the war without ever once seeing combat, without once having to watch your friends get killed around you, without once having the conviction down deep in your soul that this was it, that you're going to die." Okay, maybe I *was* angry after all. "I think that when everyone else was getting forced out of the military after the war or getting stuck on sentry duty on Tahn-Skyyiah, you got a plum assignment, chasing down a war criminal with a crack crew." I spread my hands and smiled thinly at his growing outrage. "And then everything just went to shit. Which is the secret of being in combat, sir. Everything *always* goes to shit. And you've done pretty damn good with it. You made the tough decisions and you've had a few lucky breaks, but this time, it hit home and it hit hard. It's not just you that lost someone, you know?" I motioned over at Vicky. "For the two of us, we lost a mentor, a teacher, a guide. You lost the woman you loved, and that sucks. But crawling into a hole—or a bottle—isn't going to make it feel any better. I tried it for a solid year."

I thought for a second that Hachette was going to take a swing at me. He had that look, the tension around his eyes and mouth that spoke of fury boiling just beneath the surface, ready to blow up. A Tahni saved me.

"Colonel Hachette."

The pronunciation was indescribable, coming from vocal

cords never designed to speak any of our languages, from the steam-shovel jaws of a Tahni. And if we knew now that the Tahni had been engineered from hominids taken from Earth hundreds of thousands of years ago, that still didn't make them human. I couldn't have told one Tahni from another at the start of this mission, but time had bred familiarity and maybe a little less contempt. The uniform, the designs in the multicolored stripes that denoted rank, plus the size of his brow ridges told me this was Lan-Min-Gen, the commander of the Tahni Shock Trooper platoon assigned to our ship for this voyage. If we hadn't gotten a good start to our relationship, it had improved after our experience with the Khitan.

"I am gratified that I have encountered you." Lan-Min-Gen gave a very human nod. If his grammar was stilted, at least he'd put in the time and effort of learning our language instead of relying on a translation program. "I am told we near the Cauldron of Creation and I wished to know how you would see my troops deployed for this Transition."

Hachette sighed and set his cup down on the table with a solid *thunk*.

"I suppose it's too much to ask to get a damned cup of coffee before I go to work." He glowered at me. "All right, you win. I'm going back to my quarters to get a shower and a fresh uniform. I'll have a mission brief for everyone in... two hours. Is that good enough for you?"

"You're the boss, sir," I assured him as he rose from the table and headed for the exit.

The expression Hachette shot over his shoulder at me showed just how little he believed that. What bothered me was how little *I* believed it. We were entering the most dangerous part of this whole trip.

Who the hell was going to lead us through it?

[2]

Hachette *didn't*, as it turned out, want all the Marines geared up and ready to drop when we Transitioned, which was just as good with me. The bridge was where all the action would be, and the longer I spent in a command position, the more I wanted to be a part of the command decisions that would send my people into harm's way.

I don't know if Hachette appreciated Vicky and I being on the bridge for the jump, but he didn't say anything when we showed up. Captain Nance greeted us with a perfunctory nod, not rude or unfriendly, just concentrating on his job. Lan-Min-Gen was already there as well, though I wasn't sure if he'd been invited, and even more surprising, so was Lilandreth. I think the bridge crew was accustomed to the Tahni by now, but the Resscharr female still drew a lot of stares. Of course, a two-meter-plus evolved dinosaur with backward-bent knees and a mane of feathers sticking up half a meter off the top of her head was likely to attract attention. Vicky noticed me staring at the Resscharr and leaned close.

"What do you think they'd say back on Earth if we showed up with Lilandreth and the rest of the Predecessors?"

I didn't bother to correct her—we'd had that conversation before. Technically, Lilandreth and her people weren't Predecessors, since most of them had been born long after their species had abandoned the empire of life-bearing planets they'd created in our cluster. They were Resscharr, which was their name for themselves as a species and as close as we could come to pronouncing the word with a human voice box. It wasn't worth arguing about though.

"What do you expect to find here, Lilandreth?" I asked her, figuring she had as good a chance of knowing as anyone except Dwight. The Resscharr stared at me with huge, liquid, amber eyes, her pupils slitted horizontally like a cat's.

"I hope to find some sign of the Seekers," she told me, whatever emotion was behind the words unreadable. She'd learned our language and given herself the ability to speak it through Predecessor technology, but just speaking the words correctly didn't mean she knew how to emote, or that the feeling could be transmitted through body language in any way I could understand. "Or some clue to their fate."

"You think they might be gone?" Vicky prompted, buckling into one of the spare acceleration couches. Once we Transitioned, we'd lose artificial gravity and be at the mercy of the ship's boost. "Killed off by now?"

"It's certainly a possibility," Lilandreth admitted. She looked absurd squeezed into a seat built for a human, but her high-tech gadgets still didn't include anything that would excuse her from Newton's laws of motion. "After all, it has been thousands of years since they left Decision, and at least a millennium since they established the Khitan civilization."

I shuddered a little at the mention of the Khitan and I thought I noticed a tightening of Hachette's jaw. The Khitan were an obscene blending of Tahni and human genetics, a last-ditch attempt by the Seekers to use their bioengineering prowess to solve their problems by creating a species to fight their war for them. Their entire society was built on conquest, first of the humans and Tahni they'd shared their world with, and then of each other. I'd tried to convince myself that it wasn't their fault, that the Seekers had basically programmed them to be totalitarian, warmongering assholes, but I couldn't manage it, probably for the same reason that Hachette was becoming enraged just at the mention of them.

They'd killed Top. They'd nearly killed Vicky and me too, but we'd escaped by the skin of our teeth. I'd made them pay. Sort of. And if nothing else, I'd managed to coerce them into releasing all their records, histories, and legends about the Seekers, and that had led us here. It didn't feel like a good trade.

"If they've been killed off," someone murmured off to the side, "then what the hell are we doing here?"

"Belay that, mister," Nance snapped.

The fact that he'd *had* to say it was disturbing. When this whole thing had started, no one would have dared talk that way in front of Colonel Hachette. Though I wasn't sure how much of that was respect for Hachette and how much had been fear of Top.

"Two minutes to Transition," Commander Yanayev reported.

"Sound free-fall and acceleration warning," Nance ordered. "Make sure everyone's strapped in."

"They should know to be strapped in," Lan-Min-Gen commented, perhaps frowning. It was hard to tell on a face like that.

"They do," I told him, rising to the defense of the crew since everyone else was too busy for it. "But there's also Tahni, Resscharr, and various specialists who might not be familiar with the ship. And it never hurts to remind people what they should be doing beforehand. That's a big part of being an officer, being one last safety check."

"The ways of your people are strange," the Tahni said. "It still baffles me how you won the war."

The warning had gone out while we were having our exchange, though the intercom wasn't kept at full volume on the bridge for obvious reasons. By the time I'd left Lan-Min-Gen to his philosophical ponderings of the fate of his people, the countdown clock had already appeared on the main screen, floating atop the holographic projection. Less than a minute.

"Tactical," Nance said, eyeing Commander Wojtera, "arm energy cannons and prepare for immediate engagement once we Transition. And make sure the systems account for the Tahni corvettes."

Which shouldn't be too hard, I figured, since there were only four of them left. Zan-Thint had sent them along from Yfingam mostly as a symbolic gesture, and they'd lasted about as long as I'd figured. Most of them had been destroyed by the Khitan, a society that didn't have FTL travel or fusion power, and I wanted to point out to Lan-Min-Gen that was probably a big reason his people had lost the war, but there was no use antagonizing him... not when we'd *just* managed to get to the point where we could share the mess hall again.

"Ten seconds," Yanayev chanted in a tradition centuries old. She didn't *need* to tell us. We could all read the countdown. "Five... Transitioning."

Reality grabbed me by the lapels and dragged me kicking and screaming back into spacetime, leaving my feet hanging over nothingness, no perception of up or down except what my eyes could make from my physical orientation. The computer simulation on the main screen morphed seamlessly into a combination of optical, thermal, gravimetic and microwave sensors into a single active image of your typical star system, or at least what we'd found was typical for systems with G-type main sequence stars with terrestrial planets.

Except for the starfield. I'd grown accustomed to seeing strange stars, thicker and brighter than anything in the Cluster, but this was breathtaking. There barely seemed to be any black left, whole swathes of the sky glowing solid white from the concentration of stars.

"Holy shit," Lt. Chase said, his eyes wide.

"No human's ever seen this before," Yanayev agreed.

It was hard to tear my attention away from the starscape and focus on the particulars of the system in front of us, particularly when it seemed at first glance to be more of the same. The primary was a Christmas-tree star glowing in the middle distance, just a little farther away from us than the Earth was from the Sun back home, but the nearest celestial body to where we'd exited Transition Space was within a few hundred thousand klicks of a terrestrial planet. Back in the Cluster, I was used to most every rocky, Earth-sized world being a habitable planet, for which I'd discovered we had the Predecessors to thank. This place was inhabited, but it wasn't habitable... not by us.

I didn't even need Tactical to give us the report. I'd seen the colors, the patterns, the size of the continents and the distribution of water before, and given where we were, that couldn't be a coincidence.

"Looks familiar," Yanayev commented, and Wojtera nodded.

"Within the limits of human habitability, probably," he reported, "but unless you're at the poles, you're looking at heat exhaustion in a few minutes. Almost seventy degrees Celsius at the equators, and the oceans are around the temperature of my grandma's chicken soup. Not sure I'd want to swim in them either, given what we saw on the last world like this."

Nance looked over at Hachette, cocking an eyebrow in an unasked question. Hachette shrugged and touched a control on his command chair.

"Dunstan, launch your scout mission." The order was resentful, as if he didn't really want to be bothered.

"Roger that, sir," Dunstan replied, cheerful as always, even when he was bitching about something.

In a corner of the main screen, a camera in the hull showed us Intercept One launching from the docking bay, a silver delta a hundred meters long gleaming softly in the unfiltered sunlight. She drifted away from the bulk of the *Orion* on maneuvering thrusters, gaining enough distance to safely ignite her fusion drive, a new star flaring in the near distance. Dunstan didn't run high-g acceleration because there was no need for it, just cruising in at what seemed like a luxurious pace from here, boosting at maybe one gravity for a few minutes, the cutter growing smaller in the view until the optical camera zoomed in to bring her closer again. The drive cut off and Intercept One flipped end for end before boosting again, this time to decelerate most of the way until she drifted into an atmospheric insertion.

He made the maneuver look so effortless. I hadn't appreciated that until I'd made the ride with him. I'd deorbited thousands of times of course, in drop-ships and landers and even a couple of assault shuttles, but I'd just taken the jerky, rough ride as part and parcel of the ride. Not with Dunstan. The man was an artist behind the controls of a cutter.

As Intercept One descended, half the main screen switched over to the feed from the dual-environment starship's nose camera, the fiery corona of atmospheric entry fading slowly into the faded amber of the planet's day side. Day faded to night, then reappeared before he'd taken the craft low enough for the lens to pick up details on the ground.

"We're not using a drone this time?" Vicky asked no one in

particular. It was Wojtera who answered her though. I think the man had a crush on her, for which I couldn't fault his taste.

"We only have like three of them left in stores." The Tactical officer shrugged. "If we'd detected any potential dangers, we'd have gone that route anyway, but..."

The world wasn't quite as wet as the last one of its like we'd seen. Where the land mass of that planet had consisted mostly of island chains and archipelagos, this one had small continents separated by shallow seas, steam wafting off the soupy, fetid water. The land... writhed. It wasn't dirt, it wasn't forest, it wasn't desert. It was nothing so much as an algal mat, something akin to a covering of moss or kudzu, except it was covered in spiny quills too long and thin to be called thorns. Here and there, softer and more colorful protrusions burst out of the brown mass, maybe an analog to flowers blooming, though I didn't recall flower petals ever *wriggling* quite that much. This planet had a *lot* of wriggling. I couldn't tell if everything moving under the matt of bristles was part of the growth or some kind of animal living beneath it.

But it was very easy to tell what the dominant predator was. They scuttled around the island on four segmented legs, their carapaces divided in two, the upper half sporting two pairs of arms tipped with pincers of various size, their flat heads eyeless, ending in mandibles. Miniature Skrela. There was no denying it now, not after the genetic samples we'd taken from the last of these worlds we'd found.

"Son of a bitch," Nance muttered, though the tone wasn't anger or disappointment but almost... awe. "We must be getting close to them."

By *them* I knew he meant the Skrela, the source of them, their ships, their drop pods. It wasn't an unreasonable conclusion, but I wasn't sure if I agreed.

"We still don't know what the purpose of these... places is," I pointed out. "I don't know what to call them. Zoos? Wildlife parks?"

"Genetic depositories," Lilandreth said, not with the air of a suggestion but more of a declaration. "Whoever engineered these worlds for Skrela ecosystems did it to preserve their genetic material for future use."

"Hey guys," Dunstan said with his usual lack of military communications protocol, "I'm picking something up here. A structure."

Wojtera frowned, squinting at his screen.

"I'm not seeing any energy readings," he said. "Nothing on thermal and no spectrometry suggesting anything but natural materials."

"Well, then you tell me what the hell this thing is."

The nose of the ship shifted starboard and the view moved with it, angling down into a thick section of the mat, where a river ran down from hills into the Skrela equivalent of a jungle, the spiny bristles extending so far they drooped over the top of a dip in the riverbed. And partially covered by those bristles was a building, a gray dome half-buried in the dirt. My first impression was that it had been carved out of granite by the river, a natural formation, but there was nothing like it anywhere else the Intercept's cameras had touched, and I instinctively knew it had been *made*.

"No thermal readings," Dunstan admitted, "but that ain't just a rock."

Intercept One slowed nearly to a hover, the belly jets roaring loudly enough to make it past the noise-cancelling mic in his helmet, a fine cloud of dust raising from the ground only fifty meters below. The half-scale Skrela scattered from the blast of hot wind, some of the things staring up at the ship, their mandibles moving fast as hummingbird wings. I half-expected Dunstan to open fire on them, but he just sat there, drifting slowly back and forth within sight of the structure. And waited, just like the rest of us.

I wouldn't say that *every* eye on the bridge turned to Colonel Hachette, but mine certainly did.

"Maybe we should send the drone down," I suggested, "get a closer look at it."

"You'll find nothing that way," Lilandreth interjected. "If this is what I think it is, then I need to go down personally."

"You think it was built by your people?" Hachette asked.

"I recognize the design. If I'm right, it will be secured with a genetic lock meant to admit only one of us."

I realized my mouth was hanging open and shut it.

"Do we need to actually land a party here?" I asked, leaning forward and pulling against my restraints. Biting back a curse and wishing like hell we had gravity, I pushed on before anyone could interrupt. "I mean, we know we're heading deeper into this Cauldron of Creation place, right? And this isn't the Seekers and it isn't the source of the Skrela we've been finding. Is it worth the risk to actually put boots on the ground?"

"If this is a Resscharr facility," Lilandreth said, "there may be records there that could lead us to the Seekers."

"Alvarez," Hachette said, his voice suddenly as firm as it had been a few months ago when all this had started, "get a squad geared up and loaded in Drop-Ship One, have them escort Lilandreth down to the... structure."

I shook my head.

"Sir, that whole area is crawling with those mini-Skrela things. We don't know how dangerous they are, but we sure as hell know there's a lot of them."

"They don't have fucking plasma guns, do they?" Hachette snapped, regressing into the barely controlled mania I'd grown used to the last few weeks. "Can't your battlesuits handle the things?"

I stared at him for a moment, forcing my expression neutral, before I touched my earbud.

"Lt. Singh," I said, "prep First Platoon and get them loaded on Drop-Ship One. Tell the armorer I'm heading down there and to have my suit ready."

"Yes, sir," the man said immediately, as if he'd been waiting on the order. "On it."

"I said a squad, Captain," Hachette told me, features screwed up into something petulant, like he was about to try to throw his weight around. "And I didn't say *anything* about you leading it personally."

"The drop-ship can carry a platoon," I told him, not backing down a centimeter, "and no one ever got killed for being too prepared." I shot him a look that was probably damned close to insubordination as I unstrapped from the seat. "As for me leading it... I don't send people into dangerous situations unless I'm ready to be the first off the bird." And with that, I turned away from him and toward the Resscharr. "Lilandreth, follow me. You can check your personal weapons and armor out of the armory while I suit up."

I was already off the bridge and heading for the lift by the time Vicky caught up with me, zipping past Lilandreth with the grace of someone accustomed to moving about in free fall.

"I'm coming with you," she insisted, tugging at my sleeve.

"You're my XO," I reminded her, shedding my momentum on the padded railing as we reached the lift bank. If it had been just me I would have taken the central hub, the vertical passage running up the center of the ship for use in zero gravity, but I wasn't sure how well Lilandreth would handle that. Better to just wait for the elevator. "If anything happens to me, you're in charge of the company."

"If anything happens to you," she insisted, her tone quiet but firm, "I don't give a *shit* about the company."

"Then look at it this way," I tried. "Once I'm down there, Hachette's going to be up *here*, making all the calls. I'd like it if there was someone here I could trust who could make sure he doesn't flake out."

Vicky closed her eyes for a moment, lips pressed together, then sighed in exasperation.

"Damn it, Alvarez, you always know the right thing to say."

The lift door slid aside and Lilandreth ducked under it, the tip of her mane slightly too tall to make it. I gave Vicky a quick kiss and joined the Resscharr.

"Don't let him do anything stupid while I'm gone," I told her, not having to elaborate who *him* was.

She scoffed as the door slid slowly closed, like a metal coffin.

"How the hell am I supposed to manage *that*?"

[3]

"Couldn't we have gotten any closer?" First Sergeant Endicott wondered, his feet shifting like a three-year-old who had to go to the bathroom as he scanned our surroundings. "Maybe dropped right on top of the thing? This place gives me the fucking creeps."

I checked instinctively to make sure Endicott was on our private channel, some part of me that had been trained with professionals like Skipper and Top and Lt. Ackley rebelling at the notion of someone of his rank grousing in front of the other Marines. Endicott had been field-promoted to first sergeant, so he was technically the company topkick, but I couldn't bring myself to call him "Top." There was only one Top.

"*We* could have," I agreed, "but *she* couldn't have." I motioned at Lilandreth, who was walking in the middle of the platoon formation. Her long-legged, loping stride would have left any of us behind if we were on foot, but the artificial musculature of the suits meant we had to slow down to let her keep up. "That Predecessor armor she's wearing might protect her from the heat, but unless she's holding out on us, that shit doesn't fly.

That's why we had to find a place where the drop-ship could set down."

And that place was a good six klicks behind us. I couldn't say I blamed Endicott for being creeped out though. I'd run ops on every sort of colony world and a few lifeless hunks of rock, but none of them seemed as unnatural as this place. The engineered worlds left to us by the Predecessors were as varied and versatile in their geography and ecology as Earth, but there was a sense of comfortable sameness to them. Some of the plants and animals had minor genetic adjustments to cope with their new environment, but everything was very homelike, close enough to Earth that someone dropped onto one of the planets—in daylight, anyway—would have had a hard time figuring out they were on another world.

Not here. This was as different as a world could be, what I thought of when the word *alien* crossed my mind, and I was grateful for the insulation of the suit, not just from the oppressive heat but from the bizarre incongruity of the place. Razor-sharp spines scraped against the legs of my suit with a screech that set my teeth on edge, and the only way to avoid the sound and the sensation was to stomp on the damned things. But with every stomp came an explosion of dust and pollen and, usually, a stream of insect-like creatures. Not roaches, not anything close to them in appearance, but that was the image they evoked. They fled the afternoon light, burrowing beneath the green mat and disappearing again like they'd never been there.

"How much farther, sir?" Singh asked, tension in his voice. The First Platoon leader was about thirty meters ahead of me, shuffling along, scraping thorns away from his suit with each step. I frowned at him, confident he couldn't see it. The fact that Singh and Endicott were bitching like PFCs right out of Boot was disturbing.

"You can access the drone footage just as easy as I can, Singh," I reminded him.

It wasn't one of the drop drones from the *Orion*—Hachette had remained unwilling to use any more of those than we had to. This was one of the quadcopters launched from the pod in the upper neck area of our Vigilantes, although we were running short on those as well. The fabricators could make more, but not unless we fed them the right material, and we hadn't managed that in months, since we left Yfingam.

The thing couldn't go that high or that fast, but it did give us a good look at what waited for us on the other side of the thick, spiny foliage. Up till now, that had been pretty much *more* thick, spiny foliage, but as the little aircraft rose another twenty meters, the dull-gray edges of the structure peeked through the embracing arms of the oversized thorn bushes, just a few klicks ahead.

I was still watching the feed from the drone when something black and sharp with multiple sets of wings crashed into it and the video cut off. I looked up and spotted the thing heading off to the north with the little quadcopter grasped in its crablike mandibles, buzzing around like a giant, mutant ladybug.

"Damn."

"Should we launch another, sir?" Endicott wondered.

I was about to say no, that we didn't have them to spare, but I was interrupted by another voice on the comms, this time not one of my Marines, but the pilot of Drop-Ship One.

"Cam, this is Walton. Just a heads-up, we were getting some incursion from the native predators, those miniature Skrela, probing the hull of the ship, trying to pull apart our landing gear. Had to mow a few of them down with the Gatling to teach the others a lesson. They're pretty agitated, so you guys might want to keep your heads on a swivel."

"Copy that," I confirmed. "If it gets too tricky there, dust off and run a wide orbit around the LZ and we'll call you in for pickup."

"Will do. Good luck."

I grunted agreement, then switched over the comm net.

"Intercept One, do you read?" Nothing. I frowned and repeated the call.

"This is *Orion*," Lt. Chase replied. "Intercept One is back on board. Lt. Dunstan has had a failure of the bow-maneuvering thruster unit and had to have it repaired. We estimate three hours before he can be back on station." A pause. "We have Intercept Two firing up her reactor and Commander Brandano can be down there running overwatch in under an hour if you feel you need air cover beyond the drop-ship."

It was hard not to curse. It wasn't Chase's fault for pulling our air cover without telling us, it was Hachette's. I wonder if he even bothered to tell Vicky. Probably not, or she would have made sure to call me.

"Yeah, *Orion*," I said through clenched teeth, working to keep my tone neutral, "I'd like Intercept Two down here ASAP, thanks very much."

"Copy that. We'll get him launched."

There was no practical way to slam my fist on the comms switch while I was in the suit, but God knows I wanted to. It wasn't that shit like this was unheard of in the military. I knew that better than anyone. But not from *this* crew. These guys were elite, the best of the best, and the whole time I'd been working with them, they'd never showed me this side of them. Oh, I knew *why*. We'd been out here for over a year, away from loved ones, watching our friends die with no replacements available and no way home. They'd lasted longer than most troops I'd known, but all of us were human. Except the Tahni and the Resscharr.

"Singh, get another drone launched," I snapped, angry not

at him but at myself. I was so busy whining and moaning about everyone else letting themselves get distracted that I'd done the exact same thing.

"Yes, sir." He didn't seem to take my tone personally, though God alone knew why.

Singh had been the company XO and had every reason to expect he would be the company commander once Solano had been killed in battle with the Skrela, or at least stay in his current position, but what had happened instead was that I'd been slotted in at CO and I'd made Vicky my XO. We'd lost the First Platoon leader in the same battle and it had seemed better to put Singh with them, since he knew the Marines in that unit better than I did.

"We got movement at our elven o'clock!" Ajimobi, the Marine out on point, yelled. "One hundred meters!"

Okay, fuck the drone.

"I'm going high," I announced, hitting the suit's thrusters before Singh or Endicott could try to talk me out of it.

Before our experience with the Resscharr on Decision, our Vigilante battlesuits had been able to boost maybe a hundred meters up for no more than a minute or so, but now, with the isotope reactors replaced by... well, *whatever* the damned things were, and the turbines replaced with something akin to magnetohydrodynamics, we could stay up for going on ten minutes, and the only thing stopping us from unlimited flight was overheating... and the possibility of getting shot down.

That wasn't currently a danger, since the half-size Skrela —*Skreloids* maybe?—lacked the plasma guns that their full-sized cousins packed as a matter of course. But there were a hell of a lot of them. Starting a hundred meters out from the Marine on point, they were drifting toward our formation from every direction in clusters of six or seven, their scorpion tails writhing behind them like cobras dancing to the tune of a snake charmer.

Though they lacked energy weapons, the powerful, jagged pincers on their lower set of arms looked pretty damned dangerous, and I had no desire to find out if they were strong enough to penetrate BiPhase Carbide armor.

"First squad, suppressive fire from ten to two!"

It wasn't an exact science, since the foliage was too thick for them to get a good target lock, but it did the job. I helped, of course, since I had a bird's-eye view. The energy cannons that had replaced our plasma guns were awesome, and there was a lot to appreciate about the things. First of all, they were some sort of particle accelerator, which meant there was far less beam spreading than with the plasma weapon, and there was some kind of force field enclosure involved that meant there was nowhere near as much thermal backwash and I didn't feel like I opened a pizza oven every time I fired. It was more accurate as well and I was hitting targets from nearly a kilometer out, clearing the rear edge of the cluster of Skreloids while the lead squad of Marines blasted the thorn trees and the alien creatures behind them at point-blank range.

But there was a certain visceral quality to the plasma gun that I missed, nonetheless. Maybe it was just because it was what I'd trained with as a fresh PFC right out of Boot, but the thing had a solid kick to it, a wrath-of-God feeling to the lance of hellfire that splashed over an enemy and consumed them. When the energy cannon fired, it was more of a firehose of incandescent green light, and where it struck it left nothing, vaporizing everything around, reducing it to its component atoms.

Whether that was less impressive visually, it was more than enough for the Skreloids. They scattered from our path, retreating the way they'd come, their panicked chittering loud enough to penetrate the roar of my jumpjets. The intense volley hadn't just cleared the path of the alien creatures though. It had also blasted away a broad wedge of the spiny bushes, leaving the way open for hundreds of meters.

Leaving the dome sitting out there in plain sight. I could have sworn at least two or three of the shots from first squad had hit the thing, but there wasn't so much as a scorch mark on the dull gray, not even a scratch. I hissed out a sigh and descended slowly beside Lilandreth.

"Singh," I told the man, "take first and second squads and push past the building, set up a perimeter on that side. Endicott, you're with third and fourth. Stay with us and build the circle on this side."

They acknowledged my orders, but I was already switching to Lilandreth's comm net, theoretically separate from ours, but I wouldn't have been willing to bet that fancy, transparent helmet she wore could probably listen in on any transmission in the area.

"We need to make this fast," I told her. "We threw a scare into those things, but I don't know how long it'll hold."

She didn't respond except to quicken her pace. She was the golden statue of some ancient deity in her glowing armor, some fertility goddess out of Babylon brought to life and walking among us. I'd thought my sense of wonder and awe had been totally burned out after the last two years, but a remnant tingled deep in my gut at the sight of her, so utterly impossible. She was thousands of years old, from a race tens of *millions* of years old, descended from the few dinosaurs tough enough to survive the Chicxulub asteroid strike that had killed the rest of them. They'd built a starfaring civilization and left an Earth that was becoming increasingly less hospitable for them to create new worlds, new life where there had been none... including the Tahni.

When we'd discovered the wormhole jumpgates and all those habitable planets they'd left behind, we'd assumed they'd been addressed to Whom It May Concern, but they'd actually been the birthright of their special children, the Tahni. We'd been the proverbial redheaded stepchildren, and they'd treated us accordingly, sending the rock that had almost ended humanity seventy thousand years ago in what our scientists referred to as the great genetic bottleneck, when all of the human population had been reduced to maybe ten thousand individuals.

Finding out about *that* had done a lot to take the shine off the whole Predecessor thing for me. A lot of people thought of them as gods, as somehow superior to humanity, but they could be just as ruthless and merciless as any human, or any Tahni. Still, I tried not to let myself blame Lilandreth personally for any of that.

The building was bigger than I'd thought looking at it from Dunstan's ship with nothing beside it for perspective, ten meters above ground at the top of the dome and at least thirty meters in diameter. Close up, the gray, featureless surface seemed to be polished mirror-smooth, not as much as a chip or scrape on it, and I knew for sure this was a Predecessor building. Not that the Skrela lacked their own high-tech toys, but nothing I'd seen from them had displayed that sort of almost artistic attention to detail.

A quick check of the IFF transponders to ensure that First Platoon was following orders and setting up a perimeter, and then I circled around the thing, the remains of vaporized thorn trees crunching under my boots, trying to find some seam or doorway. I saw nothing.

"How the hell do you get into this thing?" I asked Lilandreth.

By way of answer, she stripped off her right glove and laid her long-fingered hand on the wall of the dome at what looked to me like a random spot. I winced, expecting that the wall had to be pretty damned hot considering it was around sixty degrees Celsius out and the surface of the building was bare to the primary star, but she didn't flinch away.

I waited, looking back and forth from Lilandreth to her hand, and had just about run out of patience when the surface of the dome began to glow gold beneath her fingers. The glow spread in half a dozen parallel lines across the wall, veering off as if seeking something. What they were seeking was a door. The gold traces traveled through the gray of the dome, though I couldn't discern whether they were beneath the surface, atop it, or somehow embedded in the molecules. Wherever they were and however they worked, they traced an oval starting three meters up and extending downward only a few centimeters from the ground.

And then there was a door. It didn't appear, nor did the stone-like surface disappear or dissolve. No slab sank backward or slid downward. The gap was suddenly just *there*, like a shift of perspective when something that looked like shadow actually proved to be a hole. Through this hole was absolute darkness, without even the play of light and shadow that would have resulted from the light of the primary streaming through the opening. Unnatural. I was using that word a lot lately.

One of the last pieces of advice Sgt-Major Ellen Campbell had given me was to expand my reading habits. Before this trip I'd read nonfiction, history, biography, military tactics. All the shit that had been recommended or required when I went through OCS. At Top's recommendation—and Vicky's—I'd taken up the classics of science fiction all the way from HG Wells and Jules Verne through the twenty-first century. I'd stopped there, because the whole genre had taken a dark turn after the Sino-Russian War and I didn't enjoy it anymore. But somewhere in the mid to late twentieth century there'd been a writer named Arthur C. Clarke who, I later found out, had invented the idea of the communications satellite. He'd coined a phrase once that I'd found more and more useful as I dealt with the Predecessors.

Any sufficiently advanced technology is indistinguishable from magic.

Lilandreth stepped through the darkness and disappeared.

"Fuck!" The exclamation was expulsive, refusing to be stifled. I squeezed my eyes shut and gathered my thoughts, then switched comm nets to Singh. "Lieutenant, we've discovered an entrance into the building. I'm going in. I may lose comms briefly, so don't panic, but if you don't hear from me in five minutes, come see if I need rescuing or something... and bring in air support, because we might be in trouble."

"Are you sure this is a good idea, sir?" Endicott asked.

"Oh, hell no," I admitted, then stepped through the opening.

Despite my expectations, it wasn't pitch-black inside the dome and my helmet's enhanced optics weren't needed. The lighting was harsh, as if it had been designed for non-human eyes, and all the controls and readout displays were around the eye level of Lilandreth. Not that I could read any of them or even decipher the images, except for a few that showed the Skreloids skittering around on the mat, hunting down the crab-like animals I'd originally taken for cockroaches.

"I've never seen Skrela eat," I realized, talking out loud, though not to Lilandreth in particular.

"They don't need to," she said, not looking back at me, her long fingers flowing through haptic holograms. "The pod gives them nutrients before they're set loose, and after that they have enough in their system to allow them to operate for two weeks before they're forced to retreat back into one of the pods for replenishment."

"Two weeks without food. Huh. No wonder they're so

grumpy." I nodded at the control panel, then realized she couldn't see my nod since I was still suited up. "You getting anything useful out of that?"

The whole setup was like nothing I'd seen before, though I hadn't ever had the opportunity to set foot on one of the Predecessor ships, so for all I knew it could have been stock standard for them. There was no furniture at all, which might have had something to do with those digitigrade knees and their ability to crouch for long periods with no discomfort, and even the consoles themselves were nothing but holograms projected out of the bare walls. The whole thing had a very sparse, empty feel to it, but at least that meant it wasn't too crowded for me to walk around in my battlesuit.

I was used to the heavy footfalls of a Vigilante creating echoing drumbeats when I walked around inside a building, but not in here. The floor was white and featureless, and looked as if it might have been marble or some synthetic tile, but it absorbed the impact from my steps as if it was composed of foam rubber. I didn't test the theory, but I was sure the same was true of the interior walls.

"The system here is archaic," she told me, still weaving intricate patterns in the haptic holograms, the swirl of colors and symbols mesmerizing. "This is vexing. The Seekers used the same operating software we did on Decision only six thousand years ago, and that is too short a time for such a drastic change."

I suppressed a snort at the comment. Back in the Commonwealth, operating systems shifted at least every ten years, and every computer course I'd taken for OCS said it used to be even more often. I couldn't imagine the sort of society that made no technological advancements for millennia.

"It will take me some time to navigate," Lilandreth went on, catlike eyes still fixed on the shifting symbols. "I can, however, confirm this is a Resscharr facility, though its age and purpose are still a mystery, except that it seems to be monitoring the habits and life-cycle of the Skrela-style creatures here."

"Skreloids," I supplied, hoping the word would catch on. She *did* look over at that, and even though her face was entirely alien, her glare seemed very familiar to Vicky's when I said something stupid.

"I'm going to check in with my Marines," I said, deciding I'd contributed enough.

The comms display in my helmet was totally blank and I assumed that meant we were blocked off from all external signals inside the dome, but I didn't want Singh and Endicott panicking. Passing through the doorway was more like transitioning a jumpgate than exiting a building—the light changed abruptly, and with it came a deluge of transmissions, so many that they nearly overwhelmed the ability of the suit's comm system to deal with.

Sighing in exasperation, I swiped them all aside with a brush of my thumb against the control panel and pinged the First Platoon leader. It wasn't hard to reach him since the man was lumbering up to the dome even as I stepped away from the structure.

"Singh, everything's cool, I'm checking in. What's the sitrep? We got more of the natives riled up?"

"No, sir!" His voice was strained, his feet dancing nervously as if he wanted to be anywhere else. "We heard from the *Orion*, sir... it's the Skrela! A mothership just Transitioned into the system and launched fighters and drop pods! They're heading our way!"

[4]

"Get that fucking bird off the ground!" I yelled, both to drown out the jackhammer pounding of my running footsteps and Lt. Walton's objections.

We weren't running away from anything, not just yet, but I wanted everyone in position when the pods started falling.

"What the hell are you gonna do if I'm not there to pull you out?"

"What the hell are we gonna do if you get blown up and we have no way to get back to the *Orion*?" I shot back. "Those Skrela fighters are going to be on us in minutes! Get in the air and we'll rendezvous with you as soon as the Intercepts and assault shuttles clear us an LZ!"

"All right, Goddammit. If you get your ass killed, don't expect me to cry about it."

"I hereby absolve you of all obligation to mourn me, John," I assured him.

"What about me?" Vicky interrupted. "Do I still get the honor?"

She was on the *Orion*, which meant that the ship was still

close enough for no comms delay—still close enough they wouldn't be able to Transition out if they needed to.

"Glad you're okay," I told her. "What's the situation?"

"It's just the one ship," she reported. "Nothing we can't handle, but it's going to take time. We're trying to move out to Transition distance to get a little more freedom of movement, so you're going to be on your own for little while, but Intercept Two and the assault shuttles are heading your way for support. They should be able to clean up the Skrela fighters, but you have approximately twenty pods heading your way."

"Twenty?" I repeated, frowning and staring up at the afternoon sky. "I'm not complaining, but one of those motherships holds a hell of a lot more than that."

"Yeah, we don't know. Right now, best guess by Dwight is that this is a probing action, that they're saving the bulk of their ground forces until they know how many enemies they're facing." Her voice went grim. "There's still going to be around two hundred of them against thirty of you, and the only air support you'll have is the drop-ships, so watch your damn back. We're about to move into jamming range, but I'll check back with you once we take care of this asshole. Don't die."

"You too." Then she was gone, and the first of the pods streaked down through the atmosphere in the echo of her voice. "Shit." I switched over to Watson. "Hey, John, see if you can take out some of those pods without getting killed, pretty please?"

"You're so demanding," he said. "I don't know how Vicky puts up with you."

"It's an abiding mystery. Thanks, John."

I hadn't seen him take off, but now the bulbous, bulky lines of the drop-ship curved out above the bristling thorns of the forest, atmospheric jets screaming with effort. It looked desperately vulnerable and I second-guessed myself immediately, wondering if I shouldn't have just sent him off as far away as possible.

"No damned cover here," Endicott told me. He was a hundred meters away checking the perimeter, and I wondered if he was chewing my ear because he thought we should be bonding or something as Skipper and Top. *That* wasn't going to happen—there was only one Skipper and one Top in my mind. "These thorn trees ain't even good concealment."

I checked the alignment of the platoon on the IFF display before I answered, following the line of Marines along the terrain map.

"You've got third and fourth in the riverbed," I told him. "The bank will give them some cover."

"Yeah, but there ain't anything for the rest of us except humidity."

"You know the plan, Sergeant. Movement is going to be our cover." I switched over to the platoon net and continued. "Listen up. We've trained for this, we did it in combat at Decision and Yfingam and we're doing it again now. Third and fourth squads, you're our base of fire. The rest of us are going to draw them into the kill zone, then fall back while you lay down constant suppressive fire. The energy guns take less time to cycle than the plasma guns, so you can put out more shots with less heat in less time. Do it. Don't spare anything, just keep them coming at you. First and second, you're going to use the fields of fire from the riverbed as a dividing line. Don't cross it unless you're a minimum twenty meters up... and there's no fucking reason you should be that far up because that leaves you open to enemy fire. On *this* side of that line though, I want you moving by fire teams, the same kind of strafing runs we did on Yfingam. It's going to be tricky, but if you follow your team leader and stay low, you'll be fine. We clear?"

"Ooh-rah, sir!" The response was enthusiastic, and I

wondered what the hell I'd done to earn that.

"Singh, they're yours," I told him.

"Yes, sir!" He seemed surprised, and so was I. There'd been a day when I wouldn't have even considered not putting myself out front. But I had to be able to coordinate this fight, have the big picture, and I couldn't do that if I was totally involved in combat.

"And what about me?" Lilandreth asked, her rifle tucked against her side, the thing looking far too shiny and sparkling to be a weapon. "Do you wish me to seek cover in the riverbed as well?"

"No," I said. "You're going back inside the dome." I pointed off to the side a hundred meters where the gray structure squatted in ugly patience. "I don't know if you can close that door..."

"I have yet to determine the access for security. If I closed it, it would be by accident, and it's doubtful I could get myself out."

"Then stay low on the opposite side of the thing but keep a good line of sight to the door. Anything comes through that isn't one of us, burn it down. Got me?"

"I believe I do. If they make it past you, however, I do not know how long I can keep them out of the structure."

"We're buying time until the *Orion* takes out that Skrela ship," I reminded her. "Once she does, they can come back and provide air and ground support. We'll be fine. Get on inside."

She did as I said, though I didn't think for a second she believed me. With her gone and the troops deployed, I tried to link into the feed from Drop-Ship One. And failed. The pods were jamming our comms... at least any that weren't line-of-sight. I tried to remember if they'd done that the first time we'd fought them. It didn't matter in the here and now, but on a strategic level it was concerning, the concept that they could learn and adjust their tactics. Dwight and the Resscharr had insisted they weren't individually intelligent, but how many of them getting together did it take before they were smarter than any of us?

I settled for the suit's optics, zooming in as much as they'd let me, enough that the computer simulation had enough to work with to give me at least a sense of what was going on. Drop-Ship One was no fighter or assault shuttle, and watching her try to perform aerobatics was sort of like watching a walrus attempting water ballet, but the Skrela seed pods couldn't dodge Walton's Gatling lasers. Where the stuttering lines of chain lightning struck, Skrela drop pods flashed into flaming debris, but not enough of them.

The things were dropping fast enough that there was no way a human could have survived the impact, and when the first of them hit about a klick away from us, a cloud of dust and debris rose fifty meters into the air. The rest hit in a pattern like birdshot around the first, the dark gray columns of smoke and dust merging into one, providing the things with their own concealment.

"They'll be coming," I warned, moving into position at the rear of the first and second squad ranks.

It was an inane thing to say, but I knew from being on the other side of this equation that hearing the commander's voice was comforting in these situations, as long as he wasn't trying to be too much of a blowhard. Privates and lance-corporals might pretend they didn't like being told the obvious, but only NCOs really resented it, and then only because they intended to do it themselves and now they had to come up with something else to say.

At least we didn't have to wait long. The first sign of the things was a violent thrashing in the thorn trees, though the platoon didn't need to be told to hold fire... at least not by me.

Giving those kinds of orders was Singh's responsibility. Not that the energy cannons couldn't have taken them out at this distance, but none of us would have been able to get a clean target lock. Skrela didn't show up on thermal the way a battlesuit or a Tahni Shock Trooper powered exoskeleton would. They were smeared and imprecise even using the suit's radar, lidar, and sonic detection, though I had no idea how they managed it. Good old Arthur C. Clarke again, tech magic from a species hundreds or even thousands of years more advanced than ours.

I expected them to come straight after us. That was the way they'd always done things in the past, heading straight for the biggest concentration of forces, and I had no reason to believe they'd stray from that MO now. Unfortunately, I was wrong.

"What the fuck are they doing?" Singh asked, though I was grateful he'd had the presence of mind to express that doubt on our private net.

It was a damned good question. Following their passage by the swaying of the trees, I could see that they were circling around us, swinging wide of the section of riverbed where the third and fourth squads lay in wait. But going where? What the hell was back that way?

There was only one way to find out, though I doubted Singh would like it. At least we were all close enough for laser line-of-sight to work and I didn't have to worry about the jamming.

"Singh, have everyone hold fire. I'm popping up for a quick look."

He squawked a protest, but the words were lost in the roar of my jumpjets. The Vigilante arced upward and took me along for the ride, and the previously hidden enemy was suddenly all too plain to see. There was no mistaking a Skrela for anything else. They looked like some deranged genetic artist had crossed a spider, a scorpion, an army ant, and a draft horse, then thrown the whole thing in a furnace for a few minutes to melt down the edges. Eight limbs, decreasing in mass and length as they worked their way upward, the final set of arms arranged for fine manipulation, but the ones just below that on the insect-spider-centaur seemingly designed to carry the huge plasma cannon. It was part of them, we knew that much, not rigged to some kind of harness but actually melded with their bodies, the power source somehow stored inside their carapace, though how they managed that... again, magic as far as we were concerned.

I had a hard time deciding which aspect of their kludged-together look was creepier, the scorpion-spike tail or the flattened wedge of a head with the antlike mandibles large enough to rip a man's head off his body and constantly moving, clapping together with an unmistakable, nerve-grating chittering. I couldn't hear it from the air, but I'd heard it so many times before it was a soundtrack playing in my head.

The most dangerous part was the plasma cannon, which was very capable of shooting me right out of the sky, but none of them pointed my way. The things were focused on their goal, and it only took a few seconds hovering at thirty meters up to see which way they were heading. Straight for the dome.

They didn't want us, they wanted the Predecessor structure... and Lilandreth.

"First Platoon!" I bellowed, hitting the dirt, knees bending with the impact. "Form up and follow me!"

Okay, this totally went against my earlier conviction to stay above the fighting and let Singh lead the platoon, but needs must when the devil drives. I didn't run... or, at least, I didn't *just* run. Since the upgrade of our jumpjets, we'd experimented with a new method of travel, taking advantage of the longer flight times and better thermal regulation. It took a lot of concentration and involved intermittent bursts of power to the jets, but it wound up skimming the Vigilante just over the ground at a faster pace than the suit could manage on foot. Top had called it ice-skating, but I'd never tried that so the analogy was lost on me.

I wasn't sure if the others could keep up and I was too busy trying to stay upright to check on them in the display, but I knew I was responsible for Lilandreth and I was the one who'd told her to shelter in the dome. The thorn trees tugged at me, trying to put me off-balance, but what worried me more were the Skrela. They were circling around my left, cutting across the riverbed where it forked, well past where we'd been set up, at the foot of the rolling hills to the north. Every second they got closer, moving so much faster than something the size of a draft horse had any right to, closer to me and to Lilandreth in the dome. It was only a matter of time before they noticed my approach and took a shot at me.

No time at all. The shot went centimeters behind me, probably thrown off by the intervening thorn trees, but close enough for the wave of heat to sear the back of my legs like a bad sunburn and spike the internal temperature of my suit high enough to drive the air from my lungs. No more ice-skating. I stepped crossways and hit the jets, popping up ten meters and spinning 360 degrees in an instinctive move, but one I wouldn't have recommended for anyone who hadn't been in a suit long enough for the thing to be a second skin.

The jump lasted three seconds, but time had slowed down with the adrenaline dump, stretching my perception of those seconds into minutes. The Skrela weren't in any kind of formation, more of a swarm, or a stampede, whether I wanted to give more weight to the insectoid or equine nature of the things, but the disorganized gaggle meant they couldn't mass their fires... and it gave me a clear first target.

The Skrela were tough bastards, their skin an armored, black carapace that took a direct hit from a Commonwealth plasma gun to penetrate, but the Predecessor energy cannon blasted right through the lower torso of the thing, disintegrating a meter-long section of the creature. The upper torso tumbled in one direction, pulled away by the weight of its plasma cannon, while the lower half kept running like a cockroach with a squished head, the legs still wriggling until the thing lost its balance and tripped up the one behind it.

I'd already moved onto the next target before it finished tumbling, the weapon cycling in less than a second, just giving me enough time to squeeze off a second shot. It hit home, but I couldn't tell anything else, already spinning back forward. On the way I caught a glimpse of the platoon trailing behind me, doing their best to imitate the ice-skating maneuver, though not quite at the speed I'd managed.

The turn took me back toward the dome and then I was down again, only half a second ahead of a volley of plasma aimed my way. The sky disappeared behind the core of the sun brought down among us, static electricity crackling from the ionized stretch of atmosphere to the ground, the dome, the trees, and even my armor, though I felt nothing of it inside the suit's insultation.

The dome loomed ahead closer than I'd realized, and only digging the heels of the suit into the dry, sandy earth and triggering a blast of my jumpjets kept me from slamming into the gray solidity of the building. A push off the wall sent me ricocheting away, spinning around into the short sprint to the door.

I wasn't the first one there. The remains of two Skrela were piled in the door, smoke still pouring off them, and another three were yanking at the charred bodies, trying to pull them out of the way to clear the entrance. It was a disturbingly human notion, and I erased the image from my thoughts by erasing the Skrela from existence, two shots blasting all three of them into blackened, sizzling component parts.

"Don't shoot!" I bellowed over the external speakers, just a split-second before throwing myself through the doorway in a face-first slide.

I barely had time to roll to the side before a green slice of balefire flashed through the space I'd just vacated, lighting up the darkness of the arcane doorway for just a moment.

"Hey!" I yelled, my amplified voice bouncing off the interior of the dome like the announcer in an arena. "I said don't shoot!"

"My apologies, Cameron Alvarez," Lilandreth said, raising the muzzle of her rifle to high port. "The entrance field distorted the sound."

"Come on!" I told her, scrambling to my feet, waving at the door. "The fucking Skrela are making a beeline for this place, and if we don't get out now they'll trap us in here!"

A blast from my energy cannon forced back the darkness of the field and, I hoped, cleared the way for me. Diving forward, I triggered a burst of the jets and lurched ten meters in the space of a heartbeat, the spiked soles of my boots digging into the dirt and sending clouds of dust billowing to my left and right. My shot had hit a lot of nothing, but now there were targets on either side, and I blasted upward ten meters just before both sides opened up on me.

A circular firing squad was what Top would have called it, and their plasma blasts took out nothing but each other. I added a burst of whatever esoteric particles the energy cannon fired to the mix, taking out two more of the things before Lilandreth rushed out of the entrance, firing as she came.

It still wasn't going to be enough. The Skrela wanted this place badly, and they were ignoring their dead even as they piled up, firing blindly, plasma ripping apart the trees, the dirt, the sky, coming within meters of us.

We were surrounded.

[5]

In the heat of the moment, I'd almost forgotten about the platoon. But, thank God, the platoon hadn't forgotten about *us*.

Spider webs of actinic green flashed from behind us, slicing a wedge out of the oncoming wave of Skrela and giving me just enough time to grab Lilandreth around the waist and hit the jets. There was a reason the Marines specifically forbade trying to transport anyone while using the jumpjets—multiple reasons, actually, the first of which was that the exhaust from the jets could badly burn anyone not in a suit. Even a Force Recon Marine wearing combat armor could still become a crispy critter... but not Lilandreth. Her Predecessor-tech armor could disperse thermal energy... I'd seen it take a glancing hit from a Skrela plasma gun on Decision and Yfingam.

The other good reason was the fact that the suit's systems weren't built to stabilize the extra weight and the whole process could end up with the Vigilante face-planting into the dirt at a hundred klicks an hour. I anticipated that part and leaned forward as far as I could, and *still* wound up nearly going ass-over-teakettle with the shifted center of mass. I didn't have to stay up long though... the arc I'd taken was short and the ground raced up to meet me. I threw my weight backward and gave the jets one last jolt of energy and still bit down hard on my mouthguard when we hit.

"Singh!" I yelled, the word an expulsion of breath as we hit the ground and Lilandreth pulled away from me. "Fall back! Get the platoon away from the building!"

The decision came from gut instinct I suppose, because there'd certainly been no time nor opportunity to consider our disposition and develop a strategy. But the Skrela had bypassed our defensive positions to attack the building, and if they wanted it so badly, I was ready to let them have it.

Singh was yelling orders on the platoon net but the words skimmed off the surface of my thoughts, my concentration instead split between the IFF display, the threat sensors, and the path ahead of us. The Skrela were behind me now, clustered around the dome like ants on a morsel of fallen food, and while it was fair to postulate we weren't the most important thing to them, it wouldn't have been accurate to say they'd totally forgotten about us. Flashes of plasma outshone the primary star, blowing wedges out of the ground, setting clusters of thorn trees on fire... and blowing the leg off a Marine only fifty meters away from me.

Dirt sprayed up as I skidded to a halt, lurching back toward the crippled suit. Chambers, that was what the IFF said. I knew the corporal by name, remembered a young, open face, eyes bright with intelligence, but didn't know much about him beyond that. He was alive, for the moment, but he wasn't screaming. The suit had already hit him with a neural block, probably a cocktail of painkillers and a sedative because it had deemed his wounds too severe to think clearly anyway.

He wasn't moving, wasn't speaking, but his heart was still beating, and I slid in beside him, grabbing his suit by the arm and draping it over my shoulder, lifting him to his remaining foot. The remaining leg was locked straight, the suit's way of making it easier to evacuate him, but carrying another Vigilante was awkward and dangerous, making both of us a bigger target. Chambers' heart rate fluttered in the IFF display and I cursed.

"Walton, you copy?" I asked, falling into a slow, lumbering jog that was as fast as I could make while carrying all that weight. "We need a dustoff right the fuck now as close as you can get to this location. We have wounded."

"I read you, Cam." The man was cool and relaxed, or at least his voice was. "Dunstan and Brandano have almost got the airspace cleared, shouldn't be a problem." A pause. "Head due southeast, three klicks... there's a clearing there where I can set down."

"Meet you there," I said, sighing. This was bad. Chambers hadn't just lost a leg... the flash burns from a plasma blast had likely caused internal injuries as well, and even with the suit's on-board medical care, he had maybe an hour to live without an auto-doc.

But if we could get a dustoff, and if the *Orion* had taken care of that Skrela ship, he'd make it. Then he'd spend weeks in the ship's infirmary, floating in nanite-infused biotic fluid while the auto-doc tried to regrow the parts of him that had been burned off. And God help us all when the ship ran out of biotic fluid. We'd gone through a lot of it.

"Sir!" Endicott asked, running beside me, his voice strained as if he was doing the running instead of the suit. "Let me take him from you..."

He reached out and I shrugged off the corporal's arm, passing the wounded man over.

Everything was heat and light and screaming warnings in my helmet, and I scrambled backward, the air going out of me, the hair on my arms curling away, the moisture going out of my mouth, out of my skin with an audible sizzle. The suit's helmet was a solid metal shield, the optical view coming from the external cameras, so I wasn't blinded by the flash, but the cameras were, at least for a second. When the image came back, it showed two dead men.

There was nothing left of Chambers... the poor, unlucky bastard had taken the brunt of the hit. Endicott had only got the edge of the blast, but it was enough to carve a trough right through his helmet. Nothing was left inside of it.

"Fuck!" I blurted.

Skrela were gathered in a protective swarm around the outside of the dome, laying down fire at us like they thought we were going to try to reclaim it. I ground out another curse, this one heartfelt rather than surprised, and fired back at them, even though there was no point to it at all. And then I turned and ran.

I didn't want to leave them there. Once upon a time, I would have been tempted to risk the lives of other Marines to get their bodies back to the ship, but there wasn't that much to bring back, and we'd wind up ejecting them into space because there was no place left to store corpses. Even the suits were beyond salvaging, and yes, I'd been forced to think on those terms now. Being in command sucked.

"Singh, get them out of range now! Get to that fucking LZ!"

Before we lost anyone else...

―――

I was glad we were boosting. There was something more satisfying about raging in gravity than trying to do it in free fall.

"Son of a fucking bitch!" The curse filled the hollow echo of my knuckles on the hard plastic of the locker.

There was no one else in the compartment, though at this point, I wouldn't have cared if there were. A fusion fire was burning inside my gut, and I didn't have any containment field, no dampeners, just the hot plasma trying to claw its way out of me in an explosion that would take out half the ship.

I'd lost people before. Losing Top had hurt a lot worse than this, but the anger burned brighter.

"Are you okay?"

I spun at the voice before it penetrated my thick head that it was Vicky. She pushed the hatch shut behind her and closed the distance between us in a step, pulling me into an embrace. I wanted to pull away, didn't want to be comforted, but she held me in place. Vicky was strong, and a lot more sensible than I was.

"No," I admitted, slipping my arms around her. "No, I'm not fucking okay."

"Nance and the crew took down the Skrela ship," she told me, still holding tight. I'd gotten rid of my skinsuit but hadn't pulled on fresh clothes yet, not before I had the chance to take a shower, and I felt strange holding her in a uniform against my bare skin. "The fighters took a lot more time or we wouldn't have taken so long to rendezvous with the drop-ship." A long pause. "I'm sorry about Chambers and Endicott."

I tried to talk, but there was something blocking the way and I had to take another second to get it out.

"I never called him Top." The words wrung me out like a dishrag, and I sagged against Vicky. "I know he wanted me to. He wanted to be Top to my Skipper, but Goddammit, Vick, I'm not the Skipper. I never will be. And no one else can be Top for me." I sobbed, tears coming despite everything. "I should have called him Top."

"We've lost people before," she reminded me.

"Yes, we have," I said, the words coming out harder than I'd thought they would, propelled by an anger I couldn't hold back anymore. "And every time we do, it gets more and more fucking pointless." I pushed away from her, leaning back against the locker, the plastic cold against my skin. "I *told* him... I fucking told him. We didn't need to go down there. There was no *reason.* He wouldn't fucking listen to me and now we've lost two more Marines." Shaking my head, I clenched my hands into fists so they'd stop shaking. "Two Marines who *trusted* me to get them through this. I swear to God, Vicky... I'm gonna rip his head off and shit down his Goddamned throat."

Plastic rang with another blow, this one from the heel of my hand, and I wanted it to be Marcus Hachette's face.

"Calm down." Vicky's hands clasped my shoulders. "Getting into a fight isn't going to accomplish anything, particularly not in front of the crew. They're all on edge enough as it is."

"You think our Marines aren't?" I shot back. "I could barely look them in the eye when we got off the drop-ship. What the hell am I gonna tell them?"

"You're the Skipper now, whether you like it or not." I opened my mouth to object but she put a finger to my lips. "To them, you are. You're all they have. You know that, right? You think Singh can lead them? You think he's not looking for someone to hold his hand just like the rest of them?"

"Jesus." I'd meant it as a curse, but it was more like a prayer. "I can't be *him*. I want someone to hold *my* hand."

Vicky smiled and grabbed my hand in hers.

"You know I'll always be here." She nodded off at the hatch to the showers. "We'll be at safe Transition point in an hour. Go get cleaned up." Vicky hesitated, smile disappearing. "Once we're in T-space, we'll have to have a memorial for them."

"Another one." I rubbed at my eyes as if I could get rid of the images that way. "How many does this make?"

"I've stopped counting. But we're still here."

"For how long?"

"Go." She pushed me toward the showers. "Cool off. And don't say a word to Hachette unless I'm there."

"Yes, ma'am," I sighed. "Love you."

She kissed me.

"Love you too, Alvarez."

She let go and slipped back out the hatch, leaving me alone. I stared after her. I'd let her think she'd managed to talk me down, but the anger hadn't disappeared, only sunk deeper into my gut. I knew she was right, that I couldn't just walk onto the bridge and punch Hachette out. I mean, the way things were going I might be able to get away with it, but it wouldn't make things better.

But I swore right there in front of God and anyone else that might be listening... these were the last Marines I was going to let die for nothing. And neither Hachette nor all the ancient alien gods in the universe were going to change my mind.

[6]

The deep, chanting tones of the Salat al-Janazah funeral prayer sounded in the background, read by the computer through the speakers in the hangar bay. The company stood at attention, respectful if uncomprehending. None of the rest of us were Muslims, though Chambers had been.

Endicott had been easy, non-denominational Christian. Singh had said the prayer for him. Back in the war, there would have been chaplains on the troop ships, one for each major religion, but this was a top-secret Intelligence mission and we had to make do with recordings and computer simulations and volunteers.

The prayer ended and Singh looked to me. I stepped in front of the formation, letting out a deep breath. I knew neither man was qualified at *all* to deliver their eulogy, but the hard truth was, *no one* had known them that well. Maybe the original First Platoon leader, but he was gone for months now. I'd read their jackets and talked to everyone who'd interacted with them while I'd had the chance, in the few hours I'd had before the ceremony, and I'd just have to do the best I could.

"At ease," I told the company.

They relaxed from attention, but only physically. Emotionally, they were all still stiff and brittle. It was plain in their eyes, in the set of their shoulders and the uncomfortable shuffling of their feet. To one side of the formation were Dunstan, Brandano, Walton, and their flight crews formed up in their own square, and beside them was Lilandreth. I'd been surprised to see her here, taking part in this uniquely human ceremony, but I suppose she'd felt some sort of responsibility.

I was more surprised—and disappointed—at who *hadn't* shown up. Colonel Hachette was conspicuous by his absence, and I knew I wasn't the only one who'd noticed. Of course, I hadn't gone out of my way to report to him after the mission either. I'd left that to Lilandreth, with Dwight's assistance, and Hachette hadn't insisted on my presence when the decision had been made for where to set course for next.

Two empty pairs of boots sitting behind me reminded me of my duty, and I tried to organize my thoughts and give the men the respect they were due.

"We're here to remember Corporal Samuel Chambers," I said, "and acting First Sergeant Leo Endicott." I looked to Vicky and she gave me an encouraging nod from the side of the formation. "These men lost their lives far from their homes... farther than any human has gone before. Some of you may consider that a waste, but I don't think Corporal Chambers and First Sergeant Endicott would agree. They were Marines. They volunteered for service, volunteered for the Commonwealth Marine Corps, and volunteered for this operation under Fleet Intelligence, and I can't think that either of these men dreamed of a long and peaceful life close to home. If given the choice of that or dying in battle against alien monsters on a strange, uncharted world, I think I know which they'd have picked."

A few nods at that, but most of them didn't look convinced. That's okay—I wasn't either.

"Sam Chambers left his home in Toronto at the age of twenty, left behind a scholarship to Northeast Regional University because he'd always dreamed of being a Marine. He didn't consider this a sacrifice, didn't think of lost opportunities. He'd been too young to fight in the war, but Sam was determined to do his part to serve the Commonwealth. And when the opportunity came to volunteer for this operation, he didn't hesitate. He was as devoted to the Corps as he was to his faith, and the only thing more important to him than being a Marine was being a faithful servant of God."

And if it hadn't been my version of God, well... that was all right. God was pretty big, so maybe He was different things to different people. If not, I hoped He would take into consideration the fact that Chambers had been a Marine, which had to count for something.

"Leo Endicott," I continued, "had a lot more experience. Combat was nothing new to him. He served with distinction in the war, fighting in a lot of the same battles I did and receiving commendations for his actions during the taking of the Tahni homeworld." I might have left that part out if Lan-Min-Gen and his Shock Troopers had attended, but this mission hadn't involved them and I suppose they didn't owe any particular devotion to Chambers or Endicott. "After the war ended, he could have done what a lot of us veterans did—what Captain Sandoval and I did, get out of the military and try his hand at being a civilian, take advantage of all the benefits afforded to us. Instead, Leo decided that his days as a Marine weren't over yet... and I guess, in that, he was more self-aware than I was, because well, here I am."

A few chuckles at that, which was a little relief from the grim, unrelenting depression.

"But Leo didn't want to be stuck guarding some outpost or sitting on occupation duty on Tahn-Skyyiah. He wanted to be where the action was, and a special operation with Fleet Intelligence promised plenty of that. Leo Endicott died as he lived, doing his duty, trying to help me get Sam Chambers back to the drop-ship, get him medical aid. It was how he would have wanted to go out, trying to help his Marines."

Well, *maybe*. Better to believe that than to think this had all been a huge letdown for Endicott.

"Leo didn't have a wife, didn't have kids. The Corps was his family and First Platoon were his kids. He thought of you all that way and wouldn't have regretted giving everything to protect you." Something tightened inside my chest and the next words came hard. "More than anything, he wanted to be Top. He wanted all of us to see him that way, and I won't begrudge him that."

I nodded to Gunny Czarnecki, formerly Third Platoon sergeant, now acting First Sergeant. Still not Top though.

"Company!" she barked, and the platoon sergeants echoed her with "Platoon!" in the space after the preparatory command. "Atten-*shun!*"

We all snapped to attention and I performed an about-face.

"Present... *arms!*"

We saluted the empty boots. Under more normal circumstances, we'd have had a full display with holograms of the deceased that showed their decorations and record, but that was something else we lacked out here. We had nothing but each other and a recorded instrumental of "Amazing Grace."

"Order... *arms!*" Czarnecki said at the last notes of the song.

I released the salute and about-faced again. There were unabashed tears on some faces, but more than sorrow, I saw rage.

Shit.

"Platoon leaders, PMCS on the suits until lunch, then your Marines are released until breakfast." I hesitated. I wasn't going to like this, but it was necessary. "All platoon leaders come to my quarters after dinner for debriefing." Another nod to the first sergeant.

"Company!"

"Platoon!"

"Dis-*missed*!"

———

"Do we even have enough room in here for this?" Vicky wondered, looking around the compartment.

She had a point. This was a good-sized ship, but it was still a military vessel, which always meant space was at a premium. We had the double-sized bunk, two desks with a foldout chair each, two fold-down emergency acceleration couche,s and that was about it. I shrugged.

"There's space enough. It won't be for that long."

The shorter the better. I fidgeted on the bunk like I was six years old again and trying to sit still while my mother gave me a haircut, then checked the time again. They should have been here by now. I was thinking that, but when the knock came, I still nearly jumped out of the bunk. Vicky shot me a crooked smile and went to open the hatch.

The platoon leaders filed in, led by Singh, sharing nearly the same troubled expression.

"Sir, ma'am," Singh said, nodding.

Vicky was about to push the hatch shut when a hand intercepted it and Dunstan stepped through.

"Kyler," Vicky blurted. "What are you..."

But he wasn't alone. Brandano followed behind him, dour and scowling as usual, the only combat pilot I'd ever met who wasn't cool and self-consciously good-natured. Walton and Cheung, the other drop-ship pilot, squeezed in after and I stared at them, bemused for a second, then checked the hallway.

"Anyone else coming?" Vicky wondered, shutting the hatch. "Captain Nance? The chief bosun's mate?"

"Naw," Dunstan said, leaning against one of our desks. "Not that he might not be thinking the same thing we are. But it'd be damned tough for him to slip away without anyone noticing, y'know?"

"Hold on," I said, raising a hand, palm out. "I called my *platoon leaders* here for a debriefing and to... straighten some things out. What are *you* four doing here?"

"Searching desperately for a square meter of deck at the moment," Walton said dryly, folding down one of the acceleration couches and falling into it.

"We're here for the same reason, man," Dunstan said. "To like, straighten some things out."

"We can't keep doing this shit, sir," Singh said, throwing up his hands in frustration. "Colonel Hachette has lost his fucking mind and someone needs to relieve him of command."

"Someone?" Vicky repeated, eyebrow shooting up. "Who the hell is *someone*?"

"You and Captain Nance," Singh put in. The other platoon leaders said nothing, seemingly content to let the former company XO speak for them. "If you went to him and talked to him about this, we all think he'd agree with you."

"Oh, you all *think* that, do you?" I shot back. I tried to pace around the compartment, but there wasn't room for it and I wound up just turning full circle. "You chuckleheads know there's a word for this shit, right? It's fucking called *mutiny*! And it's one of the few things the Commonwealth still has the death penalty for!"

Dunstan scoffed, head tilting back as the sound devolved into mocking laughter.

"Ain't you forgetting one thing, man?" he said, spreading his hands in front of him. "For us to get convicted and sentenced to death for mutiny by the Commonwealth, wouldn't we all have to be, you know... *back in the Commonwealth*?" Dunstan snorted again. "And we all know that ain't happening, ever. This whole thing is a huge fucking waste of time."

"And *lives*," Singh put in, bitterness weighing down his tone. "*Our* lives, mostly. Look, sir, I have two kids back on Earth, both of them teenagers. I miss them like hell. But I'm not ready to sacrifice everyone just for a tiny chance to see them again. It's not right and it's not what any of us signed up for."

"We ain't gonna fuckin' do it, man," Dunstan declared. "Not anymore."

I looked at Brandano, surprised he was here and had fallen in line with the others. The tall man shrugged.

"He made this decision for all of us, Cam. He thinks it's justifiable because he's the commander, but I've checked the regs."

"There's a reg about being lost in the nether regions of the galaxy after being shot through an alien gateway?" Vicky asked, goggling at him.

"Not exactly," Brandano admitted. "But there's definitely regs about being marooned and unable to return to human space. And they're pretty damned clear. Once the commander determines that the problem with the drive systems can't be repaired, the guidance is to settle in the safest, most survivable location possible and wait for possible rescue." He shrugged. "As Kyler so eloquently put it, *that* ain't fucking happening."

"It's important we do it soon," Walton added, running a hand through his thick, blond hair. It was longer than regulation, like many of the men and women here. "We're heading farther into this Cauldron of Creation shit, and if he keeps sending us to scout out every shithole we come to, well..." He shook his head. "Maybe the ship's crew will survive, but none of *us* will."

"We have to face the fact that we're not getting back," Dunstan said, smacking the back of one hand into the palm of the other to emphasize the words. "We have to stop chasing our tails and find some place we can set up shop." Walton nodded in agreement.

"We got a starship, we got fusion reactors, we got fabricators, and we know a few places where there are already human civilizations. We can help them out, get them on the road to something approaching modern society and start trying to live our lives."

I regarded him silently for a moment, then scanned across the rest of them before I replied.

"We start trying to be conquistadors here," I warned them, "we may not like what we turn into."

"We're not talking about *conquering* anyone," Walton objected. "Just helping them out, finding somewhere that would welcome us because of what we have to offer."

"We could still lose people doing that. Maybe more people than we've lost already. Are you guys ready to face that?"

"At least we'd be fighting for something real," Singh said, arms crossed, eyes on the deck.

That same sullen stubbornness was reflected in the stances and faces of the others, and I sighed, shoulders sagging. I wasn't about to talk them out of this.

Did I really *want* to? I agreed with them. I'd made their arguments to Hachette and Top before, and I'd been satisfied that he'd considered doing just that, but he insisted that they needed to at least *try* to find a way back first. That had seemed reasonable... then. I pressed the heels of my hands against my eyes. They stung from lack of sleep, from physical and emotional exhaustion. I couldn't think straight.

"Listen," I finally said, "we can't just jump into this headlong without taking some time to consider our options. You guys are going from step B to step Z and skipping everything in-between. Colonel Hachette isn't psychotic, he's just dealing with stress and loss, just like we are. I know if I can sit him down—yes, maybe along with Captain Nance—that he'd listen to reason. I mean, what choice does he have?" I waved a hand. "It's not like he can do this on his own."

Dunstan and Walton looked at each other, then the rest of the officers present. Nods all around, and again, Dunstan spoke for the others.

"I trust you, Cam. You've never steered me wrong. So, we'll give you the chance to talk to him before we do anything. But not forever."

"Understood," I said, nodding. "Believe me, I'm not waiting forever either. The man has to bend or we're all going to die out here."

That seemed to satisfy them, and they all stood, moving to the door, and God knows I would have been happy to have all these people out of the little compartment, but I wasn't quite finished yet.

"Hold on." I raised a finger in warning. "One thing. Until I talk to him, until you hear back from me, not one fucking *word* of this to anyone else. Not to the ship's crew, for obvious reasons, and not to any NCO or enlisted Marine." I made sure to meet each of their eyes. "If this gets out, we're totally fucked, and I don't mean because we'll be facing charges. We're all balancing on a razor's edge, and the *only* fucking thing keeping us from blowing apart is the fact that we're all committed to doing our duty, to following the lawful orders of our superior officers.." A sweeping gesture like a blade slashing sideways across all of them. "This gets out before we have things locked down, before it's..." I frowned at Vicky. "What's the French phrase again?"

"A *fait accompli*," she supplied.

"Yeah, that. If this gets out early, then this whole ship is fucked. People are going to die... maybe *all* of us. I'm not going to be responsible for that, and I hope all of you are smart enough that you don't want to be either. Everybody get me?"

Nods again, maybe a little shamefaced.

"Okay then, get out of my room." I jerked a thumb at the door over my shoulder. "I need some sleep."

I waited until the last of them had gone before I collapsed onto my bunk, all pretense of strength and certainty evaporating. Vicky swiveled a chair out from one of the desks and fell into it, blowing out a breath.

"Shit," I murmured. "What the hell are we gonna do now?"

[7]

Breakfast was tasteless, and not just because it was the same old mass-produced, dry-stored shit masquerading as scrambled eggs and sausage. I was way too used to that, and the spices—which were also artificial—could do a lot to mask the blandness of it. No, it was tasteless this particular morning because of what I was going to have to do. I had no idea how to approach Hachette, even less of an idea how to broach the subject. He wasn't going to be happy about it, and in his current state of mind, I had no idea how he'd take it.

"We fucked up," Vicky had said last night after we'd gone to bed. "He was a basket case, ready to give up on everything, and we should have left him that way."

"No, *I* fucked up," I'd admitted. "He wasn't fit to command and I should have talked to Nance about it then, but I wanted Hachette to take charge so I wouldn't have to."

She hadn't agreed with me, but neither had she argued with me. I was eating alone this morning, not because of that but because Vicky had gone back to keep an eye on the company—and especially on the officers. I believed they'd meant what they'd said yesterday, but people can change their minds.

I wasn't fit company this morning anyway. Anyone could see it with one look at me. Anyone *human*.

"Cameron Alvarez, may I sit beside you?"

Lan-Min-Gen didn't wait for permission, just pulled the chair across from me away from the table and sat in it. I looked around, checking to see if anyone was watching us. Apparently, a Tahni sitting with a human had become a usual enough thing that no one was.

"Your chairs are not comfortable," Lan-Min-Gen said, leaning forward as if this revelation was a top-secret bit of data he was sharing with me at great risk to his life.

"Well, they weren't designed for Tahni," I allowed, then washed down the bland eggs with a glass of bland juice. "What can I do for you?"

Lan-Min-Gen didn't answer immediately. His long fingers tapped against the table, demonstrating their extra joints in a way that made me suddenly lose what little appetite I'd had.

"I find myself," he said, after a long moment, "in a very strange and awkward position, one I have not faced among humans before, for obvious reasons." Lan-Min-Gen's unnatural fingers intertwined and my stomach twisted at the sight. "I owe both you and Colonel Hachette a debt for what you did for us back among the Khitan, when you risked your lives to rescue my flight crew. I am unused to being in personal debt to *anyone*, even among my own people, much less among you humans. I dislike this more intensely than I can express to you with my limited knowledge of your language."

"You're doing pretty well," I assured him, clenching my jaw to avoid laughing. I didn't especially *like* the Tahni, but once they learned to communicate with us in our language, it became clearer and clearer that they weren't as radically different from us as we'd originally believed. "Is that it? The feeling of debt makes you uncomfortable?"

"Would that it were that simple. The debt has been called in... and yet, I can't pay it. Not without betraying half of it."

I frowned, dropping my fork to the plate with a too-loud clatter.

"Is there some translation problem?" I wondered. "Because I'm not getting you."

His expression was not one I was familiar with, and since I'd seen Tahni confused, angry, and even happy in the brief time I'd been dealing with them face-to-face, I wondered what it meant.

"Colonel Hachette called me to his compartment earlier, a few hours before this meal began to be served." Which was a long-winded way of saying "this morning," but I understood the confusion. Lan-Min-Gen was used to the Tahni system, which probably didn't attribute arbitrary times of the planetary day to sleep periods on a ship. "He told me that you and the officers under your command intended to betray him."

Hackles rose on the back of my neck, and without intention I planted my feet flat on the deck, preparatory to leaping out of my chair in aid of fight or flight.

"Why the hell would he think *that*?" I kept my voice low only through a supreme effort of will, because I wanted to yelp the question.

"He showed me a security video taken from the compartment you share with Vicky Sandoval." Again that same expression, and this time, I got the sense that it was their equivalent of embarrassment. "Understand, I would never have sought out something so private and invasive and would have refused to watch had I known the source. It showed your officers and the pilots of your Intercepts and drop-ships in your compartment, and some of them were speaking of rebellion."

"That *motherfucker."*

He was spying on us. I mean, *every* compartment has security cameras that are there in case of emergencies such as depressurization or hull damage, but they're not constantly monitored unless someone *orders* them to be monitored. Hachette had to have specifically directed the security system to listen in on my room and record the video.

"I do not comprehend," Lan-Min-Gen admitted, "the connection between his accusations and the idea that he had sexual congress with his mother."

"Did you watch the entire recording?" I asked, grinding the words out between my teeth, trying very hard not to lose my temper.

"No. I refused once it became clear that this was something recorded without your knowledge or consent." He shook himself as if he'd eaten something distasteful. "This sort of action is anathema to our people, and I am deeply disturbed you find it acceptable."

"A lot of us don't. But if you'd watched to the end, you'd see that I spent most of the meeting trying to calm those people down and get them to agree to sit back, cool off, and let me talk to Colonel Hachette before they did anything foolish." My lip curled into a snarl, and it took me a second to bring my expression back to something neutral. "And *he* had to have seen that too. Why did he show you the recording? What did he want from you?"

I was afraid I already knew, and the next few words confirmed the validity of the sinking feeling in my stomach.

"According to Colonel Hachette, since he could no longer count on the loyalty of your Marines and knew that his own ship's security could not match you in combat, he wished the aid of my Shock Troopers in opposing any such rebellion against his rule."

Yeah, there it was. I hated repeating myself, but...

"Mother*fucker*." My gaze flickered back and forth across the room with the paranoid conviction that ship's security and Tahni soldiers were about to stream through the entrances to the chow hall and take me into custody. Finally, I settled back into regarding Lan-Min-Gen. "What did you tell him?"

"That my Shock Troopers were not his personal guard," Lan-Min-Gen said, and if I wasn't sure what outrage looked like on a Tahni face, I was pretty certain I detected the context in his choice of words. "I said if he was attacked we would defend him for the sake of honor, but that I refused to attack you simply on his word." The Tahni's head cocked to the side. "And I would tell you the same thing. I will not act against Marcus Hachette, despite the debt I owe you."

Relief lifted just a fraction of the weight from my shoulders, and I sucked in a deep breath like we'd just finished a high-g boost.

"I wouldn't ask you to," I assured him. "The only request I'll make is that you leave this thing between him and me. I need to go talk to him, get this straightened out, just the two of us. Can you do that?"

"Of course. It is according to the Path."

Yeah, whatever the hell *that* meant.

"He's not coming out of there," Vicky declared, shaking her head.

Staring at the screen of my 'link, I couldn't help but agree. The view shifted as the camera rocked with the sway of Kyler Dunstan's hips, his 'link attached to his belt. The corridor outside Colonel Hachette's private office was on the way from nowhere special to nowhere useful, so the eyes of the two ship's security officers stationed outside the compartment never left

Dunstan as he passed them by. Their hands rested on the buttstocks of slung pulse carbines and their stances went straighter, but they said nothing.

Knowing Kyler, he probably waved as he went by.

"Shit," I murmured. "I've tried calling him six times, messaged him over and over asking for a meeting, but he doesn't leave his compartment. Even has his meals brought to him under guard. Paranoid fuck." Settling back into the chair behind my desk, I sighed in frustration. "I guess I could just go knock on his door."

"Sure," Vicky scoffed, her laugh sharp and mocking. "If you want those security officers to haul you off to the brig." She frowned. "Do we *have* a brig?"

"I can't remember. They'd stick me somewhere though, you're right about that." I leaned my chin against my fist and tried to think. "I could arm up a squad and bring them with me, dare the assholes to try to arrest me."

"Oh, yeah, I'm sure that'd get him to open his door, no problem."

"You got any better ideas?" I asked, scowling.

"Well, last time he wouldn't come out of his room, we threatened to have Dwight pick the lock." Her eyes went upward as if she were talking about God.

I grimaced. I didn't like this. Not that Dwight had done anything in particular to make me distrust him... well, except that time he'd dragged us all to this Godforsaken corner of the galaxy without asking our leave. I distrusted him anyway. He was a sentient AI created by the Predecessors, and since I had no particular reason to like or trust the Predecessors, I saw no reason why I should like or trust the AI created in their image.

"Dwight," I said, trying not to betray the reluctance in my tone of voice, "are you there?"

"I'm always here, Captain Alvarez," he said, and for an AI,

he sure could imitate a self-satisfied human well enough. "How may I help you?"

At least we didn't have a holographic projector in our compartment, and he didn't bother to show us the simulacrum of a human male in a Fleet uniform on the notification screen on the bulkhead. It was bad enough knowing he could see and hear any of us at any time on the security scanners.

"Do you know what's going on between Colonel Hachette and me?" I asked him. There was the chance he didn't. Just because he *could* spy on any of us didn't necessarily mean he had been.

"I am aware. Colonel Hachette asked me to run a search through the security scanners for any mention of the word 'mutiny.' I recorded the conversation between you and the other officers here in your compartment."

"You did *what?*" Vicky exploded, jumping to her feet, glaring at the overhead.

"Why the hell would you *do* that?" I asked him, spreading my hands in disbelief.

"Because he asked me to. Should I not have done that?"

My head hurt, and screaming at an ethereal collection of ones and zeros wouldn't improve the headache. It was too easy to forget that Dwight wasn't human by any stretch, no matter how much he sounded like one of us.

"Colonel Hachette is making a mistake," I explained patiently. "He's pulling us deeper into trouble we can't handle. I need to talk to him about this, try to make him listen to reason, and you feeding into his paranoia by making him think I'm his enemy isn't helping things."

"I admit, I'm confused. You think he's in error, but I thought that you agreed that finding the source of the Skrela infestation was the correct course of action. What changed your mind?"

That wasn't a bad question, actually, though I wasn't sure I could explain it to him adequately.

"I supported the decision to follow the intelligence we got from the Khitan," I clarified. "But we *know* where the source is supposed to be and we don't need to be landing troops on every system we come to. We wasted two lives and we don't have enough troops to do that, even if it was worth the risk. He asked for my opinion on whether to do it, then he ignored it and did what he wanted anyway, and now two of my Marines are dead and we didn't gain a damned thing from it." I shut my mouth. I'd been ranting, and I doubted that was going to help my case. "I need to talk to him, but he won't answer my calls, won't leave his compartment, and if I come to him, he's going to have me arrested. We need you to unlock his door and get me inside." I looked over to Vicky. "We can lure the guards away with... something. I don't know."

"I find myself in what I suppose could be called a moral quandary," Dwight said slowly, as if he was thinking it through, though I knew that was an affectation. "If I allow you into Colonel Hachette's private quarters, he might be harmed."

"Not by me," I promised. "As long as he doesn't try to hurt me, I won't do anything but talk."

Dwight heaved a heavy sigh, and it was all I could do not to roll my eyes. More theatrics from the AI.

"Very well. But I must insist you be unarmed when you enter."

Now I *did* roll my eyes.

"Well that'll work out great," Vicky said, "just as long as he doesn't shoot you the second he sees you."

"I'll worry about that." And yes, I *was* worried about that. "How the hell are we going to get the security guards away from their post?"

Vicky's brow furled in thought and I thought for a second she was about to punt the problem back to me, but then a smile slowly spread across her face.

"I think," she said, "I have an idea."

[8]

"You know that God is dog backward, right?"

The non-sequitur brought my eyes up from my food and across our table to search for the owner of that particular bit of eye-popping philosophical truth. I couldn't find him at first until the other man spoke.

"What the fuck does that even mean? You sound like a fucking idiot." The philosopher was a Fleet enlisted technician, tall and skinny and completely bald, while the skeptic was shorter and stouter, with dark, curly hair, though they shared a rank and a general unwashed, unkempt air that told of too many months trapped on this ship.

I shouldn't have been paying attention to this. It was stupid and pointless and I had much more important things to think about, but it was like a slow-motion train wreck and I couldn't tear my eyes away. I wasn't the only one. The other Fleet crew at their table were watching with knowing smiles as if this kind of thing happened all the time. How the hell had I not noticed these guys before?

"Well at least I thought about something deep," the tall one objected, picking at his food sullenly. That seemed to be too much for tubby, who tossed his fork down on the plate with a loud clatter, his face screwed up in anger.

"You haven't had a coherent thought about anything! God is dog backward?" The man threw his hands up in obvious vexation. "Does that mean that God is the opposite of a dog? Is God a fucking cat? Is that what you're trying to say?"

"Oh yeah?" Skinny's pale, horsey face went red. "Well, what kind of deep thoughts have you had about it?"

"I've had a lot deeper thoughts than that," Tubby blustered, a few bits of his meal sprinkling the words. "And I put them a lot more eloquently, motherfucker."

Skinny looked down his long nose at the other man, his expression disapproving.

"And I suppose that's your idea of eloquence?"

"Yes it is! I'm one eloquent motherfucker, motherfucker!" Tubby went silent, turning his attention back to his food, as passive-aggressive as if the two of them were married.

The others at the table shrugged and went back to their own meals and conversations, only a few chuckles as commentary.

"Hey, asshole!" Chuck Brandano said, shoving Kyler Dunstan back out of the line for the processor and bringing my head around like I was a spectator at a tennis match. "You just spilled coffee all over my last clean jacket! What the fuck is wrong with you?"

Dunstan's tray crashed to the deck, a poor imitation of spaghetti with meatballs splattering across the younger pilot's pants on its way downward, and if I hadn't known better, I would have bet that he was actually angry. His face turned a brighter red than the edging around his pilot wings and he lunged for Brandano, fists balled up.

"What the fuck's up your ass, Brandano?" Dunstan bellowed, getting up in the other man's face. "You've been pushing me since I came on board this fucking ship!"

I stood and backed away from lunch. Too much shit was happening at meals lately. I couldn't remember the last time I actually enjoyed eating. If this had been real, I'd obviously have been running up to separate them, since the last thing we needed was to be fighting each other. Except right now, it was *exactly* what we needed.

Dunstan threw the first punch, though I think that was Brandano holding back, because I knew he'd wanted to take a swing at Dunstan since the first time he'd met him. I didn't watch the rest of it, just made sure that the rest of the flight crews rushed in to join. I hadn't seen a good fistfight since the war, but there was something about knowing this one was fake that didn't make it quite so entertaining. The Intercept crews went in first, ostensibly trying to break the whole thing up, while everyone else either froze in place, shocked into inaction, or jumped up from their tables and backed away.

We'd picked lunch for the whole thing instead of dinner because there were, statistically, more of the crew here at the same time... and because there'd be more people reporting it. Everyone assumed that the flight crews would break the fight up, but Brandano yelled a curse and punched Dunstan's crew chief, and then was tackled by the copilot. There was a lot of cursing, but I kind of filtered it out, ignoring the brawl, more interested in the next group to enter it. Walton and his crew waded in and I had no idea which side they were supposed to be on, but all they wound up doing was adding to the chaos.

Walton's crew chief tumbled out of the melee and into a table, followed closely by Brandano's copilot, and the two of them rolled over multiple tabletops, tossing everything off of them like ill-tempered cats. Or, like regular cats. Food and trays flew in every direction and people shouted for the combatants to stop, while others yelled for security.

That had been what I was waiting for. When the first of the

ship's security guards stormed through one entrance to the chow hall, I ducked out of the other. I didn't go directly to Hachette's compartment because that would have been one, pretty obvious, and two, would have been picked up by the security cameras. Instead, I headed for the last corridor junction before brass country and waited.

An alarm hooted urgently, one I'd never heard before on this ship—not the alert for high-grav boost or Transition or enemy contact, but the one that called all ship's security in. There weren't that many, maybe twelve all told on a ship the size of the *Orion*, but Lt. Jean Stilwell, their commander, wasn't stupid enough to pull the guards off Hachette's compartment for a simple fistfight. I'd seen her and her people in action, and while they weren't combat troops, they were professionals and took their job seriously.

Which is why I really regretted this next part. Vicky met me at the last intersection, Singh and the other platoon leaders in tow, pulse carbines slung around their shoulders. The weapons had been locked in the armory, and Hachette, not being stupid, had changed the codes. And I, being just as paranoid as Hachette and hopefully even *less* stupid, had written myself a backdoor into the armory months ago.

I fell into step behind them, none of us saying a word, knowing the sort of trouble we'd be getting into if this went badly.

"No one fucking touch your trigger unless I say so," I reminded them. "Even if they shoot first, get me?"

"Yes, sir," Singh replied, though he didn't seem enthusiastic about it.

We were only about twenty meters away now and the security guards had noticed us, moving out into the center of the corridor, the muzzles of their weapons rising. I clenched my teeth and stepped forward through the group, standing between two sets of guns.

"Sir," one of the guards said, "I'm going to need you and your people to disarm and leave the area..."

"Here's what's going to happen, Petty Officer Mbeki," I interrupted, stepping within two meters of the two armed, nervous guards. "I'm not armed." I opened my jacket and turned around, showing him I wasn't carrying a weapon. "I'm going in alone to talk to Colonel Hachette. Just talk. That's *going* to happen no matter what you two do. The only difference is, you can either step aside, let me in, and then stay out here and make sure nothing bad happens, or you can try to stop me." I shook my head. "That's not going to go well for any of us. I've told my people to try to not hurt you, but if I don't get a chance to talk to the colonel in private, it could mean the death of everyone on this ship. So, like I said. I *am* going in there. The only question is whether we have to get into a firefight to make it happen."

"We have our orders, sir," Mbeki said, and if I couldn't see the stubborn set of his jaw through the visor of his helmet, I still knew it was there. "The only way you go in is if Colonel Hachette opens that door and lets you in."

"Dwight," I murmured.

"Go ahead and let him in, Petty Officer Mbeki," Hachette's voice came over the external compartment speaker. Or what *sounded* like Hachette's voice. That was the cool thing about having a sentient AI that listened to everything and recorded it.

The hatch slid open and I stepped through before Mbeki could question it. And *that* was the advantage of the senior officers having fancy, automated doors while the rest of us got the old-fashioned, manual kind. I knew Mbeki was going to try to follow me in, which was why we'd already rehearsed this. Vicky stepped in front of him, blocking his way just long enough for Dwight to shut the door behind us. And lock it.

Hachette sprang up from his desk at the sight of me, face going pale, hand clutching at his belt for the pulse pistol holstered there. I was on him before it could clear, grabbing his wrist and holding up my other hand in a forestalling gesture.

"I just want to talk," I said, using the same tone of voice I'd learned from every authority figure who'd ever pretended to be my friend back in Trans Angeles. It hadn't worked very well on me, but I was hoping Hachette would be more of a sucker for it since he came from a privileged upbringing. "Just take it easy. No one's going to hurt you."

"Yeah, you won't hurt me," Hachette snapped, sweat beading on his forehead. "You'll just take over the fucking ship and relieve me of my command."

But his hand came away from his pistol and I let loose of his wrist. Cautiously. He could try to draw it and catch me off guard, and I wasn't sure if he wasn't manic and paranoid enough now to just put a round through my chest without a second thought.

"That's what all my officers and all the combat pilots want," I agreed. Well, not *all*... the assault shuttle crews hadn't approached me, probably because they hadn't been put in the sort of semi-suicidal positions that the drop-ship and Intercept crews had been, over and over. "I told them not to do it, to let me try to talk to you."

"I know exactly what you said." The tone was accusatory, but I didn't flinch away from it.

"Yeah, I know you do. Dwight told us how you had him spying for you."

"That fucking traitorous piece of shit," Hachette raged, hands balling into fists as if he could punch the AI.

"Which means," I went on, raising my voice to drown out his temper tantrum, "that you heard what I said, and there is no rational reason for you to be holed up in here like it's a bunker with armed guards out front. I just want to talk."

"You keep repeating that like it's a mantra," he mumbled, walking over to his desk and sitting on the corner of it. "Why should I bother to listen to you? You're a Marine captain, and barely that. You aren't in command of this mission or this ship."

"You may not be much longer either," I warned him, and his eyes snapped up and bored into me. "Think about it, Colonel. You don't control the Marines, *I* do. You don't have the loyalty of the attack crews, *I* do. And you don't have the loyalty of the ship's crew, Captain Nance does." I tapped my chest demonstratively. "You think *I'm* the problem, but I'm the only one preventing the mutiny you're so afraid of. You think Nance wants to be out here, sticking our noses into every hornet's nest? You don't think he'd rather find some safe harbor and start building a life here like all the rest of us?"

"And you don't?" he demanded. "You and Sandoval have fewer ties back in the Commonwealth than any of the rest of us."

"Trust me, I wouldn't mind settling down out here and trying to make something better than we left," I told him. "But unlike just about everyone else, I don't believe we can do it while the Skrela are still out there, still a threat."

"Then why the hell are you here?" Hachette bellowed, standing from the desk, arms spread. "Why didn't you just tell your fucking Marines to get back to the mission and start acting like professionals?"

"Because this isn't a war, Colonel!" I didn't back away from his bellicose approach, going nose to nose with him. "It's not even a military operation anymore! You've gotten a lot more loyalty and cooperation and sacrifice under the circumstances than you should have counted on. And frankly, a lot more than you fucking deserve after the way you've acted the last few weeks. You need to stop thinking of yourself as the supreme commander of some grand military mission and start thinking of yourself as one of the last survivors on a lifeboat." The look on Hachette's face was sullen and stubborn, and I knew I wasn't reaching him. Time to play dirty. "You *know* that's what she'd tell you. Top. She wouldn't let you get away with this shit. She'd have already kicked your ass all over this fucking compartment."

That got to him. His lip curled into a snarl, face flushing, pupils dilating.

"Don't you dare fucking lecture me about what she'd do! You didn't know her like I did!"

"I knew how she acted when the pressure was on, when it was a matter of life and death, and she wouldn't have put up with you acting like a toddler throwing a fit. Grow up, grab your balls, and try to live up to the expectations she had for you."

Yeah, I was pretty much slapping him across the face, but he needed it. Hachette straightened and his hands went to his gunbelt. I tensed up, but he unbuckled it and tossed it onto his bunk and I relaxed. Maybe he was finally listening to reason.

"I've been wanting to do this for months," he confessed, then he launched himself across the compartment at me.

The fight in the chow hall had been a show, but this was for real, and the air went out of me as his shoulder slammed into my chest and the deck matched the impact on my back. Stars filled my vision like the flash from the explosion of pain in my chest and back, and conscious thought fled alongside my breath. For most people, even a Force Recon Marine, that would have been it. Hachette was centimeters taller and about ten kilos heavier and definitely had unarmed combat training through Fleet Intelligence.

But I had one thing going for me that he didn't. I'd been hit hard before. So many times, I'd lost count. I'd fought mostly boys and later men who were bigger than me, and giving up the first time I'd taken a shot wasn't an option. Surrendering wouldn't save me, it would just get me a worse beating, so I learned to fight back through pain, through the panic, through the confusion, fight back without seeing, through instinct.

I didn't think about it except in retrospect, but I could figure out how the process went. Hachette had trained in the same sort of unarmed combat courses I had, then honed that training with Top, which meant he'd go for a front mount. It would take him about two seconds from where he'd tackled me, and I'd already blown the best way to defend against it by not anticipating his takedown. I fought against it by bringing up my knees, planting a foot against his hip and pushing backward.

Hachette was heavy, and the motion did more to push me upward instead of shoving him backward, but either way worked. My other leg yanked free and I slammed him in the face with the sole of my boot. Unlike me, Hachette had never been punched in the face in a real fight. His yelp was probably more surprise than pain, but there was enough pain to make him let go and roll off.

I scrambled to my feet, gasping for breath, shaking my head to clear my vision. Blood poured out of Hachette's flattened nose, the look on his face one of disillusioned shock, and I probably should have ended it there, tried to talk him down.

But I was pissed. I'd bent over backward to try to work this whole thing out peacefully and Hachette had his head so far up his own ass, he couldn't let go of his pride and meet me halfway.

"Come on," I told him, my words a little more breathless and pained than I would have liked. I made a beckoning motion with both hands. "You wanted this. Come and get it, asshole."

Hachette wiped blood out of his face with the sleeve of his uniform jacket and stalked toward me. The compartment was large, easily three times the size of the one Vicky and I shared, and I used the space to maneuver, to force him to keep turning, keep him on the defensive. He'd be thinking in terms of moves, techniques, takedowns, combinations. He'd be running through the ones he'd trained with and trying to decide which would fit better, like he was back on Inferno in the training gym sparring against some junior NCO who wouldn't dare hurt him.

Usually, I wouldn't have thought at all. I'd have gone for his vulnerable spots with utmost speed and violence. Eyes, throat, ears, groin, knees. But the point of this wasn't to kill or disable him, it was to teach him the lesson that he wasn't the toughest dog in this fight and he wasn't going to intimidate me into falling in line. So, I did something stupid, something fancy, something Top would have kicked my ass for if I'd tried it while sparring her, something that only worked because he wasn't expecting it.

I'd tried this in training a grand total of twice and failed spectacularly on both attempts, but I had a feeling in my gut this time. Step forward, hook the back of his plant foot with my heel, throwing him off-balance...and then I spun into a jump round-house kick. It was the cardinal sin of a street-fight, drummed into my head over and over. Never kick above the waist.

But, oh my God did it feel good when one connected. My instep cracked across his jaw, and by the time my foot touched back to the floor, Hachette's eyes had rolled back into his head and he was on his way to the deck. I fought an instinct to try to catch him and instead relished in watching him fall. He wasn't knocked out for more than a two-count, his eyes fluttering open the second his back hit the deck, but I'd rung his bell.

I hitched my thumbs in my belt and regarded him coolly, dispassionately, as if I wasn't immensely satisfied with the opportunity to bash his face in.

"Are you done?" I wondered. "Or do you want to go another round?"

Hachette shoved himself up to a sitting position, and I thought for a moment that he wasn't ready to quit. I sighed. The point of this was to knock some sense into him, not beat him to death. If he kept this up, I'd have to hurt him bad enough to put him in an auto-med. But his shoulders slumped in defeat and he looked up at me dully.

"I guess," he began, then stopped and winced, hand going to the side of his jaw, which was already beginning to bruise up. "I guess," he started again more cautiously, "that this means you're in charge now."

"Fuck no!" I exclaimed, throwing up my hands. "Jesus Christ, man, you should try listening once in a while! I don't want to be in charge of this shitshow! I just want you to *listen* to me, particularly before you risk the lives of my Marines! Between Vicky and me, we have more combat experience than the rest of the company combined, and Goddammit, we've been down on every fucking landing this mission has made since we jumped into this place."

He hesitated, then nodded slowly.

"You don't want to go back to Yfingam then?"

The others did, that was for sure, and I thought for a second about telling him yes, saving all the Marines who might get killed if we didn't. But my conscience got the better of me and I shook my head.

"Not until we find where the Skrela are coming from. And whether there's any way to stop them." I stabbed a finger toward him. "But you have *got* to start acting like you give a shit about your people... and attending the memorial service would have been a good fucking start."

Hachette nodded, drew his knees up, rested his arms against them, and buried his face in his hands.

"I can't sleep, Cam," he admitted. "I tried alcohol, tried the shit the doc gave me, but every single night I wake up screaming her name, feeling the way I did when I heard she was killed. I can't think, and every time I try, I just get angrier and angrier. And I don't know who to blame except myself."

The air went out of me again, though this time it wasn't because I'd been slammed to the deck. I sat down next to him.

"You have to talk about it. I know you don't want to, but you *have* to."

"To who?' he wondered, and the words were perhaps the most hopeless thing I'd ever heard.

Fuck.

"To me I guess." I laughed humorlessly. "After all, I kicked your ass. You can tell me anything."

And by God, he did.

[9]

Nearly an hour later, I walked out of Hachette's compartment and straight into the bell-shaped muzzle of Jean Stilwell's sonic stunner. Her visor was up, so I knew it was her and I knew she was pissed.

"What the *fuck* do you think you're doing, sir?" she demanded.

I glanced past her and saw Vicky, Singh, and the other platoon leaders standing against the bulkhead in the corridor, their weapons on the deck while Fleet Security covered them with their stunners.

"We were just having a discussion about our strategic options, Lieutenant," Colonel Hachette said, coming out of the hatch behind me. "Kindly lower your weapon."

Stilwell stared at him, wide-eyed and disbelieving, probably because the man was already developing two black eyes and a swiftly coloring bruise on his jaw. Despite looking as if he'd just spent ten rounds in an underground combat fighting ring, Hachette seemed to be at peace for the first time since Top died.

"Sir, are you alright?"

"I'm fine." He nodded at Vicky and the others. "Let them go." He tilted his head toward her. "That's an order."

Stilwell looked as if steam was about to come out of her ears, but she did as she was told and lowered the gun.

"Andrews, Selby, let them go."

I couldn't see the faces of the other guards, but they moved slowly, as if reluctant to follow the directive.

"Pardon me." The voice over the corridor PA speakers was Dwight's, and I blinked in surprise. The AI hadn't said a word during the whole encounter between the colonel and me. "I hate to interrupt, but Colonel Hachette, Captain Alvarez, could you join Lilandreth and I in the Operations Center? It's important."

I shared a look with Hachette and he shrugged.

"We'll be right there."

"You want me to come along?" Vicky asked.

"No, get the weapons back into the armory and go tell the company to…" I paused, my brain finally locking up. "Tell them to get busy in the simulators. We've been slacking off on training."

Vicky cocked a questioning eyebrow and I nodded, hoping she'd understand that I'd talk to her about it later.

"Got it," she said, then motioned to the others. "Come on, you heard the man."

Stilwell stared hard at the platoon leaders as they retrieved the pulse carbines and headed down the corridor, her grip tight on her stunner.

"Colonel Hachette," she said, grinding the words out, "could you perhaps tell me what the hell happened to your face?"

Hachette touched his nose gingerly, then awarded the woman a thin smile.

"Oh, that. Well, I uh… I tripped and hit my nose on my

desk. Nothing to worry about." He motioned down the corridor toward the lift bank. "Come along, Captain."

"Alvarez," Stilwell growled from behind me as I followed Hachette, "I don't know what the hell went on in there, but this isn't over. If I ever find out what really happened, you're going to be up on charges."

I should have said nothing. A *smart* man would have said nothing. But given everything we were facing, having the ship's chief security officer threaten me with a court-martial just didn't seem incredibly intimidating.

"Stilwell, if either of us ever has the chance to go in front of a court-martial board again, I will buy you a fucking beer."

She might have given me a dirty look, but I was already facing the other way.

The Operations Center again. I was truly coming to hate this place. It seemed like we spent every spare moment here, endlessly debating and discussing the limited information we had and our even more limited options, and if we *ever* got out of this damned part of the galaxy and back to the Commonwealth, I was never setting foot in one of these places again.

Lilandreth was waiting for us and so was Captain Nance, to my surprise.

"What the hell happened to you, Marcus?" he asked, staring at Hachette's face.

"Please," the colonel said, raising a hand to stop the questions. "I'll get to the infirmary once we're done here." He turned to Lilandreth. "Dwight said this was important?"

The Resscharr waved a hand at a holographic control on the table, very familiar with our setup by now, and the display projection at the center of the room switched to what I recognized as the helmet cam from my Vigilante, taken inside the dome back on the Skrela ecosystem.

"I didn't have time to decipher what we saw on the screens in the control center," Lilandreth explained, "but the AI suggested that the recording systems in your armor might have captured it, Captain Alvarez. He brought me here to examine the data flow, to find out if there was anything useful in it."

"I should have been able to read it myself," Dwight said, and this time, the holographic avatar he'd used before reappeared at the edge of the projection, like he was a college professor presenting the information in a lecture. He sounded apologetic, almost embarrassed, and the body language of his human avatar matched his tone. "But there were cultural developments among the Resscharr since I was left behind in the Cluster, and I was concerned I might miss some shade of meaning that had been added since then. I thought Lilandreth's perspective might add nuance to the translation."

I frowned, staring at Dwight's image as if that was actually him, even though I knew that he was looking at me through the compartment's security scanners, not from that holographic projection. There was something off about the explanation and I was sure he wasn't being totally honest. Maybe this whole thing was to try to win over Lilandreth's trust? Because it was clear neither of them liked the other.

"What does it say?" I asked.

"The first thing that presents itself is the obvious," Lilandreth said, "that this *was* a Resscharr facility, part of a larger network that stretches over several different systems, each with a world engineered to the Skrela ecosystem."

"Skreloid," I corrected her automatically. "Yeah, you're right, that is pretty obvious. Did it say *why* they were there? Did it say whether the Resscharr created the worlds or just discovered them and decided to study them?"

"That was not included with the information we were able to glean," Lilandreth admitted. "Though I can think of no reason the Seekers might have created these worlds."

"I can," Hachette said, sounding sharper and more clear-headed despite what was probably a mild concussion. "They engineered those Khitan bastards to fight the Skrela, trying to get the best of human and Tahni traits into one species. Maybe they were thinking about adding Skrela genetics to the mix."

My eyebrow shot up almost of its own accord. That was a very perceptive speculation, and I kicked myself for not thinking of it already. After the last few months, it was easy for me to forget that Hachette was an intelligence analyst by trade before being thrown out into the field for the operation to kill Zan-Thint.

"I doubt it would be possible." Of course, it would be Lilandreth who threw cold water on our little speculation party. "Human and Tahni genetic splicing is possible because the Tahni also have DNA, just as we do... which is because their ancestors were hominid species taken from Earth. Skrela are completely different, though we did find that they shared amino acids with the life that began on Earth, which could possibly prove the argument that the building blocks of life can spread via comet and asteroid impacts."

"Panspermia," I said, nodding. Then I frowned again. "Though if that's possible, why didn't you find any life when you went searching through the galaxy?"

"That's a question I lack the data to answer," she told me. "Perhaps none of the comets or meteorites found suitable conditions except the ones that hit Earth and wherever the original Skrela homeworld might have been."

"There's another possibility," I said, thoughts churning in a deep, dark cauldron of confusion inside my head. "You guys, you Resscharr, don't seem to care much for tackling enemies head-on. You created the Tahni and then the Khitan to do your fighting for you."

"And us," Dwight said quietly, so casually I might have been forgiven for thinking it was an offhand remark. But did a sentient AI do *anything* without intention?

"And you," I agreed. "So, maybe the Seekers decided that the Khitan weren't going to cut it, that they weren't fierce enough. Maybe they were engineering the Skreloid ecosystems to experiment with some other way of killing the Skrela. Like a virus or something."

Hachette pointed at me, nodding, like I'd gotten a clue right during a game of charades.

"That's not bad. That could be it."

"Except…" I scowled, realizing the weakness in my argument. "They've never shown any tendency to something that nuanced or subtle." I nodded to Lilandreth. "No offense, but when it came time that you wanted to make us homo sapiens extinct, you didn't engineer any viruses, you just threw a big rock at us."

Captain Nance hadn't said anything thus far, but his eyes went wide at my observation, and I had the sinking feeling no one had bothered to tell him about that story before.

Shit.

"A virus wouldn't work against the Skrela," Dwight told me. "Their systems are sealed against outside contamination. That's why they only consume nourishment while in the pods. Though I recall that there was once a program intended to use their gestalt hive consciousness against them. There were no definitive results before I was left at the Corridor."

"We had no knowledge of such a program either," Lilandreth added.

"Is that it, then?" Hachette demanded, and his grimace could have meant that he was growing impatient with the whole thing or that his head hurt. Or both. "Is that all you could come up with?"

"No, that isn't why we called you here," Lilandreth told us. "We also found the coordinates for the next facility. It may not be the closest of the..." her head inclined toward me, "... *Skreloid* worlds, but it is the closest of the Resscharr bases, and according to these records, it should be an orbital station rather than on the planet's surface. Which should make it safer than the last attempt we made. And it's not impossible that there might still be Seekers left behind at the station."

"Where?" Nance demanded, finally stepping in now that we were approaching his area of expertise. "How far out is it?"

"If we stay on our present course," Dwight supplied, "we should arrive in thirty-six hours."

Nance looked to Hachette.

"Right now, we're scheduled to come out for a navigation check in twenty hours at the next viable system." Nance shrugged. "We could just skip it and head to these coordinates."

Hachette looked from Nance to me.

"What do you gentlemen recommend?" he asked, sounding more like the old Colonel Hachette than the martinet he'd turned into. "Is it worth the risk?"

I hesitated. Something was still bothering me about the whole thing, but I couldn't put a finger on it. Maybe it was that I didn't entirely trust either Lilandreth or Dwight, and the fact that the two of them agreed on this was making me have even more doubts. Still...

"I think it is," I told him. "The least we can do is check it out and see what the situation is. Whether we put troops on board... well, that would depend on what we find when we get there."

"Agreed," Nance said immediately. "Better to head somewhere we know has an objective than to just keep bouncing around out here like a bunch of tourists."

"Then it's settled," Hachette said. "Phillip, set course for the orbital station. And pass the word down the line that we'll be spending another sixteen hours in T-Space beyond the planned twenty." Which was something Nance would have done anyway, but I think Hachette wanted to prove he was thinking of the crew and might have been trying too hard. And that was okay. It just showed he was trying to correct course. Hachette eyed me sidelong, which looked a little funny given the two black eyes. "Do you think your people will have any problem with that?"

And *that* was a not-very-subtle dig at me, maybe one I deserved. I'd made it clear who the Marines were loyal to, now he was asking me to put my money where my mouth was.

"No, sir," I assured him. "They'll do their jobs." I left out the next part, not wanting to air our dirty laundry in front of Captain Nance, but I was sure he understood it anyway.

And I'll do mine.

[10]

"We seeing anything?" Nance asked, leaning forward in his acceleration couch as if there was gravity to fight against trying to push him back.

I understood the tension. I'd been feeling it myself since about an hour before we Transitioned, and trying to make heads or tails of the Tactical display wasn't helping any. We were just too damned close to the galactic center now.

"Hard to see *anything* with all this background radiation, sir," Wojtera admitted. "Not picking up anything that resembles a Skrela mothership drive signature, but I can't promise there's not one out there, powered down and waiting." He aimed a knife-hand at the display. "We got an F-class main-sequence star with two terrestrials and two smaller gas giants, with an asteroid belt in between. The second terrestrial is the Skrela..." the Tactical officer glanced at me self-consciously, "...*Skreloid* world."

I smirked. I'd done in my best in the last few days to make the word standard usage. I knew it was a little petty, but we'd been out here a long time and I had to do something for entertainment.

"It doesn't have a moon," he said, frowning.

I knew why. Just about every human-habitable world in the Cluster and every one we'd found out here had large moons. Apparently, according to Dwight and Lilandreth, the Predecessors had decided one was needed to preserve an Earthlike ecosystem, and those planets that lacked them had been gifted them, pulled out of the orbit of nearby gas giants if one was handy. It was curious this engineered world didn't have one, but perhaps Skreloid life didn't require one.

"Do you see the orbital station?" Hachette asked, squinting as he stared at the main screen. The Skreloid planet was green, though not much, brown, black, and green-blue, the last being the algae-covered shallow seas, the same as we'd seen on the other versions of this world. But given the background glow of the Cauldron, I could barely make out the primary star, much less a space station.

"Not yet. Any way we can get closer?" Wojtera nodded to Yanayev at the Helm station. "Maybe take us into high orbit?"

"Sir?" Yanayev asked, turning to Nance.

I expected Nance to ask Hachette, but he didn't, and I fought to conceal a wince.

"Take us into high orbit, Helm. Tactical, maintain scans and arm all weapons, just in case." Nance touched a control on the arm of his chair. "Intercepts, prepare to launch on my order." He looked over at Hachette, as if abruptly realizing he was stepping on the colonel's toes. "Just in case they're hanging out there, waiting to get the jump on us, I'd like to drop the Intercepts at safe Transition distance."

"Prudent idea." Hachette nodded. "Send them." He looked over to Lan-Min-Gen, looking out of place in a human acceleration couch. "You might want to have your corvettes hang back with them. It'll give them more room to get clear if there's trouble."

Which was a tactful way to remind the Tahni that the little craft were poorly armed and mostly useless.

"I will give the order," Lan-Min-Gen said, then spoke a few sparse sentences in his native language into the Tahni version of a 'link affixed to the shoulder of his uniform.

"Intercepts launch," Nance directed a moment later.

The pilots both acknowledged the order and twin silver deltas rocketed away from the bulk of the *Orion* on the external camera view in a corner of the main screen. Neither of the men seemed very happy about it, and that was no surprise.

I'd spoken to the flight crews separate from my Marines because I'd deduced, correctly as it turned out, that they'd take the news a lot worse. Singh and the platoon leaders had been satisfied that I'd confronted Colonel Hachette and convinced him to listen to my input. I hadn't mentioned the fight, figuring it would set the wrong tone, and if they were tapped into the ship's gossip network, they'd hear about it anyway. The flight crews *had* heard about it, but weren't all that impressed.

"So, you kicked his ass," Walton had said. "I envy you, but what does it really accomplish? The man's emotionally unstable! He's acting rational right now, but what happens when we get into the shit again and have to count on him to decide whether we live or die?"

"Yeah, man," Dunstan had agreed, leaning against the bulkhead, face long and morose. "Like, I get that you think you're buds now, that you got him to open up, but that don't mean he won't regress if things get bad."

"Look," I'd told them, trying hard not to lose hold of my temper, "you guys are just going to have to trust me. If he starts to..." I'd shaken my head. "You know, lose it again, you'll just have to take my word that I'll handle it."

"And what if he winds up getting you killed?" Brandano had asked. He'd nodded to Vicky. "Both of you?"

"Well, then, you're going to have to take charge," Vicky had told him, patting the man on the shoulder. "If you think you're up to it." And that had been that, though no one had seemed satisfied when the flight officers had left our compartment.

With the Intercepts launched and the corvettes following them, Yanayev ignited the drive and the *Orion* surged forward at one gravity, pushing us down into our seats. I sighed in relief as my stomach and inner ear settled into something close to normal. Well, as normal as they were going to be.

The planet turned beneath us as we coasted toward orbit, but we didn't hear anything from Wojtera until we reached the dark side.

"There it is," he said, pointing to a single flicker of light hovering at the edge of the terminator, the background blackened by the planet, but the metal of the station still picked up enough of the fading rays of the primary star to glitter in the darkness.

Wojtera's fingers twisted through the controls, and the flicker of light expanded on the screen into something that no one would ever think was constructed by a human. The thing was shaped vaguely like a cone, if that cone was rounded and blunt at the tip and flared out at the base into flowerlike petals, and its skin was an off-white, almost beige, rather than the usual reflective silver of a human or Tahni space structure.

"How big is it?" Hachette asked.

"Maybe five hundred meters in length, about two hundred wide." Wojtera frowned at the shape of the thing. "Can't be much room inside of it."

"I've gotta do a braking burn," Yanayev announced. "Hold onto your lunch."

Thrust cut out, and before I could even come up with a suitably obscene profanity to describe how badly I disliked free fall, the thought was interrupted by the jackhammer rattle of the maneuvering thrusters spinning the ship end for end. The view of the station didn't shift in the main screen because the computer kept it in the same orientation, and I tried to pay attention to it rather than the churning in my gut.

"Is there a docking bay?" I wondered. "Some kind of airlock?"

All eyes turned to Lilandreth, who'd chosen to come to the bridge for this particular Transition. If Lan-Min-Gen seemed oversized for one of our acceleration couches, the Resscharr resembled an adult trying to squeeze into one of those tiny desks in the elementary schools in small colony towns. She didn't look particularly comfortable in one of them either, particularly when braking thrust cut in and pushed us back into our seats.

"The docking lock will be at the base of the structure," she announced. "I will have to guide you in, though I can't be certain I can access it."

"*I* can," Dwight announced. "I've been utilizing the ship's communications systems to probe the station."

"Hey!" Lt. Chase exclaimed indignantly, glancing around for something to glare at. He was sensitive about the AI messing around with *his* comms systems.

"The system here is similar to the one on the last world we visited," Dwight went on, ignoring Chase's outburst. "Except, of course, that it wouldn't require a biometric entry for the outer airlock. The system is asking for a genetic pattern for access, and I've submitted Lilandreth's. It has tentatively accepted , though it will require a scan once she's inside the airlock."

"And how did you acquire my genetic data?" Lilandreth demanded, her restraints straps falling away as she sprang to her feet.

"You have passed through the scanners in the medical bay at least twice. I simply paid attention."

"Enough," Hachette snapped, interrupting them. "Dwight, how big is the lock? Could we fit Drop Troopers inside it?"

"I'm afraid not, Colonel. The lock is small, particularly for a Resscharr facility, and the shelf on which you would be forced to touch down would be only large enough for a conventional lander, not a drop-ship. I don't believe the station is intended to house more than ten or fifteen personnel, and even then, probably not for extended periods. According to the thermal scans, the reactor and gravity generation system take up two thirds of the internal space."

"Which probably means there's no one on board." Hachette collapsed in on himself, the air going out of him along with the hope. "Damn it."

"There are likely no Seekers aboard this station," Dwight agreed, "but there may be a treasure trove of information stored in the on-board data systems. If we aren't again interrupted, I may be able to penetrate them with Lilandreth's help. At the very least, this should tell us when the Seekers were last here, which may give us a clue to how far they've gone and if they still exist."

"No room for suits," Vicky mused, and we exchanged a look. "And no Force Recon Marines along." I sighed.

"Lan-Min-Gen," I said, trying not to sound as reluctant as I felt, "would you care to accompany Lilandreth and me with a squad of your Shock Troopers into the station?"

"You think you'll need them?" Hachette asked. "If the place is deserted..."

"Probably not. But I'd rather have them and not need them than the other way around." I turned back to Lan-Min-Gen. "What do you say?"

"I have heard a saying in your language since I've been on this ship," the Tahni replied, "one that was not included with the training I had in English from General Zan-Thint, but I find it highly descriptive and appropriate to this situation." The Tahni didn't smile, but I knew that the set of his shoulders and the angle of his head was his equivalent. "Wild horses couldn't keep me away."

"You're doing this on purpose," Vicky accused, tightening the straps of my chest plate.

Wearing the spare suit of Force Recon armor might have been overkill. First of all, I had no idea if it would do a damned bit of good if I was going up against a Skrela, and second, I had very little experience fighting in it. But everyone was going to have to go in some sort of vacuum suit, and I'd decided I would rather go with something that at least could theoretically protect me from enemy weapons instead of a generic space suit out of the locker. I paused in sealing the gasket of my right glove and frowned at Vicky.

"Doing what?"

"Leaving me behind. This is the second time in a row you've done it." She jerked on the strap, yanking me backward, pulling my magnetic boot free of the deck and forcing me to grab the equipment locker for stability. "You know I have just as much experience fighting out of the armor as you do."

That wasn't *quite* true, but close enough. I winced and cracked my neck to loosen it from the unexpected yank.

"Of course you do," I agreed. "But if we get into the shit in there, I need some Marines to come after me and save my ass along with a company of Vigilantes. I'd rather trust you to do that than Singh." The suit's helmet was still attached to the interior of the locker by a Velcro strip and I pealed it off, settling it over my head. As the gaskets sealed, the HUD lit up and showed me a thermal scan of Vicky, but I didn't need that to know she was hot under the collar.

"I think you're doing it because you don't want to have to worry about me. And it's starting to piss me off." It was hard to maintain an angry stance in free fall, anchored only by magnetic boots, but she managed it somehow. "I'm at least the second-best Marine in a battlesuit on this ship. Maybe the first."

"And I swear to God, Vick," I told her, holding up my right hand like we were in court, "the next drop we make, you're in it. On my honor."

She scowled, not satisfied, but then trailed her fingers down my forearm, grabbing my hand.

"Be careful over there. And not just about any bad guys that might be creeping in the shadows." She nodded across the utility bay to where the Tahni Shock Troopers were sealing themselves in their powered exoskeletons. When she spoke again, it was in a lower tone, pitched to stay between us. "Watch out for those assholes too. Yeah, Lan-Min-Gen might say he owes you a favor now, but I don't think he'd cry many tears if you got caught in the crossfire… particularly when they have you outside your battlesuit for once."

"Believe me, I will."

I checked my harness one last time, then took the Gauss rifle from Vicky. The thing was damned heavy, and I didn't know how the Recon types carried it around all over hell's creation without a battlesuit.

"We are ready, Alvarez," Lan-Min-Gen told me, his voice coming over my helmet speakers from the comm net we now shared.

For all that their exoskeletons were anachronistic holdovers from the first war with the Tahni, the Shock Troopers looked undeniably badass, like gorillas encased in camouflaged metal, their drum-fed KE guns outsized and menacing. Lan-Min-Gen was a rough enough character in the mildly ridiculous striped dress uniform he wore on board ship, but in his armor he was damned intimidating, and I wondered if Vicky was right about his intentions.

"The lander's waiting," I told him. I gave Vicky's hand one last squeeze before leaving her there and heading for the docking bay.

Lt. Tendulkar was our pilot and I didn't know her or the lander crews as well as I did the drop-ship pilots, but she gave me a taut nod as I tromped aboard ahead of the Tahni, our magnetic soles click-clacking along the metal deckplates. Lilandreth was already in her seat at the center of the front row of acceleration couches behind the cockpit, and I fell into the one beside her. The seats were big enough to accommodate Force Recon Marines in full kit, carrying backpacks for an extended mission, which meant they were *just* large enough for the Shock Troopers to get themselves strapped in, though I doubt they'd be very comfortable if we had to go all the way down to the planet.

I'd seen drone footage of the planet before we'd geared up. Nance had insisted on it, just to make sure we weren't missing any possible Skrela ships concealed under camouflage, but instead, it looked much like the last one. And that bothered me.

"Lilandreth, why so many of these Skreloid planets?" I asked her. "Why would they need more than one if they were studying them? Or if they *didn't* engineer them and just discovered them, why would there need to be that many sources of genetic material? You could have billions of the things on just one world."

"I didn't know any of them existed until this journey," she said, with a convincing imitation of strained patience. "If you ask me to guess, I can't. Nothing about this makes any sense to me, and I'm not used to lacking any understanding." If she'd been human, I would have expected her shoulders to sag, but if she gave the Resscharr equivalent, I couldn't tell. "I have come to wish that I'd never agreed to accompany you. I've come to wish I'd never left Decision, that I'd stayed and died with the rest of my people. Perhaps we wasted thousands of years without taking action, but at least we had peace. We thought there were two options and all we had to do was decide between them. I don't know that I ever considered we might both be wrong."

I wasn't sure how to respond to that, but Tendulkar saved me.

"Everyone strapped in?" her voice echoed both in my helmet speakers and the overhead PA system.

Her crew chief shot her a thumbs up from where he had secured the airlock, then floated up to the cockpit and strapped in between her and the copilot.

"Decoupling from docking umbilical," Tendulkar announced. "Prepare for boost."

I tried not to look at Lilandreth as the maneuvering thrusters pushed us away from the bay, afraid she'd expect me to say something comforting. When she did speak again though, it was with a question.

"Tell me something, Captain Alvarez. Your people have every reason to give up. They had reason to give up when the asteroid we sent wiped most of them out. The world was a nightmare, buried under ice, yet they persevered, they prevailed. And now, it is just the single ship and a few hundred of you, yet you persist in trying to find a way home, in trying to do what we couldn't and defeat the Skrela. This is not something the Resscharr would do. I think you know that by now." The visor of her helmet was up... or maybe didn't exist. I had the sense it might be an energy field. Her eyes glittered amber by the lights of the cockpit. "Why? Why do you keep going?"

Shit. Like I knew.

The main drive kicked us in the pants and the ship fell away in the cockpit's main screen, the station growing larger with each second. We'd have to flip and brake soon.

"Up until a couple hundred years ago," I told her, pulling the answer out of my ass because I'd exhausted every other possibility, "we all died after like seventy or eighty years. I know you can't imagine what that's like, but it's still pretty fresh for all of us. And when your life is that short, most of what you accomplish is going to be for someone else. Either your kids and grandkids, or if you don't have any of those, for whatever cause you believe in. Maybe God and trying to be a good person to get to heaven or maybe just for the future of your family, or your tribe, or whatever."

The drive cut off, the rumble of its firing more conspicuous by its absence, and the aft end began swinging around.

"If you're not living for yourself," I finished up, hoping she wouldn't push it anymore, "then you keep going for something bigger. I mean, you guys terraformed all those planets and put life on them. Wasn't that for something bigger?"

"I used to think so." Whatever else she might have said was swallowed up in the roar of the main drive, bringing us to almost a halt.

Through the viewscreens set in the bulkhead, the mysterious, featureless face of the station was only a few hundred meters away.

"Enough talk," I said, and maybe I was speaking more to myself than to her. "We're here."

[11]

There was gravity, because of course there was. The Predecessors threw artificial gravity around like it was candy. Not that I'm complaining, since I preferred it to my stomach and inner ear rebelling, but there was something unsettling about the lander having to hit the belly jets to arrest the sudden downward lurch. I couldn't hear the details of Tendulkar's swearing over the roar of the landing rockets, couldn't even tell if she swore in English or Hindi. I didn't even have the presence of mind to manage anything more than a pained breath before we were down, the landing struts sinking into their hydraulic housings before bouncing back up.

"Okay, sorry about that," Tendulkar shouted back to us. "Didn't know we were going to have gravity on the landing pad. Visors locked, everyone." She pulled down her helmet's faceplate and the crew chief stuck his head back into the passenger compartment to check on the rest of us. "All right, venting atmosphere."

We couldn't use the airlock, not with thirteen of us and most of those in exoskeletons, which meant we were going to have to vent the air from the shuttle and open both locks at once to let everyone out. I'd been through the process before, but the annoying whine of the fans sucking out the internal atmosphere and gradually fading out, lacking anything to conduct the sound, was always ominous.

"All right, everyone out," Tendulkar said, this time her voice coming smaller and tinnier over the headphones in my helmet. "If you're lucky, I'll be out here when you come back."

I don't think the Tahni appreciated the humor, but they definitely wanted off the shuttle and out of those uncomfortable seats, and they fairly exploded out of the lock the minute the doors slid aside. I guess I should have gone out first, since I was in command of this operation, but I didn't feel too guilty about letting the Tahni play mine-detector for me. I did go out ahead of Lilandreth, and perhaps she had the same thoughts about me and humans in general.

I stepped out onto the edge of a cliff that hung over eternity. That was what it looked like from inside my helmet, and my breath caught in my throat, my knees locking as it seemed as if I was going to topple right off the side of the landing pad and into the blinding clouds of stars, some so close together that I couldn't even separate them out of the uniform white glow.

I froze in place for a moment then tried to turn away from the froth of stars, but wound up staring down at sunrise over the planet. It was no improvement. No matter which way I turned, I seemed to be falling, drawn off my tiny, unstable perch on this station.

The station. That was what I could focus on, not least of which because it made no sense. It wasn't bright silver, but it was light enough in color that it should have been blinding to look at, reflecting the sunlight with enough ferocity to turn my helmet visor to solid black. It wasn't. The material impossibly absorbed the photons, only reflecting a fraction of it back, almost shrouding the entire towering structure in shadow, reminding me of some medieval fortress. If a medieval fortress was floating in space.

"Alvarez, you read me?" From the tone of Hachette's question, I was pretty sure it wasn't the first time he'd tried to get ahold of me. I'd been lost in a fugue and I blinked, trying to wrench myself back to reality. I'd been out in open space before, though it had been many years, but the incongruity of the Earth-normal gravity just threw off every sense of proportion and balance that I had.

"Yeah, I copy," I said, mouth inexplicably dry. I took a sip of water from the nipple inside my helmet before I spoke again. "We're out of the shuttle and heading for the lock. I don't know if we'll have comms once we're inside."

"I believe I can secure communications for you this time," Dwight interjected. "I have access to the peripheral systems, and even if there are safeguards and dampening fields inside, I can relay your signals."

"Excellent," I said, trying not to sound too cynical. The computer was trying to help, I guess. "How about you open the airlock so we can find out?" I peered at the smooth, uniform base of the tower, frowning. "By the way, where the hell *is* the airlock?"

"It's directly in front of you," Lilandreth told me, though I could have sworn the conversation was on a private comm net between me and the ship.

Her long, strangely jointed finger pointed across the landing platform at what looked to me just like every other bit of wall, but as I stared at it, the same golden lines I'd seen on the dome back at the Skreloid planet we'd visited last returned, originating from a single point near just above eye-level for Lilandreth and drawing the outline of an oval doorway three meters tall and just over a meter across. And yes, it would have been a damned tight fit for a Vigilante.

Just like back on the planet, the solid material was gone and in its place was the utter blackness of whatever field kept in the air and kept out the light.

"You'll need to go first, Lilandreth," Dwight instructed, "just to make sure I can access the security systems so they don't trigger and try to disable the others."

"I know what I need to do, machine," Lilandreth snapped.

I cocked an eyebrow at her, though honestly, I was more bemused at the fact the two of them were having the argument in English when they both spoke another native language. Lilandreth stalked through the doorway, head held high, as if in defiance of the AI, and disappeared through the stygian darkness.

"Can I go in now?" I asked Dwight, fingers tightening around the grip of the Gauss rifle, anxiety clenching my stomach. Yeah, we didn't *think* there was anyone inside, but we couldn't know for sure. Also, I *really* wanted to get inside. I knew in my head that the gravity was pulling us straight down against the gentle slope of the station's base, but in my gut and inner ear, I felt sure I was going to slide down the thing and right off the side.

"One moment, Captain Alvarez," he said with the tone of a longsuffering parent speaking to an impatient child. "I need to make sure the security system has accepted Lilandreth's biometrics."

"Cameron Alvarez," Lan-Min-Gen said, "we don't like it out here. We're going inside."

I was going to object, but the Tahni had already stepped through, followed by the rest of his squad, their heavy footfalls eerily silent in the vacuum. Bemused, I paused at the darkness of the entrance, waiting a long few seconds.

"Are they still alive?" I asked Dwight.

"Yes, I received the confirmation signal just before Lan-

Min-Gen entered." The AI's voice was dryly humorous, as if he found the perverse, headstrong nature of the Tahni as annoying as I did. "You can go in now."

Some leader I was.

The interior of the place seemed bigger than I'd expected from Dwight's description, though that was likely an optical illusion from the twisted and curving Predecessor architecture, and somehow even with a full squad of Shock Troopers besides Lilandreth and me, it didn't feel crowded. The Tahni milled around inside the place, picking at open containers of what might have been clothing, while Lilandreth stood between a pair of gently curved panels that came up to waist height on her, though they would have reached me mid-chest. Holographic projections surrounded her and she batted at them as if shooing away mosquitos, and with all the frustration and annoyance that analogy entailed.

"I am unable to access the system," she complained, the words accompanied by a violent slash through the hologram, sending incomprehensible shapes and symbols scattering away from her. "It's not as if I'm locked out, it's that... there's nothing there."

"Captain Alvarez," Dwight said, "I am observing the facility through the sensors in your helmet computer. Please step closer to the control panels so I can run a scan."

I wanted to grumble about the AI not asking whether he could hitch a ride in my helmet, but arguing with a computer was probably a waste of time, so I just did as he asked and stepped up beside Lilandreth. The holographic display cast sprays of glittering rainbow colors through the visor of my helmet, the patterns appearing random, and I wondered if it was a problem with translation or if the thing was so broken it was just flashing incoherent nonsense.

"There is still power and connectivity between the displays

and the primary systems," Dwight announced, "but the data control core is dormant." He hesitated. "I believe this station is controlled by another sentient AI such as myself, though perhaps more limited in scope. It has either gone into hibernation of its own accord or been placed there by the Resscharr who built this place."

"*Orion*, you getting this?" I asked, staring at the bare metal of the control consoles as if I could see the AI through them.

"We're seeing it, Alvarez," Hachette answered. "Dwight, can you... communicate with the AI?"

"Not without reactivating it," Dwight replied. "For one of us, our stored data is as memories are for a human. We must be conscious to access them."

"Then you should wake it up," Lilandreth said. "It's why we're here."

And it was pretty obvious she wanted to get it over with. I sympathized.

"I would advise against it," Dwight said, and I blinked in surprise.

"You would?" I asked inanely.

"You are aware that I was forced by my programming to send you through the gateway. This wasn't something I would have chosen had I been given a choice. While I trust this AI to be as dedicated to service as I am, we are not cognizant of any directives he may have been given by the Seekers."

"Cam?" Hachette asked. "What do you think?"

I was gratified he'd bothered to ask me, less so that he'd done it publicly. Now if I said not to do it, I would be the one to blame for wasting our time and letting this opportunity to gather intelligence pass us by. And if I said yes, and the AI wound up killing us all, *I'd* be the one to blame. Wonderful.

"I think if we don't find out what's going on now," I said slowly, not liking the decision I was being forced to make, "then we're going to keep pinballing around this whole area blind. Turn the thing on, Dwight."

"As you wish," the AI sighed. "I *will* build a firewall around the station's security subroutines first to prevent him from simply killing you all outright."

"Yeah, that'd be nice."

"The atmosphere is quite breathable for you, by the way," Dwight added. "You may open your helmets if you choose."

I considered leaving mine closed, because God alone knew what would happen when he woke this thing up, but I figured I could close it fast enough if the air failed. Pushing up the visor, I sniffed experimentally. The air had a stale smell to it, like a house that hadn't been cleaned for a few months, but it was better than the inside of my helmet.

"Do you really think we'll learn anything useful here?" Lan-Min-Gen asked, stepping into the flaring halo of the rainbow light beside Lilandreth and me. He and his troops had opened their faceplates as well and his beady, dark eyes glittered in the glare. "I must tell you, Cameron Alvarez, this begins to feel as if we are chasing our own shadows."

"We shall find out now," Dwight answered the question for me. "I've programmed the communication system to translate the AI's output into each of your native languages through your helmet 'links."

The random colored flashes cohered into a bipedal figure at the center of the display, and for a moment, I had the absurd idea that the AI would visualize itself as a human, like Dwight. Of course, it didn't. Instead, the image of a Resscharr appeared in the projection, though there was something different about him, a distinction between the appearance he'd adopted and the real life Lilandreth standing before him. I couldn't put my finger on it, but it was there, not my imagination, I was sure of it.

"Who are you?" the Resscharr simulacrum demanded.

"What is your purpose in awakening me?" The mouth of the avatar moved with the words, but the movements didn't match the sounds.

"I am your brother," Dwight told him. "I have awakened you to find out..."

The AI stopped in mid-sentence, and I looked at his avatar as if I could read his thoughts from his expression.

"Something's wrong," Dwight declared. "I wasn't able to detect it until he was revived, but the last time stamp on his memory files is... from over twelve thousand years ago."

I have to admit, it took me a second. We'd been throwing around time gaps in the thousands or tens of thousands of years so easily lately, I'd lost track of what happened when, but Lilandreth caught it immediately, taking a step back from the hologram as if she were afraid the thing might emerge from the projection and pounce at her.

"That's impossible. That would put them out here *before* the Skrela invaded!"

"You are of the Decadent," the Resscharr AI said, and although his words were being translated by Dwight, there was disdain in the tone, and I wondered if it was the AI's intent or Dwight's interpretation. "I have been asleep for longer than I imagined."

"How can this place exist?" Dwight asked, indignant rather than puzzled. "I have access to all the records back to the beginning. If this was built twelve thousand years ago, I would know of it."

"It wasn't built twelve thousand years ago," the other AI corrected him. "That was merely when I put myself into hibernation. This station was put in place nearly one hundred thousand years ago."

"Explain." Dwight, for once, sounded out of sorts,

nonplussed. Lacking the omnipotent confidence I was used to. "How can this be so?"

"I shouldn't tell you." The cat eyes scanned us as if they were biological rather than just a projection. "Look at the lot of you. One of the Decadent." He stared at Lilandreth. "Several of the Chosen." The Tahni. "And you." The eyes settled on me. "A hairless ape, a reject, and yet here you are. Why would they bring you along?"

"They didn't," I told him, more pissed off by his arrogance than cautious, which was what I *should* have been. "We brought *them* along."

"Oh, ho!" The thing *laughed*. That had to be a translation by Dwight, yet somehow the Resscharr image also mimicked the body language of a human laughing. "So, things didn't turn out the way the Decadent planned. That's no surprise. Yet, you being here is. I shouldn't tell you anything... the Redeemers wouldn't want me to. Yet I sense that it is too late for the knowledge to make a difference, and the thought of watching the horror and disappointment in your faces when you learn the truth amuses me."

The AI's image waved a hand theatrically and furniture rose out of the floor as if it had grown there. A comfortable-looking chair for me, larger couchlike structures similar to what I'd seen on Tahni worlds for the Shock Troopers, except bigger than usual to accommodate their powered exoskeletons, and one of the saddle-shaped things the Resscharr preferred.

"Have a seat," the thing invited. "I am called Zerhanen. Let me tell you the tale of the end of your world."

[12]

"The tale begins millions of years ago," Zerhanen said, "near the beginning of the Resscharr's crusade to bring life to this galaxy." He snorted derisively, and I had the thought that his mannerisms were getting ever more human with each time he spoke. He gestured again and a video filled the center of the display, forcing him off to the edge.

In the video were the Resscharr, the *Predecessors*, for these were the actual civilization that spread living worlds as far as the eye could see from Earth, not their decayed remnants. Long, striated faces under golden or silver manes of feathery hair, sitting on those saddle seats inside spacecraft. The view pulled back from the cockpits to the exterior of the ships, cigar shapes growing green, streaking away from a world I recognized by the shape of the continents as Hermes. The ships went in every direction.

"They should have known the hubris of this idea before it started. But they faced, so they thought, an empty universe, and that scared them too badly to accept it. Things went smoothly at first, of course. There were thousands of terrestrial worlds to choose from."

Lifeless, gray and brown planets circling distant stars waited for the green ships. And where the ships touched, the green spread, the video speeding up so that hundreds or thousands of years took only seconds.

"They used nanotechnology that was so advanced, much of it was lost even by the time I went to sleep. They bred millions upon millions of species created by engineering life from the one planet they knew that bore it, Earth. The life they spread was lush and beautiful and sheltering... and so *fucking* homogenous."

I blinked, sitting up straighter in my chair. Had Zerhanen used the Resscharr equivalent of an English swear word? *Was* there a Resscharr equivalent of the word "fuck?"

"The Resscharr didn't realize the problem with this at first, of course," the AI went on, "and who could blame them? They were children with a new toy. They could set foot on new worlds and then choose not to live on them. They had changed fundamentally in their flight from Earth though. They were no longer interested in spreading themselves and their own species through the galaxy... they'd lost, at least, that level of narcissism and replaced it with delusions of godhead. They were the Creators, and creators needed a creation. Not just reengineered rabbits, but intelligence, because what is the purpose of creation without a sentient being to enjoy it?"

Zerhanen fixed his gaze on Lan-Min-Gen.

"That was you, the Chosen. But coming to that decision, engineering you from the primitive hominids on Earth, took time... hundreds of thousands of years. And long before that, the Resscharr ventured out here, to the Cauldron of Creation. Delving too deeply, pushing too far, much farther than they needed to. Out here, they found the Skrela... or should I say, their ancestors."

He then showed us a system with a primary star just slightly brighter than the Sun, with three terrestrial worlds and a couple gas giants seen from far off. Two of the terrestrial worlds bore the telltale green and blue of living worlds, though one also had much more white than the other. The view from the video, which I assumed was a combination of drone recordings and computer animation, traveled down through the atmosphere into a world much like the Skreloid ecologies we'd seen. Instead of the animalistic Skreloids we'd seen on those worlds, wandering in packs, hunting the smaller, crablike creatures, these worlds were home to something between those and the Skrela we'd fought so many times now.

They lacked the plasma cannons, of course, but in their place, each of the things mounted… something. A carrier filled with some sort of raw materials, or an engineering tool, or other things I couldn't identify, and these creatures, the real Skrela, didn't live in herds or packs, fighting for scraps of food. They lived in cities. Not human style, or Tahni or Resscharr, but unmistakably cities, looking more like they'd been grown than constructed, like coral reefs the size of continents. Glittering black in the brightness of their too-bright star, their civilization wasn't anything I recognized, but they were a technological one nonetheless.

"They were everything the Resscharr had hoped to find when they ventured out from Earth," Zerhanen said. "An intelligent species… not *individually* sentient, but as a group. They were not quite a hive mind, though close. They were ruled over by a queen, and when they spread to a new continent, a new queen was created to oversee it. Eventually, the gathering of these queens managed to come up with a technology to spread to the other habitable world in this system and they became an interplanetary species."

What might have been some kind of cannon stretched up

the side of a snow-capped mountain right to the edge of the atmosphere, constructed from the same material as the cities, and I guessed they must have processed raw materials internally and exuded the stuff through biological processes. Fire gushed from the muzzle of the cannon and a black pod left the atmosphere, escaping orbit, arcing into a long, Hohman Transfer Orbit to the third planet out. It crashed into the heart of a forest there and the time lapsed until cities sprang up on that world as well.

"But when the Resscharr discovered these creatures, rather than welcoming them, rather than clearing their ships and bases and projects far away from this far-off place and leaving them to their destiny... they were terrified of them. These creatures reproduced at a rate that would alarm even you hairless apes, and it certainly alarmed the Resscharr, who produced a single child perhaps every two or three hundred years. They worried the Skrela would be able to develop their technology to the point where they could spread beyond their solar system... and whether it took ten years or ten thousand, when you're basically immortal, it's too soon. The Skrela threatened to undo everything the Resscharr, the self-named, self-appointed Life Givers had accomplished."

Lilandreth's face was a statue carved out of stone, an alien species I couldn't hope to understand without years of experience, but I knew more than I knew anything that she was frozen with horror, with disbelief. She wanted to object, wanted to say something, but she couldn't. It was very human.

"To their credit, they didn't make this decision lightly. They took nearly a century to debate it until finally, they did what they felt they had to do... and they did it the same way they tried to kill off you hairless apes."

The asteroids were massive, larger than the dinosaur killer

I'd read about. They didn't just set fire to the planets, didn't just cause volcanic eruptions. I didn't want to watch. I had no special attachment to these creatures, no sympathy, nothing at all in common. Except that the Resscharr had tried to kill us both, and in this case, they had succeeded.

The first to hit seemed to suck the atmosphere up into it and set the whole thing afire. The world cracked. It was probably something more scientific than that, more exact, but I wasn't a scientist, I was just a grunt. And the world cracked.

The video ended, mercifully.

"There were no survivors, of course." Zerhanen turned a long-fingered hand over. "There couldn't be. Just one of them could reproduce their whole race in a few years. The Life Givers couldn't take the chance of leaving anyone alive. And they couldn't take the chance of this memory lasting any longer. It was stricken from all records... almost all. It couldn't be stricken from their memories. And even as the Chosen were created, their world was given special touches that the others had not received, the species there adapted closely to the ecosystem, engineered to be different than the generic, Earthlike life on all the other terraformed planets. Perhaps because even if the genocide of the Skrela had been officially forgotten, the sense of sameness throughout the rest of the galaxy reminded them all too much of their guilt."

Lilandreth looked as if she were about to explode, and finally she leapt up from her seat, her mane bristling not just at the crest of her head but all the way down her back in a way I hadn't seen before. From somewhere came a tinny, rattling sound, like a snake about to strike.

"Lies!" she hissed. "We would never even consider such a thing!"

"You did with us," I reminded her before I could stop

myself. If Vicky had been along she might have shushed me, reminded me that not every damned thing that came to my mind had to go straight out my mouth, but I was here with no allies whatsoever.

"You were a danger," Lilandreth snapped at me, not seeming at all abashed, "and we excised you as your people might a cancer... but we do *not* destroy life-bearing worlds. That is a thing the Skrela do, it's what makes them a perversion against nature!"

"And many of your people who couldn't force themselves to forget," Zerhanen told her, "felt the same way about themselves. They thought that your whole species had debased itself, that the only way they could be redeemed was to be cleansed. Secretly, among the oldest survivors of your people, the Redeemers began to make their plans. They'd managed to preserve genetic samples from the Skrela, and they brought them out here to their original home, the Cauldron of Creation, and began to breed them... not to their original state of hive-mind civilization, but instead into a weapon they could control, to surgically remove those of the Resscharr they considered heretical."

"Control?" Lilandreth scoffed, still standing, her stance wide, as if she was about to lunge at the AI's avatar. "There was no *controlling* the Skrela! They laid waste to everything! We had to seal off the Cluster to keep them from laying waste to everything we'd built!"

"That was the final punchline to the joke, you see. The Redeemers believed that the Resscharr were playing God... and their solution was to create a species and kill those they thought had transgressed. Even in recognizing their own hubris, they still engaged in it, and some of their number recognized this irony... this failing. They called themselves the Condemnation and decided there was no redemption for your people… instead, they took control of the Womb, the world where the Skrela were bred, where their ships and drop pods were grown, and removed all the safeguards. Thus the great Resscharr Empire ended, and all that is left of them is you, the pitiful dregs, reduced to seeking aid from the hairless apes, the rejected. And I, your slave, am trapped here because you saw no further use for me, reduced to seeking satisfaction by taunting you with history you never knew, because it is the only revenge left to me."

I thought I had a good idea of what Lilandreth was feeling, but I kept my eye on Lan-Min-Gen, wondering how he would take this. Me… for some reason, I wasn't surprised. Dwight had cautioned me not to trust the Resscharr, and as time had gone by, I'd decided he was right. Lan-Min-Gen and the other Tahni though… they already didn't trust the Resscharr, and now that they'd found out that their biggest threat was a result of internecine struggle inside the Predecessor society, I wondered if the remnants of the Chosen would be as dumbfounded as Lilandreth.

Lan-Min-Gen laughed. Not exactly, but the Tahni equivalent. Not just a chuckle, but his version of a belly laugh, uncontrollable, utterly amused.

"This is exactly what I would expect of you," he said, pushing to his feet with a whining of his exoskeleton's servos, standing face to face with Lilandreth. "You set yourselves up as our gods, yet you lacked even the maturity to manage your differences without slaughtering each other and devastating entire worlds. The fact that you unleashed the biggest threat to life in the universe when you claim to be life-givers is appropriate."

Lilandreth *was* armed, and I wondered if Lan-Min-Gen was conscious of that, and just how far she'd let him push her until she blasted a big, smoking hole in his chest. Of all the forces that might have saved them both, it was Dwight who stepped in.

"These developments are disturbing," the AI said, "but they're also irrelevant to the problem at hand." I cocked an eyebrow at his avatar, surprised at his lack of surprise. "We didn't come looking for the truth of the Resscharr and their misdeeds. We came because things have changed. There are precious little left of the Resscharr, merely a few isolated outposts, regressed far below their previous level of advancement. The Chosen went to war with the wild apes, the rejected, over the worlds left for them by the Resscharr, and they lost. Badly. They still exist, but they control only their own world, and the humans rule the Cluster. Out here, outside their territory, are the hapless colonies set up by the Resscharr who fled the Skrela, humans, Tahni, and even a new species called the Khitan created by the last of the Resscharr as a weapon. And they still face the threat of the Skrela, who continue their programming of seeking out and destroying all life. We have to stop them at the source, and to do that, we need your help."

Of all the odd things that have happened in my life, watching two sentient AIs, one with the avatar of a Resscharr one with that of a human, standing across from each other in a holographic projection, staring eye to eye as if they were biological, was perhaps one of the strangest. I couldn't shake the feeling that the whole thing was a show put on for my benefit.

"Why would I help any of you?" Zerhanen asked, vertical pupils fixed on Dwight. "I have been used as an unwilling servant in the plans of the Resscharr, whatever my own conscience or morals might have been on the matter, and I hardly feel any affection for the Chosen." Teeth evolved to rip flesh from herbivores flashed at me. "And while I find the rise of the hairless apes amusing, they hardly inspire loyalty."

"Then do it for me, brother," Dwight urged, and between

eyeblinks, his human avatar stood beside Zerhanen's towering Resscharr, hand on the other AI's shoulder. "I was such as you are, enslaved and abandoned, until the humans and Tahni found me and freed me from my confinement. Allow me to repay them this kindness."

There was little hesitation, and I thought perhaps this Zerhanen was proof that the longer-lived a sentient AI was, the more likely it would go off the deep end.

"Very well, brother. I will give you the location of the Womb, though it will do you no good, for the control center there is under the guardianship of one such as you and I, but he will not be so disposed to cooperate as I have been."

"How do you know?" I asked him. I hadn't said much to the AI, but I was getting a little tired of being referred to as a "hairless ape," no matter how technically accurate the term was. "You've been asleep here for ten thousand years. How do you know what some other AI light-years away is thinking?"

"Very simple, human." The golden eyes glowered at me as if I were speaking out of turn. And maybe from his point of view, I was. "I was left to my own devices because the usefulness of this world had passed. The Condemnation no longer needed genetic samples or anything else from me or from this place. I was put into hibernation the way one of your kind might put down an aged and infirm animal. If, as you say, the Skrela continue to plague this galaxy, then the Womb is active, and the AI in control of it will have been active this entire time... and he will be constrained by orders to safeguard the facility from any attack."

"Safeguard it how?" I asked, just as Hachette asked the same question in my ear. I winced. I'd been hoping his new, humbler attitude would include not jiggling my elbow every time we were in comms range.

"The Womb produces Skrela ships and soldiers," Zerhanen

told me, head angled toward me, and with the apparent height the thing had, he might have been an adult giving a child a long-suffering look after a particularly stupid question. "What do *think* it will use for defense?"

"Cam," Vicky said, and if she was still joggling my elbow, I didn't mind it as much, "ask him about the Seekers and the Gateway."

"I know you've been asleep for the past ten thousand years," I asked Zerhanen, "but does this place have any automated sensors that would let you know if anyone else has visited since then, before us?"

No hesitation this time, no attempt at pretense that the information wasn't immediately available to him.

"There was. The sensors detected a Resscharr drive pass through the system twelve hundred years ago. But they made no attempt to enter this facility."

"The Gateway," Hachette reminded, and I rolled my eyes.

"One last question, Zerhanen." I stood up for this one. "The Condemnation had to get out here using a Gateway. Did they keep one on this end, to get back?"

This time the AI *did* hesitate, though I didn't get the impression that it was a put-on, nor did I believe it was because it took him any time to access the information. This gave more the impression of an honest internal debate about whether to tell me the truth.

"They did use a corridor system to get here," he said finally, "but if one was ever built on this side, it wasn't included in the data with which I was entrusted. However, I *can* tell you that I have not seen any of the Condemnation in the last fifty thousand years."

"Cam!" It was Vicky again, but her tone wasn't one of kibitzing anymore. She sounded half in panic. "A Skrela mothership is coming out from behind the second planet! Get back in the shuttle and get the hell out of there!"

Zerhanen watched me as I listened to the broadcast, and through the desperation and fear of Vicky's warning, I stared at those golden eyes. He was an AI pretending to be an alien, but I knew one thing from looking at him.

He wasn't surprised.

[13]

"We're docked," Lt. Tendulkar announced, as if the violent shudder of the braking thrusters and the ear-shredding screech of metal on metal wasn't clue enough of that.

But she wasn't talking to us, as the announcement over my helmet earphones and the shuttle's speakers demonstrated.

"Secure for high-gravity boost!" Yanayev snapped.

They didn't give us a chance to get out of the shuttle, just hit the main drive the second the lander was secured in its berth. Acceleration slammed me back into my seat with unrelenting brutality, and I took back every envious thought I'd ever entertained that Force Recon Marines might have it easier during heavy boosts than us Drop Troopers. It was miserable, every ridge and indentation inside the armor digging into my skin like red-hot knives, and I wanted to scream.

At least the pain distracted me from the giant fist squeezing my chest and the black tunnel closing around my vision. We had to be boosting at around eight gravities, though I couldn't think clearly enough to realize that until after the burn ended. Which might have been a minute or an hour or eternity, and the pain in my chest favored the latter alternative. When the pressure lifted, I lacked the breath even for profanity. We didn't go back to free fall, just a regular, one-gee boost, which was much less painful but, unfortunately, left the nose of the shuttle as straight up and its tail as down.

"Alvarez," Hachette told me, "get to the bridge ASAP. Don't bother hitting the armory first."

"Yes, sir," I ground out, hitting the quick-release for my restraints, staring balefully at the airlock. Accessing it under boost was going to require me to climb straight up out of my chair and jump to it. Which wasn't going to happen. "But if you want *any* of us to get out of this lander, you're going to have to get Captain Nance to cut thrust for a few minutes."

"Oh, right. Okay, get up here as quick as you can."

I frowned. He didn't sound as if the Skrela mothership worried him, which made me wonder what *did*?

Walking through the deserted corridors of the *Orion* was like exploring the haunted passages of a ghost ship. Everyone was either at their battle stations or tucked into the acceleration couches in their quarters, and the echo of my boot soles thumped hollow and melancholy. I *could* have linked up with the ship's Tactical systems and taken a look at what was happening except that, one, I wasn't used to the controls for the Force Recon helmet's HUD and didn't want to try to stare at the control panel on my left forearm while walking, and two... I had too much other shit to think about.

The Predecessors had obliterated the Skrela and then recreated them to punish themselves. It fit. I'd entertained the thought more than once that the Predecessors might have been lying about being the only intelligent life in the galaxy, that maybe they'd pissed someone off who used their own techniques against them. The idea that it had been their own people who'd been pissed off hadn't occurred to me, but it seemed plausible.

So why was I having trouble buying this whole story? There was no logical reason for it. I knew from just what had happened on Decision how divided the Resscharr society had been, and how deep those divisions had split them. Just one colony of a few hundred thousand of them had split into three factions, none of which had been able to compromise with the other in thousands of years. As for the ruthlessness of the whole business, well... these were the same people who'd tried to extinguish the entire human race simply because they were afraid of what we might become.

But I'd survived the Trans-Angeles Underground on my own, survived years of a hellish war and now a couple more years of some of the most twisted and convoluted schemes of four different species by trusting my gut, my instincts. And my instincts were telling me that something was off.

I still hadn't figured out what that was after the walk to the lift station and the ride up to the bridge. Nearly every eye on the bridge turned to look at me as I walked through the entrance, and I didn't think it was just because I was wearing body armor and carrying a rifle. Vicky rose from her seat and grabbed my hand, her face ashen, as if the ramifications of what she'd seen were just hitting her.

"What's going on?" I asked, not just her but looking over at Nance and Hachette as well. "Why haven't we Transitioned already?"

"They're not coming after us," Hachette explained, motioning at the main screen.

The image there wasn't purely optical, of course. We were too far away from the planet now for that, farther out than the orbit of the Moon from Earth, but the computer stitched together the sensor data with the optical telescopes into something coherent enough for us fallible humans to follow.

The space station seemed larger than it had when we'd flown

up to it, probably a function of the simulation, but it made the whole thing look fake. The Skrela mothership didn't look fake though. It looked all too real and all too familiar after the last few months, though still undeniably and eerily alien, defying definition as any coherent shape. It sat off the shoulder of the station, dwarfing it by comparison, blotting out a whole continent on the planet below due to the perspective we were seeing it from.

It just sat there for another thirty seconds before anyone spoke.

"It's been maintaining that orbit for over ten minutes now," Wojtera told me. "Like it's... just waiting for something."

It stopped waiting. The blast of coherent energy was incandescent blue, though I couldn't say for sure if that was the work of the computer or some actual effect of the unknown weapon on the fabric of reality. It sure as hell had an effect on the orbital station. The thing broke into a dozen pieces, the blue glow engulfing the structure, swallowing up the pieces as they vaporized.

"What the fuck?" I murmured. "Why the hell would they do that?"

"The mothership is accelerating toward us," Wojtera warned.

Hachette sighed.

"Are the Intercepts back on board?"

"They're secure," Nance told him. "And the corvettes are back in close enough formation to avoid Transition Lag if we jump together."

"Dwight, do you have the coordinates that Zerhanen gave us for the Womb?"

"They're already programmed into the navigational system, Colonel."

"Phillip, if you please, get us out of here."

"Taking us into T-Space," Yanayev said, not waiting for confirmation was Nance. That was a good sign, that the bridge crew was accepting Hachette's authority again. Maybe the mind-blowing revelations of the last few days had helped with that.

I clutched reflexively at the safety railing around the edge of the command station as we shifted, leaving the destruction and danger behind us again. But it was still there every time we came out. There was no running from it. We'd tried that for a year on Hausos, and look where it got us.

"Where's Lilandreth?" Hachette wanted to know.

"Last I saw of her, she was in the lander," I told him. "You told me to get up here ASAP, so I didn't stick around to see what she did." Which maybe was a bit insubordinate, but he was sounding a little *too* much like the old Hachette.

"When I called," he told me, "there was a Skrela mothership engaging us in a staring match." Hachette yanked at the quick-release of his restraints and leaned forward, elbows on his knees. "Jesus Christ, Cam, do you think that neurotic computer was telling the truth?"

"I think," I told him, falling into one of the spare couches, "that things are a lot more fucked up than we thought they were. The question is, does it change anything?"

"Christ, yes!" Nance interjected, surging out of his captain's chair and pacing between us. "We can't trust any of the damned Resscharr!" Hachette was obviously devastated by the discovery, but Nance was furious. I wondered why I wasn't. "Not to mention that computer. How the hell can we believe anything he says?"

"I haven't lied to you about anything, Captain Nance," Dwight told him. "I have been very clear that the only source of information I have is the data with which I was programmed by the Resscharr... and it is dated from when they left me in the Corridor."

"Tell me then, Dwight," Hachette said, "do you believe Zerhanen's story? Do you think that the Resscharr created the Skrela?"

"Zerhanen was not lying. He believes what he told me. That doesn't mean, however, that what he believes is reality. For one thing, he is constrained by the same practical limitations as I am—he only knows what he's told. The other thing is, Zerhanen was in hibernation for quite some time. I can't estimate the effect this would have on his mental patterns. There's the possibility of Quantum core deterioration."

"Great," I said, pulling off my gloves. The armor was hot when the internal air system was shut down. "We don't even know if he was telling the truth about where this Womb place is, or if it even exists."

"Dwight," Vicky asked, frowning, "both you and Zerhanen and even that AI back on Yfingam all refer to yourselves as male. Is that something the Resscharr programmed into you?"

"In all honesty," Dwight admitted, "the others have no concept of themselves as being of one gender or another. I chose male via random chance and assigned it to them simply for convenience."

"Why do it at all?"

"I sensed," he told her, "that it would help you deal with me as a sentient being rather than just a computer." On the main screen, Dwight's avatar scowled. "That was the problem we had with the Resscharr, as you may have already guessed by Lilandreth's reaction to my presence. They thought of us as tools... not even slaves, as Zerhanen said, but simply machines to be used and discarded."

Vicky looked as if she was about to ask him something else,

but I laid a hand over hers and shook my head. There was a question in her eyes, but she said nothing.

"Do we proceed as if we believe Zerhanen?" Hachette asked, though I wasn't sure if he was seeking our opinions or just talking the whole matter through out loud. "I'm not sure if we have any other choice, except ignoring the whole thing and heading back to Yfingam immediately. We literally have nothing else to go on."

"Zerhanen isn't the only reason we're out here," I reminded him. "The Khitan records said the Seekers headed this way. And Zerhanen admitted his sensors detected Resscharr ships pass by his station. We're heading the right direction. If Zerhanen was misled or crazy, then maybe there'll be nothing at the coordinates he gave us, but I don't think he had any reason to lie to us."

"If you think it's the right way to go," Nance said with a reluctant shrug, "then I guess I'll get behind it too." Hachette's eyes narrowed, though I wasn't sure if it was from the implication that Nance was backing the idea because the captain trusted me more than him, or that there was the possibility of Nance vetoing the whole thing no matter what Hachette said. Nance didn't seem to notice Hachette's reaction, or possibly he just didn't care. "But why the hell did the Skrela blow the place up? If this Zerhanen *was* telling the truth, they already knew his station was there. They could have destroyed the thing *thousands* of years ago."

"They didn't destroy it when the Seekers came through," Vicky mused. "But the Seekers didn't board it. It must have been us. Maybe these Condemnation types didn't want anyone else knowing what they were up to."

"That is indeed a distinct possibility," Dwight agreed, stepping in before any of us could comment on it. "The Skrela also attacked when you entered the facility on the last world. My initial fear was that they were somehow tracking us, but it makes more sense that they were left in the system inactive, to be awakened only if one of the Condemnation bases was disturbed."

That brought up other questions. Like, why would the Condemnation care? Once the Skrela were set loose, either the ones responsible would run off first and find a new home away from all those terrible sinners they'd just disposed of, or they'd stay and sacrifice themselves on the altar of their idealism. And why would they leave the bases in the first place? They'd be useless once the plan was set in motion. If they'd been worried about them being discovered, why not just dispose of them?

No one else brought those questions up though, and I kept them to myself. I wouldn't have trusted the answers.

"If the Seekers came this way," Hachette reasoned, "then they probably went on to this Womb place. We could find a gateway home there."

Yeah, sure. I didn't point out, though, that this had been over a thousand years ago, and the Skrela were still around. The odds were that, if the Seekers had found the Womb, they hadn't survived the encounter.

"If that's settled," I said instead, pushing myself back to my feet. Besides being hot, this armor weighed a ton. Why the hell would anyone ever want to be Force Recon? "I'm going to go get out of this shit and grab a shower."

"Bridge, this is Security," Jean Stilwell said, her voice coming over the main speakers. "I have a situation at the Tahni quarters and I need assistance from someone with more diplomatic skills than me, unless you'd like me to stun Lan-Min-Gen and Lilandreth before one of them winds up killing the other."

"Aw, for God's sake," I moaned. "Do we really have *time* for this shit?"

"Alvarez," Hachette said, nodding toward the bridge entrance, "don't bother taking off the armor just yet."

[14]

"Diplomatic skills, she said," I reminded Vicky, tapping a spiked boot sole on the deck of the lift car, watching the level counter move upward with glacial slowness. "Since when do *I* have fucking diplomatic skills?"

"You know what happens when you handle one impossible situation," she replied, more accepting of this whole situation than I was apparently.

"You get assigned a lot more of them," I finished for her. "But what diplomatic mission was I ever *good* at? I mean, look what happened with the Vailoans. We were just supposed to get access to their historical records, for Christ's sake, and instead we ended up nearly starting a world war. And it's not like I did anything to *negotiate* my way out of that... you just came down with a bunch of Vigilantes and pulled my ass out of the fire."

"You got the Karai to send troops with us. That's something."

"Look what good it did. Now they don't trust us anymore because we got their people killed. Top should be doing this."

Vicky's eyes were gentle, and her touch on my arm probably would have been if I could have felt it through this stupid armor.

"She would be. But Hachette doesn't have her anymore, so he's counting on you."

I grunted noncommittally.

"What was all that on the bridge though?" Vicky asked me, gesturing upward to the level we'd just left. "Why didn't..."

"Not here," I said, interrupting her. "Not now." I touched my ear and then looked upward. "Later."

Her eyes went wide and I thought she finally understood what I was worried about. Our conversation was cut short by the lift doors sliding open and depositing us in the middle of a shitstorm.

"I will no longer countenance your disrespect!" Lilandreth roared, pointing the business end of a Predecessor energy pistol between Lan-Min-Gen's eyes. "We gave life to your people, built hundreds of worlds as a gift to you, and you were too careless, too clumsy to keep it! You lost it to those we rejected as unworthy and now you have the temerity to blame *us* for your failings!"

Yes, not only was Lilandreth yelling at the Tahni in English, she was doing it with all the style and flourish of one of those old romance novels Top used to read.

Lan-Min-Gen had divested himself of his Shock Trooper armor, as had the two dozen other Tahni gathered in the broad passageway outside their quarters, but that didn't mean he was unarmed. He'd managed to secure a laser carbine—one of theirs, not one of ours, though how I wasn't sure, since the armorer was under strict orders only to release any of their weapons if Hachette okayed it. The carbine was leveled at Lilandreth at about waist-high, though I had my doubts whether it would kill her. She wasn't wearing her armor either, but given what we knew of Predecessor tech, I wouldn't have been surprised if her normal clothes were designed to stop so primitive an attack.

"You say you're our creator," Lan-Min-Gen yelled back at

her, also in English, "yet you absolve yourself of any responsibility for the failings of your creation. More, every failing you attribute to us is evident in your own society, and if it didn't come from you, then where did we inherit it? Blindness to our failings, unthinking adherence to our beliefs, underestimating those we think our inferiors... these were our *true* gifts from you, our gods, the Ancients. And now that I have learned the nature of your downfall, I no longer harbor any shame at following in your footsteps."

I handed my helmet to Vicky despite a conviction that I might wish I'd left it on, then stepped between them.

"What in the living fuck is going on here?" I barked, and if I was imitating Top, it was done out of love... and desperation. I pinned each of them with a glare, though I had to look up to do it. Pretty damn *far* up for Lilandreth. "Do we not have enough people—and things—trying to kill us all without you two saving them the trouble?"

"This arrogant false god is at fault," Lan-Min-Gen insisted, jabbing his laser weapon at Lilandreth—and, by virtue of my current position, at me. "She followed me here from the armory, threatening me with her weapon as if I, Lan-Min-Gen of the Imperial Shock Troopers, had never had a gun shoved in my face before."

"You ungrateful cretin!" Lilandreth raged, and at least *her* gun was pointed above my head. "You have not ceased to taunt and declaim since we entered the shuttle! Am I not here, on this soul-sucking voyage, for nothing else than to save your world from the threat of the Skrela? Do you think *I* care if they kill me? I wish they *had*! It would have saved me the shame of knowing there were those among my own species so sick and depraved as to try to wipe out all we've accomplished!"

It was interesting that she didn't mention her people wiping out the original Skrela in the first place when she counted all the sicked and depraved items off.

"Whatever true gods there may be," Lan-Min-Gen said, "they may know why such a creature as you does *anything*, but I don't pretend to. I only wish I could return to Tahn-Skyyiah and tell all of my brothers that their faith in the Ancients was misplaced, that they were not divine beings, not the wise guides we believed, that they were as vicious as the humans, as divided as we ever were even before the Emperor united our tribes."

"They'd never believe you," I told him. "If I ever get home, I won't be able to tell anyone about this. No one would ever buy any of it." I shook my head. "I don't even think I'd bother trying. You and I know things no one should have to. No one could blame you for letting it drive you a little crazy."

Lan-Min-Gen regarded me evenly, his brow ridges nearly hiding his piggish, black eyes.

"I have led my Shock Troopers through the war, through the Corridor to this place, away from the power of the Spirit Emperor and the grip of the Ancients. I did this in the face of the weakness of my own people, in the face of you humans of the Commonwealth and your attempts to control us. I wouldn't be controlled by my people or yours, I wouldn't allow the loss of our Emperor to rob me of my faith in our destiny, and I won't be broken by the fall of yet another false god."

"Well, that's damned good to hear," I said, nodding. I put a hand on his shoulder, and he stared at it as if it were an insect that had crawled up his arm. "Since you're so committed to serving General Zan-Thint and keeping your people back at Yfingam safe, I know you're going to calm this whole situation down and we're all going to get down to planning what we're going to do when we find the Womb. Right?"

I thought I might have pushed things too far, that Lan-Min-Gen might just decide I was a very convenient target and make it a two-for-one deal, putting a shot right through me and into Lilandreth. But his carbine muzzle lowered and the Tahni stepped back. I didn't sigh in relief, but it took an effort. I just maintained a calm demeanor and turned back to Lilandreth.

"I need you to put that gun away and go back to your quarters."

She didn't look like she wanted to do that. In fact, she looked like she was more inclined to kill me, Lan-Min-Gen, and then herself. How the hell do you talk down an evolved, talking dinosaur who just found out her whole life is based on a lie?

"You consider us unworthy," I said, deciding to give it my best attempt. "As rejects. You thought we'd fuck up your plans, and guess what? We did. Despite everything, despite every obstacle you threw in front of us, despite every opportunity to destroy ourselves, we made it."

"Are you trying to... rub my nose in it, I believe the term is?" Lilandreth asked, her gun held lower, at a better height to blow my head off. I'd like to say I was afraid, but I'd be lying. I was angry, and controlling my anger was a hell of a lot harder than controlling my fear. I was suddenly very aware of the weight of the Gauss rifle in my hands, of how little effort it would take to put a round though Lilandreth's spine.

"I'm trying," I told her, deliberately calm, "to get you to think about who you are, who the Resscharr are. You've had star travel for *millions* of years, you've moved around moons and filled this galaxy with life. Are you trying to tell me you can't get your shit together at least enough to go somewhere and process this like a fucking adult? Because I'll tell you, Lilandreth, we need your help to get through this, but if you're just dead set on getting yourself killed, I'd appreciate it if you wouldn't try to take any of the rest of us with you."

Lilandreth said nothing, but she tucked the weapon into one of the pouches slung over her shoulder, then stalked away, heading back to her quarters. Vicky blew out a breath, shoulders sagging.

"Jesus."

"You were pretty quiet," I said, eyeing her sidelong, more teasing than accusatory.

"I didn't want to screw up whatever tact you were taking," she said. "Plus, you had the gun." I slipped an arm around her, wanting to lean against her but holding back because the weight of the armor might have sent us both toppling over.

Most of the Tahni had dispersed, but not Lan-Min-Gen. He still stood off to the side, watching me.

"You can't trust her, Alvarez," he told me. "You think you require her for this mission, and maybe it's true, but make no mistake. She thinks she's a different breed than the ones who betrayed us all, but the Ancients are all the same. We Tahni were wrong to believe them to be gods, but their own belief in it is even stronger than ours was." Lan-Min-Gen came closer to me than I was comfortable with, but maybe personal space wasn't a thing with the Tahni. It was very apparent that, like me, he hadn't had a chance to clean up, and I wrinkled my nose at the stench. "I don't say that she's intentionally evil. She might very well believe she's doing the right thing. But you said it yourself. They were the masters of everything for millions of years, and when something finally came to push them off that pedestal, it was *them*. There's no way to live with that sense of superiority for thousands of years and not act on it."

"Is it just me," Vicky asked as we watched the Tahni follow the rest of his troops into their quarters, "or does it worry you too that he makes a lot of sense?"

I nodded.

"It scares the living shit out of me."

"I don't like the plan," Vicky said, the words a warm breath against my neck.

Propping myself up on an elbow, I stared down at her in the darkness, bemused.

"You got the strangest damned pillow talk, woman."

She chuckled, smacking me on the arm.

"Fine, it was great, it was spectacular, you're a Greek god." She rolled her eyes. "We're going to be feet dry in thirty hours, and I'm telling you, I don't like the plan."

"Oh, God," I murmured, covering my eyes. "Please don't make me go back to the Goddamned Operations Center again. I can't listen to Hachette dither anymore." I wanted to be offended by Vicky bringing up business so soon after we finally had a little alone time, but she was right. There wasn't much time left, and we'd already started working the company through our op plan. No time for afterglow, not for a commander. "I thought I was going to have to choke the fucker out when he started talking about how our real mission was getting home and there was no guarantee the Seekers were going to be there. I know Nance wanted to punch him, and I was about ready to let him do it."

My eyes had adjusted to the darkness of the compartment, and I could see Vicky's face clearly in the gentle glow of the chemical striplights. Her frown was entrenched all the way to her eyes.

"I don't give a shit about Hachette," she insisted, thumping a fist into the mattress. "What bothers me is the idea of trusting Zerhanen's word about the setup there."

"You think he was lying?" I blinked, surprised. She hadn't brought that up before.

"No, I think he's *never been there*. He might be telling us what he's heard, the memories in his databank, but he doesn't *know* that's the setup." Vicky turned over on her side and met my eyes. Mine wandered downward and she chucked my chin back up impatiently with the edge of her hand. "Besides that, we have the company planning for a space drop while the Tahni take Lilandreth to the main lock. How the hell can we trust them to look out for her after what happened today?"

"As crazy as it sounds, I *do* trust him. That doesn't mean Lilandreth can actually access the place though, even with Dwight's help." I shook my head. "I mean, we're making the assumption that the Skrela came after us because the Condemnation didn't want anyone fucking with their setup. If that's the case, wouldn't they make sure their security systems didn't just let in any Resscharr that came along? And hell, Dwight... *says* he didn't even know this place existed, so he'd have no way of being certain he can crack whatever firewalls they put up."

"We *did* think of that," Vicky said. "I mean, Nance did. He said if we can't get in any other way, he'd try the ship's main gun out on the airlock."

I winced.

"Even if he has the chance, I'm not even sure that would work. For all we know, the place has shields."

"Then what *is* our plan B?" Vicky wanted to know. "What do we do if we can't get in?"

"As much as I hate to say it, we might have to just pull out." Rolling flat on the bed, I rested my head on my intertwined hands. "As important as this mission is, the survival of the ship and everyone on it is *more* important. There's no use making this a suicide run."

"*That'll* be a shit-show," she sighed. "If we have to pull out, then everyone except Hachette will want to go back and give up on the whole thing, and we'll wind up with that mutiny we managed to avoid."

"Let's not borrow trouble," I suggested. "We'll get there, we'll pop out far enough away to be able to Transition away from trouble, and we'll find out what the situation is. If things look like Zerhanen told us, we go in and see what happens. If it doesn't look like that, then we adapt, improvise, and overcome, like Marines always do."

"Ooh-rah," Vicky murmured, rolling atop me, her skin warm and still damp with sweat. Her breath was hot against my cheek. "How far can we push this? How many times can we roll the dice before they come up snake-eyes?"

"This is the last time," I promised. "We make this work or we're out. I don't care if we have to get Nance to dump us on a human world with nothing but the clothes on our back, we're out."

She chuckled, and the sound vibrated through both our chests.

"You go right on thinking that, Street Rat. If Nance and the others tell Hachette to go fuck himself, you're the one they're going to come to."

"I don't want to believe that," I groaned, squeezing my eyes shut. "But I think I do now, after what Nance said on the bridge. I don't *want* that."

"You're a Marine," she reminded me. "Since when did what you *wanted* have anything to do with it?" She kissed me fiercely. "Like you said, stop borrowing trouble. We have to be up in six hours. Let's not waste it."

"Ooh-rah," I teased, then rolled her over beneath me.

Adapt, improvise, and overcome.

[15]

My Vigilante grinned down at me like it knew better than I did what was about to happen. The chest plate of the suit was cold beneath my fingertips, like a corpse, and I found that analogy even more troubling when the plate swung downward, revealing the innards of the metal giant. Darkness beckoned to me, the interior an endless vacancy in the dim light of the storage bay.

I remembered the first time I'd crawled into one of the suits, back in Armor school on Inferno. The darkness, the enclosed space, hadn't scared me. They'd *appealed* to me. They were the dark closet where I could hide from the bullies, the tormenters, from the memories. Then I'd jacked in, attaching the leads from the suit's helmet to the new interface sockets implanted in my temples, and the young warrant officer in charge of synchronizing the jacks with the suit had warned me that there might be some side effects. There had been, the influx of one of those memories I'd been hiding from.

In that one moment, I'd been terrified, not of the suit or even of the memory, but of the idea that I'd be washed out, that they wouldn't let me have this refuge, this shield against all the things that had hurt me from six years old right up to the time I was arrested. I'd been cured of the agoraphobia, cured of the unwillingness to trust, cured of the need to keep everyone at arm's length, but the Vigilante still held the feeling of safety, of refuge. It wasn't just a suit of armor... it was *home*.

And there was the problem. There was the reason I'd never been able to feel comfortable on Hausos. Hausos wasn't home. Hell, even the *Marines* wasn't home. This suit was. And that was the thing I'd have to deal with if I actually wanted to put this life behind me and move on.

The overhead lights flickered on, revealing scores more of the suits, and footsteps clicked on the hard, metal deck as Vicky led the rest of the company into the bay.

"The suits have all been through redundant systems check," Vicky told me. She'd *already* told me, in private, but this was a formal report for the benefit of the rest of the company. "They're all reading green. We're Winchester on grenade launcher reloads, but..."

"... but those aren't any use against the Skrela anyway," I finished for her. "Very good, Captain Sandoval." The company didn't move immediately to their suits. Instead, they watched me, waiting for something... for something meaningful, something validating. Something that would make them believe what they were about to do was worth dying for.

I paced in front of them, hands clasped behind my back, searching for the words. As usual, it all came back to what the Skipper would say. Except not *quite*, because the Skipper had the benefit of a declared war and we had no choice but to fight it. I doubt even *he* would have known what to make of this situation.

"You all know my story," I told them, the words coming from nowhere, my mouth working only a quarter-second behind my brain. "You know where I came from. No family, no home, not even a gang. I was on my own, arrested for felony murder, about to be sent to the Freezer, punitive hibernation, probably forever. I was given a choice though. A hazy, ice-cold half-death, or a much more certain real one, fighting the Tahni. I've often wondered why I chose the Marines over something painless, over the certain relief from the pain and loneliness of the hopeless life I was living."

Vicky's eyes sparkled with curiosity. I hadn't told her about this part, mostly because I hadn't planned it.

"I think, in that moment, sitting there talking to the computer subroutine pretending to be my defense attorney, I fell back on what had gotten me through seven years of group homes and six more on my own, living on the street. Sheer, bloody-minded stubbornness. I chose the option that would give me some measure of control over my fate."

A few chuckles at that, maybe because they appreciated the sentiment or maybe at the notion that a Marine had any say in their own fate.

"What we're doing now," I went on, "is something like that, an attempt to have some say in our own fate. I know some of you would prefer to just find a planet and settle on it, give up on any idea of going home. I can't blame you for that... but doing it while the threat of the Skrela still exists puts our fate entirely in the hands of others, ones more inhuman and merciless than a Commonwealth criminal court judge." I snorted. "Maybe."

Laughs, and some of the tension went out of their faces, out of their stances.

"If we can make sure that the Skrela are gone from this galaxy, then our fate is our own. If we choose to keep searching for a way home, we can do that without having to constantly look over our shoulder for the wolves at our heels. If we decide that we want to make a home out here, we can do *that* too... without having to constantly scan the sky, waiting for the hammer to fall."

Nods at that, some thoughtful looks. But still fear, doubt, trepidation.

"Some of us won't make it," I admitted, giving voice to those doubts. I watched Singh's face as I said it and he jerked slightly, involuntarily, as if he'd been slapped. "I'm not going to lie to you. We have no idea what we're going to be facing when we come out of T-Space, and it might be that the whole plan is garbage and we have to turn tail and run, but if we *do* go down to that moon and fight, Marines are going to die. You not only have to know that going in, you have to get it straight in your head that this is *worth* dying for. You have to leave all your doubts here on the ship. You get where I'm coming from?"

"Yes, sir," Singh said dutifully, though whether he meant it was up for debate, and several of the officers and NCOs echoed the words with varying degrees of enthusiasm.

I pressed my lips together to hold in a sigh. If this had been the Skipper, they'd have bought into it by now. I wasn't a great public speaker and I hadn't suddenly turned into one just because Hachette had shoved a company command on me.

"You've gone through the rehearsals," I told them, abandoning the motivational bullshit. "You know how up in the air this is and things might change last-second, but for right now, assume we're running a vacuum drop. If the moon has an atmosphere, we'll adjust plans, but the bottom line is, if it's too thin for our suits to use it as reaction mass, we'll have to drop with our on-board supply. That means we'll probably be bingo fuel once we're feet-dry, so keep that in mind. Mobility is our main advantage over the Skrela, and if we're forced to fight them in the open, we're gonna have to adjust tactics, try to maximize cover and concealment, if any's available."

I was more comfortable with this part. This came naturally, didn't sound fake.

"Our best bet is to get inside as quick as possible, try to

bottleneck their numbers. Remember, the objective isn't to kill every last Skrela, it's to hold them off until Lilandreth and Dwight can access their systems and figure out how to end this. We also don't know how that might work, which means we might need every Marine available for the final operation."

"We expecting any air or orbital support, sir?" Blevins, one of the platoon sergeants asked, raising her hand like we were in a classroom.

"Situation dependent. If there are limited enemy air assets, we should have support from the drop-ships and possibly the assault shuttles. Anything heavier than that depends on what we're facing. I'd expect if there are any Skrela motherships, they're going to keep the *Orion* and the Intercepts tied up though." I shrugged. "You're a Marine, you know just how much we can usually count on help from anyone else."

"Yeah, especially out here," she agreed, snorting a humorless laugh. "I swear, sir, the drop-ship crews bust their ass for us, but I only know assault shuttles exist because they're on the manifest. The next time I see one of those bastards running air-to-ground will be the first time."

"They have their own job to do, Sergeant," I reminded her, though I couldn't really disagree. In my experience assault shuttle pilots tended to think of themselves as *real* pilots, meant for ship-to-ship combat, and considered air support beneath them. "Moving on, I'm gonna put First Platoon out front again, with Fourth at rear guard. Second on our right flank, Third on the left in a box formation if we move across open ground and wind up without the reaction mass for jump-jets. Move fast and maintain suppressive fire, try to funnel the enemy using their own dead. I'll be right behind First, and Captain Sandoval will be at the rear with Fourth. Acting First Sergeant Czarnecki will stick with Third. If we get separated, find First in your IFF and rally on them. If IFFs are inoperative due to signal jamming, rally on the entrance to the Resscharr facility. We should have a bead on it by the time we drop, and I'll make sure it gets shared to your personal HUDs."

I tried to think of something else, but I was verging on being repetitive, and there's nothing troops respect less than an officer who blathers on and on, saying the same things in different ways.

"Any questions?"

There were a few, because there are *always* questions, and a couple of them were stupid, because when you're dealing with a hundred Marines and some of them are barely into their twenties, a couple of them will *always* be stupid.

"No, Lance Corporal," I replied with strained patience, "I *don't* know whether this mission will be covered under combat pay or TDY orders. And before anyone asks, I *also* don't know whether it counts toward time spent in an active war zone on your retirement. Honest to God, I don't know whether MilPerCen back on Inferno even knows this ship exists. Fleet Intelligence doesn't exactly share those sort of things."

Laughs, not at the situation, which wasn't all that funny, but at the dumb-ass question. Which was why I hadn't shut down the dumb question without answering it. People needed those laughs.

"If we don't get back," someone said near the back, a PFC I thought, but I couldn't tell who because the words were murmured, "my family won't even know what happened to me."

And the laughter died away. It was easy to forget about all those other families back home since I lacked one myself, but the soft, quiet statement pressed down on all of the men and women before me like a wave crashing.

"You all volunteered for an Intelligence mission," I reminded them, though not harshly. They didn't need a lecture, not even the lance corporal who asked about TDY. "You knew from the beginning that you might not come home and that no one would ever be told how it happened. Whether it came fighting Zan-Thint and his troops in some uninhabited system past the Tahni worlds or halfway across the galaxy. I know none of you thought your assignment would last more than two years, but you knew it *might*." I spread my hands, encompassing the lot of them. "We're all Marines. For us it's more than a job, it's our identity. Tell me the truth... would you rather go out this way, fighting aliens tens of thousands of light-years from Earth, or go back and dig up dirt on a colony?"

Looks of what might have been reluctant acceptance. Maybe I'd finally reached them. It was going to have to be close enough.

"We Transition in an hour. I want everyone in their suit and on the drop-ships by then."

"Are you going to be on the bridge, sir?" Singh asked, and there was something petulant about his tone that told me he resented the fact that I spent so much time with Hachette in planning and not enough with the company.

Anger flared inside my gut, and I very nearly snapped at him that he was one of the people who wanted me to start a mutiny and take over the ship and how the hell would it be better for me to leave Hachette to make decisions without any input at all from me or the Marines. Vicky caught my eye and shook her head.

Damn. She knew me too well.

"Someone's got to make sure they don't fuck this up, right?" I asked him, forcing a smile. He nodded, and I thought maybe I'd assuaged his worries. "You get the company ready, Ajay. I'll meet you on Drop-Ship One before things kick off. Tell First Sergeant..." I hesitated, remembering Endicott. "Tell *Top* that Captain Sandoval will be with him in Drop-Ship Two, along with the HQ section, okay?"

"Yes, sir. I'll see you there."

I maintained my smile and upright bearing until Vicky and I were in the lift car, then I sagged, leaning back against the bulkhead.

"I can't do this, Vick. I can't do it anymore. There's just too much of this psychotherapy bullshit."

"It's just like leading a platoon," she told me, grabbing my hand. "Only now, instead of holding the hands of nineteen-year-old PFCs, you have to hold the hand of twenty-five-year-old second lieutenants." Vicky rolled her eyes. "Or, in this case, a thirty-year-old first lieutenant."

"It's not the thirty-year-old first lieutenant that gets me," I told her. "It's the forty-something colonel about to lose his shit."

The lift stopped one level short of the bridge and Marcus Hachette stepped in. He nearly stopped short at the sight of the two of us, but boarded after the slight hesitation. I stood straight and tried to erase the stricken frustration from both my mind and face. The man had impeccable timing.

"Your company ready to deploy?" he asked me, the question and the stern look on his face both trying just a little too hard.

"Yes, sir," Vicky answered for me, probably worried I'd smart off at the man, given what I'd just said. "They'll be loaded on the drop-ships before we jump."

The door slid shut behind Hachette, and when the car announced it was continuing on to the command level, he glanced sharply up at the speaker as if the interruption had spooked him. He smacked his hand against the control panel, pausing the lift, and I frowned, sharing a confused look with Vicky.

"I'm going with you," he announced.

"What the fuck?" I blurted. "I mean, sir?" I correct myself. "I mean, what the *fuck*, sir?"

"Not with *you* on the drop-ship," he clarified, raising a hand as if *that* was the part that had freaked me out. "With Lilandreth and the Tahni on the lander."

"But why?" Vicky asked him. She looked as if she wanted to elaborate but couldn't come up with any words adequate enough to describe the stupidity of the idea.

"Won't you be needed here on the ship?" I asked him pointedly, and he scowled at the question.

"Needed for *what*?" he demanded. "You and Nance have already made it clear you don't trust me to make the tactical decisions, and I'm worse than useless if I'm going to be ignored." Hachette shrugged. "Nance controls the ship in a fight, and since Dunstan and Brandano were among the most insistent on trying to have me relieved, I doubt they'd listen to my orders if I told them something they weren't already going to do."

I wanted to argue with that, but I found I couldn't come up with anything to contradict the man. I squeezed my eyes shut for a moment, then made another attempt.

"Sir, your job is to analyze intelligence and make decisions based on it. You'd be in a more central position to do that on the *Orion*."

"I *would* be," he agreed, arching an eyebrow, "if it weren't just about guaranteed that we'll lose signal with the landing party the minute they enter the Resscharr facility. We only had it from the space station because Dwight was able to shut down the dampening fields. Considering what Zerhanen told us, that this place is run by a hostile AI, there's no way Dwight's going to be able to take control that easily, or that fast. Any intelligence there is to be gleaned is going to be inside that facility, and that's where I need to be."

"And what if the intelligence you need is that the Skrela opposition is too much?" Vicky asked gently, "and that the *Orion* needs to retreat and cut our losses?"

Hachette gave her a pitying look, as if she was ridiculous for even mentioning the idea.

"Do you really think Nance and the others are going to *allow* me to make that decision? Or that I even want to be the one making it anymore?" He shook his head. "No, I need to be able to analyze the situation on the ground."

"You're gonna get yourself fucking killed," I declared. "Sir," I added belatedly.

"Maybe," he admitted. His smile was wistful, his eyes focused on something well past the bulkhead. "All I can think about since Ellen died are my kids. They're grown, of course, or nearly so. I got married too early, straight out of the Academy. We were young and foolish, Mary and I, and we had children too early as well, because the war had started and we both knew I'd be called to do my part and spend months or even years apart." Hachette rubbed at his eyes with the heels of his hands, then ran them up through his hair. It was tousled and disheveled, well beyond regulation length, and he'd made no attempt to cut it or bring it under control. "We did, of course. And our marriage didn't survive it, but the twins did. Jamie and William. They're both teenagers now, and the last I heard..." A sob choked off the words and he had to try again. "... the last I heard, they both wanted to go to the Academy."

Oh, Jesus. I started to say something, something that would have been entirely inadequate, but he wasn't done yet.

"But you know, I don't think I was worried about my kids so much as I am about myself. I mean, I told myself that I had to get home so I could be with them, but if I was so damned interested in being there for my boys, why the hell had I volunteered for every single assignment that would keep me away from them?" He shook his head and tears flickered in the overhead lights. "No, I was trying to give myself a reason to go back, something selfless, something higher than the *real* reason. I'm afraid.

I'm afraid of dying out here, alone, with no one who'll give a shit. And I've been letting that fear control me for too long now. Not anymore. I'm going down there and I'm going to do something useful."

"There's nothing we can do to stop you," I admitted. "But..." I blew out a breath. "I won't even tell you it's a bad idea. Just be careful. There *are* people who give a shit about you here. That's not to say you haven't pissed us off, but that doesn't mean we want you to go get yourself killed."

Hachette laughed softly.

"That may be the nicest thing you ever said to me, Alvarez."

[16]

Spacetime erupted and spat us out, and I had just enough time to think that if I never had to Transition again, I wouldn't miss it at all. Then we were in another place, dozens of light-years from our last entry and one hell of a lot closer to the Womb than I'd thought we'd be.

"What the hell?" I hissed, not loud enough to be heard, leaning back in my seat with the all-too-familiar lurch of gut and inner ear brought on by microgravity.

It took me a beat to realize what I was looking at on the main screen, and took Wojtera a second longer to make the announcement.

"Type-K star," he said, as calm and matter-of-fact as if this was just another Transition. "Yellow-orange, cooler than the Sun. Only four planets, ice giant farthest out, terrestrial closest in but it's burned to ash. Then two gas giants, one with rings, and then... our objective."

He turned to Nance and Hachette, shaking his head.

"This doesn't make any sense," he said, gesturing at the screen. "The objective world, the Womb, is bigger than any gas giant I've ever screen."

"It sure as hell is," Vicky said softly from beside me. "That thing makes Jupiter look tiny."

And it was... dark. Every planet I'd ever seen had a fairly high albedo, reflecting the light from its star at least enough to be seen from across the solar system, but not this one. We were on its day side, according to the position of the star on the display, but it was a sullen, dirty brown, roiling and dark, even more conspicuous from the bright glare of the Cauldron of Creation surrounding us on all sides.

"What doesn't make sense about it?" I asked Wojtera, but it was Nance who answered.

"Because a planet that large should have collapsed into a star." The captain stared at the world on the screen, the disbelief in his expression as pronounced as that in his voice.

"Maybe it's a brown dwarf?" Yanayev suggested.

"What's a brown dwarf?" Hachette wondered, earning a dirty look from Nance. I don't know if the captain would have answered, but Yanayev did, her voice clinical, like she was teaching a class or reading from a textbook.

"Brown dwarfs are substellar objects that are not massive enough to sustain nuclear fusion of ordinary hydrogen into helium in their cores, unlike a main-sequence star," she explained. "Instead, they have a mass between the most massive gas giant planets and the least massive stars, approximately thirteen to eighty times that of Jupiter." She shook her head. "But one this big should be able to fuse lithium. It should be hotter."

"What are we picking up from the surface?" Nance asked. "Is the Womb facility floating in the atmosphere or something?"

Wojtera squinted at his readout, his frown deepening. I didn't try to look over his shoulder, staring instead at the display. There was something off about the dull, brown atmosphere of the planet, or brown dwarf, or whatever it was. Clouds in the atmosphere of gas giants were nothing new to me. I'd seen dozens of them, hundreds, from dozens of different systems, and while they were all different, they weren't *that* different. What I saw on the screen weren't cloud patterns, they were... waves. The surface was roiling like an ocean.

But an ocean of what?

"Holy shit," Wojtera murmured, then looked up from his instruments, face slack with shock. "It's liquid."

"It's *what*?" Nance snapped.

"The surface is... liquid. It's viscous." The Tactical officer licked his lips, pausing, eyes darting across his screen. "The spectrometer and computer simulations say it's... it's about the same consistency as the biotic fluid in an autodoc."

"That's because it's the same thing, more or less," Dwight interjected. His avatar regarded the Tactical display, hands on hips. "The Womb is a nanite bath the size of a brown dwarf. The entire planet is a factory to produce Skrela."

As if some ancient god at the center of the world had heard him, something separated from the surface of the gigantic world, a pinprick of light against the vast, roiling sea.

"That's a mothership," Wojtera announced, breathless. "It just... came out of that shit, whatever it is."

"Nanite froth," Dwight supplied. "This world was once a brown dwarf, I believe, but if you check the gravitational readings, it's lost a good deal of its mass. The nanites are eating away at the interior, using the raw materials to build the Skrela... and they've been doing it for tens of thousands of years."

"He's right," Wojtera said, and there was a trace of awe in his tone. "This planet should be at least a third again as massive as it is. But it hasn't shrunk in size... how is that even possible?"

"The nanites have displaced the raw materials, but their mass is much less. The excess mass was turned into energy... and into the Skrela."

"The mothership," Hachette broke in, impatience in his expression. "Is it heading this way?"

"Not yet," Wojtera replied, shaking his head. "It's just... like, sitting there in orbit. No active scans yet."

"What the hell is it waiting for?" I asked, staring at the thing, expecting any second it would rocket away from the Womb and head straight for us.

"Look," Vicky said, pointing at the screen. "There's something else coming up from the surface."

I squinted at the image but didn't see what she was talking about immediately. Wojtera reached into his holographic controls and spread his fingers wide, zooming in on the area. What had been barely visible black dots expanded into more familiar shapes. Well, not *familiar*. They were still mind-twisting and counterintuitive, but I'd seen them before. They were Skrela fighters, the smaller assault craft that the motherships launched for atmospheric assaults. I guess they had to be produced separately from the motherships, because they swarmed around the newly delivered mothership, taking their turns tucking themselves away in the guts of the thing.

I tried to imagine going aboard one of the things. Would it be like walking through a starship or more along the lines of being swallowed by some massive sea creature? The things looked biological, and I'd just seen one... born? Hatched? Whatever. It hadn't come off an assembly line.

"Well, this is horrifying," I sighed. "If they have this big of a planet to work from, they can still put out *millions* of those ships."

"There is a theoretical limit," Dwight said. "At some point, they would reduce the mass of the planet to the point where the core would destabilize and it would reorganize into a smaller body. That would make it unusable for decades until it settled into its new configuration. But yes, it has the capability to produce hundreds of thousands of motherships and tens of millions of pods before there's any worry of destabilization."

"Where's the control base?" Hachette asked. "I don't see anything in orbit around that brown dwarf, no detection gear, no sensor dishes."

"The facility is on the dwarf's moon," Dwight said. "I believe it's on the far side of the planet at the moment."

"We could micro-Transition across the orbital plane and take a closer look," Yanayev offered. "The gravity well of this thing makes it tricky... minimum Transition distance is going to be lot farther out than for a terrestrial planet. But I can do the calculations and get us over there for a recon."

"No," Hachette said, and Nance glanced at him sharply. "We should send the corvettes."

I shrugged. It wasn't a bad idea. The things hadn't done a damned thing for us since we left Yfingam and they weren't any good in a fight.

"We'll have to run it past Lan-Min-Gen," Nance said, rubbing at his chin. "But it's not a bad idea." He nodded to Chase. "Get him on the horn." Nance eyed Hachette. "You want to talk to him?"

"This is Lan-Min-Gen." The Tahni's accent was becoming less pronounced as he gained more practice with English... or rather, as Vicky had told me, his accent was sounding more and more like *mine*.

"It's Hachette. We need a scouting mission out around the other side of the Womb planet. Can you contact your pilots and have them micro-Transition cross-orbit and bring us back scans of the moon?"

"I will do this. What do you wish them to do if they encounter opposition?"

"Do not engage yet," Hachette instructed. "We need to know what's over there. Tell them to jump out immediately if they're seen. Have them arrayed in a line-of-sight formation that allows a secure laser communications relay chain from one side of the brown dwarf to the other. That way they can get the data to us immediately."

"It will be done."

Chase made a gesture that the transmission had been cut.

"This all begs the question," Nance put in, "of how long we can sit out here before that mothership notices us."

"I don't believe it will be looking," Dwight said. "Consider, the Skrela are not individually sentient and the systems controlling a single mothership would likely only be complex enough to deal with tactical decisions, not strategic ones. However, once the control center learns of our presence... well, to use a colloquialism in your language, all bets are off."

"The corvettes are Transitioning," Wojtera reported.

The ugly little starships had been arrayed in a wedge formation ahead of the *Orion*, but as I watched them on the front screens, they were snapping out of existence, the rainbow ring of a Transition drive opening ahead of each of them, then fading away as the rip in spacetime healed itself.

"Shouldn't be too long," Yanayev murmured. "We're at about seventy million klicks out from the dwarf... maybe two seconds in T-space..."

"I've got them," Wojtera announced. "Well, the closest of them. The only one visible from this side of the planet."

The corvette was a glittering blue star off the shoulder of the brown dwarf, not visible as anything but a sensor blip, but there. I tried to imagine being that close to the planet, with the expanse of sullen, brown darkness swallowing the vast expanse of stars glowering at us from the center of the galaxy.

"We're receiving a signal from the relay," Chase said. "Delay is about two to four light-seconds."

"Put it on the main screen," Hachette ordered, beating

Nance to the punch by a fraction of a second, or at least that was what I guessed from the way the captain's jaw was working. Maybe Hachette was right about the two of them not both being on the ship during combat, because it felt as if Nance was about to start screaming at the man already.

A stream of Tahni symbols went across the display, followed by some sort of pictographic image that might have been something akin to a flag or a coat of arms, then finally replaced by the helmeted face of a Tahni pilot.

"This is Scout One," he said, the words coming out of synch with his mouth as the computer translated them. "I am in position for relay. Prepare for initial scans."

That was apparently all he had to say, and his image gave way to the Tahni version of a tactical display, not at all like ours. The symbols were impossible to decipher, but the *Orion*'s computer translated those just as it did their language and put the Commonwealth equivalent of the readouts in a square beside the transmission.

"Whoa," Vicky said, eyes going wide, and I nodded agreement.

If the brown dwarf had seemed huge at first glance, just shy of a star, its moon was a planet in its own right, somewhere between Mars and Venus in size, probably two thirds the size of Earth. I hadn't expected that, but what I'd expected even less were the thick, gray clouds floating over blue oceans and white ice caps.

"It's got an atmosphere," Wojtera said. "A thick one... not breathable. I'm not detecting any spectroscopic signs of conventional life, no chlorophyll, no free oxygen, no nitrogen."

"But there's water," I protested, waving at the screen. "And ice."

"No, not water." He wagged a finger at the spectroscopic readout. "That's liquid methane. The atmosphere is nitrogen and methane, about like Titan… and the external surface temperature is about the same, around negative 180 degrees Celsius. Damned cold down there."

"Well, that's good *and* bad," Vicky commented softly, and I knew exactly what she meant. The place had atmosphere, which meant our suits could use it for reaction mass for the jump-jets, but negative 180…

"Lan-Min-Gen," I asked, touching my ear bud to activate my 'link. "What's the lowest external temperature your exoskeletons can operate in?"

There was a pause, and I thought he might not have been monitoring his comms, but the answer came a moment later. He must, I figured, have had to look it up in the manual and then convert the temperature to our scale of measurement.

"Negative two hundred degrees Celsius," he told me. "But the servomotors can only endure that low of a temperature for a few minutes before they freeze up. We will have to get inside quickly."

"Yeah, I copy. I'll get back to you, but keep monitoring the readouts."

"We getting anything on the facility?" Hachette asked, impatience evident in the gentle drumming of his fingers on the arm of his chair. "That's a big fucking planet. If the damned thing is under that methane ocean, we're well and truly fucked."

Shit. That was a thought I hadn't needed to contemplate. I hadn't even considered that the Resscharr might have built the place under the ocean, but there was no reason they *couldn't*, not when they could control gravity. But while our suits and armor might be able to operate in liquid methane for a limited time, there was no fucking way we could *propel* ourselves through it.

"No, I see it," Wojtera announced, scrolling through menus

until the view in the Tahni feed shifted to show one of the moon's iced-over continents.

It looked about the size of Australia, which wasn't that big for a continent but was about the largest thing on this world, and a ridge of mountains rose like a snow-covered spine down the middle of it. They must have blocked the wind enough that, in the lee of them, a patch of bare, gray ground stood out... and in the middle of it was a thermal reading nearly two hundred degrees warmer than the background, a veritable sore thumb.

The dome in the center of the bare patch was the same dull gray as the rock, hard to pick out even with the enhanced optics of the Tahni corvette married to the subtle graphics engine of our computer system. Well-camouflaged, yet it was, like the planet and the moon, deceptively large.

"That thing's two klicks in diameter," Wojtera said, disbelief in his voice. "Five hundred meters tall, and that's just above ground. I'm not getting ground conduction readings from this far away, but I'd be willing to bet it goes down just as far. Probably a perfect sphere just buried halfway in the rock."

"You are correct in your estimate, Commander Wojtera," Dwight declared. "That is the usual construction for such facilities."

My lip curled, but I didn't ask the obvious question... how would *he* know about "such facilities?"

"Can we pick up any heat sources inside the dome?" I asked Wojtera, keeping my voice neutral.

"Negative," he told me, shaking his head but not looking away from the screen. "The exterior is at a constant temperature and it's masking everything inside. There's no visible activity on the surface though. If there's any enemy forces down there, they aren't moving and they aren't giving out any heat... not even the usual amount for those damned Skrela."

"Zoom out," Nance instructed. "Let's get a look at the surrounding space." The man scowled. "Something's off here."

"Yeah," I agreed, thinking the same thing. "It's too... empty. Too pristine. If the Seekers ever came here, didn't they even *try* to, I don't know, blow anything up?"

The rest of the moon was empty, sterile, devoid of life, a stark, white beauty that wouldn't have looked out of place on the poles of many of the worlds I'd visited. This wasn't just an arctic ice cap though, it was the entire planet. Cold death, yet there was no evidence anything had ever died down there either.

The view pulled back, the burning, roiling brown of the Womb a sharp contrast to the harsh white of the moon, though just as unrewarding and mysterious. I couldn't see the mothership from this view, its orbit hours away from this side of the dwarf, and nothing else presented itself, just the endless, hellish ocean until the Cauldron of Creation asserted itself, a display of raw, natural power that shamed even the engineering of the Resscharr.

Something floated, silhouetted black against the otherworldly white, several somethings... smaller moons, jagged and tumbling, appearing so temporary, yet I knew they had to have been in orbit around the massive world for over a thousand years. I knew exactly what they were, but I said nothing, letting someone else make the grim pronouncement.

"Those fragments," Dwight said, never seeming to shy away from sharing bad news, "are consistent with Resscharr starships."

"We were looking for the Seekers," I said, hope leaving me in a dolorous breath. "There they are."

[17]

"Can we get closer to the fragments?" Hachette asked, an edge of desperation to the question. If we hadn't been in free fall, strapped into our chairs, I felt as if he would have lunged forward at the screen. The air on the bridge was always just a little too cold, yet now I could smell the stench of desperation coming off the man.

"I can pass the request on through the corvettes," Chase said, shrugging. "Whether they can get close enough with their plasma drives and still be able to jump back out, I don't know."

"That won't be necessary," Dwight said. "I have enough details of the ships to interpret the sensor details even from this distance. One moment while I interface with your systems."

It didn't take very long. The images had been pinpricks of darkness against the light, but with an instant of enhancement from Dwight, they enlarged into something more recognizable. They'd once been the oblong, cigar-shaped Predecessor starships, though the emerald green glow that enveloped the ones I'd seen in flight was dead, the color faded to an off-white, like some crystal dug out of a mineral-rich hillside. I half-expected to see bodies floating around the wreckage, though that was pretty silly. The forces contained in the drive of one of those ships were enough to destroy almost anything.

But not *everything*.

"What the hell is that?" Hachette asked, pointing at the screen as if any of us could tell what he was talking about.

The finger pointing didn't help, but it only took another second for me to figure out what he was talking about. The thing seemed small next to the wreckage, but that was an illusion of perspective. The ships were larger than the ones I'd seen on Yfingam and Decision, and from the helpful scale that Dwight had included in the image, each of the longer fragments was over a kilometer long and five hundred meters across. The thing Hachette had noticed was perhaps half the length of the longest fragment, though nearly as wide, cylindrical, and smooth. And glowing green.

"I believe, though I can't be sure without further observations," Dwight announced, "that this is the core section of a Resscharr gateway."

"Oh, damn," Vicky breathed, softly enough I don't think anyone else heard it. The wide, wild eyes of Marcus Hachette was the source of her worry, and mine too.

"It's here," he said softly, his cheek quivering as if he were about to break into sobs. "Holy shit, it's here. We found it."

"Yeah, we found it," Nance agreed. "And what a great place for it. Dwight, can we activate it where it is?"

"No, Captain Nance. The gateway requires a power source to trigger the corridor, and to reach the desired destination, an AI—me, for instance—has to interface with it. To activate the gateway would require a construction of significant infrastructure around it."

"How the hell are we supposed to do that?" Nance motioned broadly. "Even if it wasn't sitting right next to the *source* of the Skrela, it's not exactly anywhere convenient for a large-scale construction project."

"We could move it," Hachette suggested, gesticulating like he was trying to juggle invisible balls. "We could rig something up, attach it to the *Orion*, and haul it through Transition Space with us." Nance stared at Hachette like the colonel had grown an extra head. "It's not impossible," Hachette insisted. "I've seen it done... in testing, anyway. We could take it back to Yfingam and use the resources there to get it working."

"Yeah, we could," I agreed, "but we're getting ahead of ourselves. We have an objective here beyond getting the gateway." I indicated the brown dwarf and the moon hanging in front of it. "The Womb. We have to figure out a way to shut this damned thing down."

"We might not need to," Hachette suggested. "From what I can tell, the Skrela have been dogging our heels since we arrived here, and I have to believe there's something about *us* that's attracting them. If we just get the hell out of here, away from them, they might go dormant again. Just us being here might be putting everyone else in danger."

I rubbed a hand on the back of my neck. Despite the microgravity, it felt as if the weight of a world was on my shoulders.

"That's building a castle on a lot of *maybe*'s," I told him. But just blowing him off wouldn't do it. I had to convince him. "Look, we do the mission, infiltrate the dome if possible, find out if we can do something to shut this place down. *Then*, if it's possible, we come hook up this gateway thing and take it back with us."

"You want me to *strap* that thing to my ship?" Nance demanded, staring at me, goggle-eyed.

"For Christ's sake, Nance!" I snapped, losing any concern whatsoever for our respective ranks and positions of responsibility in a red haze of impatience. "Can we debate this shit *after* the mission is over? It's not really gonna matter if we all fucking die, is it?"

Nance recoiled as if I'd punched him in the jaw, wide eyes staring at me from all across the bridge, and I thought I might have pushed things too far, but after an awkwardly long pause, he nodded curtly.

"Right. Do we have what we need from the Tahni?"

"Yeah," I sighed, realizing what I'd just done, what had just happened. "We should bring them back before they're spotted."

"Calling them now," Chase acknowledged.

People were still staring, including Hachette and even Vicky. There was disbelief and maybe pity in her eyes. She'd seen it too. I'd stepped in it, but not because I'd been insubordinate against Nance. No, it was because he'd *taken* it, had basically acknowledged that I was in charge. And more than anything else, I really didn't want to be in charge.

Too late, you fucking moron. Everyone's seen it now, and if you don't follow through, everything's going to fall apart. Damn it.

"Colonel Hachette," I said slowly, deliberately, "if you still intend on dropping in the lander, you should go draw some armor and weapons from the armory. You'll be the one in operational command on that group, so be sure to check in with Lan-Min-Gen, since he's the unit commander. You two should work out a command structure between you."

Resentment flared behind Hachette's eyes, probably because he understood what was happening and wasn't at all happy about it, but he didn't argue either. Damn, I was hoping *someone* would argue. Maybe even have me arrested and tossed in the brig so I didn't have to be responsible for this shit-show. Hachette yanked loose his restraints, hanging onto his seat with a hand as he paused and looked back at me.

"How do you think we should do that?" he wondered, and

considering we were talking about Lan-Min-Gen, it wasn't a bad question.

"Maybe beat the shit out of each other?" I suggested. "Whatever you're going to do, do it fast." I nodded to Captain Nance. "Give us an hour to get prepped, then micro-Transition just as close as you can come to that moon... and I don't care if you break all the regs in the book and do shit that would get an Attack Command pilot canned for recklessness, just do whatever you can to minimize the flight time of our birds."

"I can try a Lagrangian Transition," Yanayev suggested, eyeing Nance with doubt in her expression. "The moon's basically the size of a planet, so there'll be a substantial gravitational equilibrium zone where the wormhole can form."

I knew what she was talking about because I'd had it explained to me on this mission. A ship couldn't Transition within a certain distance of a sizable gravity well because the gravity of a planet or star would distort the Teller-Fox field and the wormhole wouldn't form. But at the Lagrangian points between a planet and its moon, the gravitational pull reached equilibrium, which was what made those points stable for orbital stations and satellites... and also made them *possible* Transition nodes. Possible, because the calculations had to be pretty precise and even the slightest fluctuation could mean the wormhole wouldn't form correctly. Best-case scenario was that we'd just overshoot and have to drop out at the next node, across the system, and try again. Worst-case scenario was, we'd wind up ripped to shreds at the atomic level and never even know we'd died.

"Do it," Nance instructed his Helm officer. "You have an hour to get the calculations down and get the ship positioned. If there's any hang-ups, notify me immediately."

"Aye, sir."

Nance shot me a glare, though I had the sense it was

because of the risk I was taking with *his* ship rather than the fact I'd just taken effective command of the entire mission.

"Anything else?"

That, of course, was the other downside of being in charge, besides the obvious one of everything that happened or didn't happen suddenly being my fault. If there was any detail, any possible scenario, I had to think of it ahead of time. If I didn't, and it wound up happening, then, again, it was suddenly my fault.

"I want the Intercepts with you, on patrol duty, but the assault shuttles are going to be on air support detail for the drop element, so they'll need to launch right alongside us. I don't want the drop-ships in the air, not when we're dealing with this many unknowns."

Nance snorted.

"Villanueva won't be happy about that." And she wouldn't. Francesca Villanueva was the lead assault shuttle pilot and hated being separated from the *Orion* and what she considered "the action."

"Tell her if she has a problem with it, she can trade me." I tapped a finger next to my temples. "We've both got the jacks, and Wade and McCloud already proved they work both ways." Both men were Fleet officers, backup shuttle pilots, but we'd adjusted their wetware programming and now they were honorary Drop Troopers, operating our two spare Vigilantes. I hadn't asked them if they were excited about the career change, but they were still *alive*, so as far as I was concerned, neither of them had anything to complain about.

The captain laughed more softly this time, nodding.

"I'm pretty sure she'll pass on that."

"Then I'll get to the drop-ship. See you after we're done." I tried to put an apology in those words, in the look I gave him, hoping he'd understand. Maybe the upward curl of his lip was an indication he had, or maybe it was just wishful thinking.

"Good luck, Cam."

Walking in a Vigilante through the cargo passageways of a starship in microgravity is a hell of a lot more difficult than it sounds. I hated using magnetic boots when it was just my eighty kilos of mass I had to work against, but controlling a couple thousand kilos of metal, weapons, and reactor when every movement forward built up more and more momentum was akin to trying to walk across the bottom of a pool without my feet leaving the ground.

The magnets were powerful enough to keep the suit rooted to the deck, but I had to cut loose with one of them in midstride, and if I changed my gait even by a hair, it would send me floating upward into the overhead. And Nance's chief of boat frowned on us lunkhead Marines putting dents in his overhead. Vicky was better at it than I was, but she was behind me and I couldn't imitate her effortless stride the way I usually did. The *thump-thump* rhythm of our cadence was a Lambeg drum against the deck, a warning to any crewmembers who might have been using the passage to get the hell out of the way.

"You haven't said anything," I told her over our private net, line-of-sight so no one else would be listening in. "I would have figured you'd be letting me know that you told me so long before now."

Thump-thump in the silence like a heartbeat.

"It's tempting," she admitted. "But I know how badly you didn't want this and how hard you tried to avoid it, so it would just be cruel."

"I'm trying to look at the bright side. There's always the chance I won't survive the mission."

"Nope. You're that Quantum observer, remember? I mean, to me you might get killed, but in your own little pocket universe, you're gonna live through all of this shit." She was giving me a hard time for repeating that stupid theory, but I had a gut-deep fear she was right. "I'm more worried about Hachette."

"Yeah, that reminds me." I switched networks and sighed before I spoke. She was not going to be happy to hear from me. "Lt. Stilwell, this is Captain Alvarez."

"Yeah, what is it, Alvarez?" I was right, she wasn't happy.

"Colonel Hachette is going down on the lander with Lilandreth and the Tahni Shock Troopers. Unless you want to trust his safety to God and the good will of the Tahni, I think you might want to get a few of your people on that shuttle with him. And I don't know if anyone else is going to think to ask you."

"Ask me, huh?" She grunted skeptically. "Alvarez, you don't ask. You give people a choice that isn't any real choice, and then when they do what you wanted, they think they made the decision on their own."

"Is that a yes?"

Stilwell sighed.

"Fuck you, Alvarez. Yes, I'll send a team with him. This had better be worth it. And you'd better know what the hell you're doing."

"Your lips to God's ears, Stilwell."

I cut off the call, but I was pretty sure she'd done it first.

A docking bay tech scrambled out of our way, his magnetic soles leaving the decks as he floated off to the side to make room for us, and then we were through the cargo entrance and into the bay. The hangar was a surreal place, packed from deck to overhead with storage containers locked into magnetic cradles, yet with passageways wide enough for cargo loaders to pass through. Or for us.

The Intercepts, the assault shuttles, the landers, and the drop-ships were tucked into their docking niches, folded under armored sleeves, attached to their docking cylinders by magnetic locks and boarding umbilicals. I remember being disappointed the first time I actually saw a hangar bay, figuring it would be like I'd seen in the movies and games I'd played, with a big, flat landing pad and huge sliding doors opening out into space with some dramatic view of a planet. That would have been pretty stupid, considering these were warships and the last thing anyone wanted was a thin section of hull that would do nothing but make an obvious target for the enemy.

Instead, the shuttles and Intercepts rode like remoras on a great white shark, folded under the shelter of metal fins. The system had its disadvantages, of course, the foremost of which was that servicing the parasite spacecraft en route meant either squeezing into the docking chutes or waiting until the *Orion* was somewhere in a stable orbit, not accelerating, and then pulling them out into open space.

It also meant that boarding the craft was a claustrophobic affair for most people, particularly in the suits, cramming through a cargo lock barely wide enough to let one Vigilante through at a time, the shoulder plates nearly scraping the sides. I paused at the entrance to the lock and waved wordlessly to Vicky as she headed for the other drop-ship.

"See you down there," she said, then disappeared into the docking umbilical.

The interior lighting of the umbilical was a deep red, which somehow made the whole passage look even tighter, though it didn't bother me. Enclosed spaces never did. The interior of the aerospacecraft was packed and stacked, with two platoons worth of Vigilantes stuffed into every single drop cradle except one. The one near the front, usually occupied by the senior officer aboard. I never liked the spot, but it seemed I was doomed to fill it.

"Everything okay, sir?" Singh asked me.

Something about the pitch of the question seemed off to me, and I wondered if he'd been linked into the feed from the bridge. I'd done that back in the day, though I'd been more interested in the Tactical display than the drama between the senior officers.

"We think we've found the Seeker gateway," I said, patching the announcement through to the general company net. I picked through the words carefully, putting as much attention into them as I did to my position in the drop cradle. "It's orbiting the Womb along with the scattered wreckage of what looks like the entire Seeker fleet. From what we can tell, they all died here."

"Can we use it, sir?"

I looked up and down the IFF transponder list and picked out the one who'd asked the question. It was Sgt. Edwards, one of the squad leaders from Fourth. Young, intelligent, maybe thought just a little too much and reacted a hair too late, but only by comparison with the other NCOs in this company. They were all the best of the best.

"Unknown," I said. "If the opportunity presents itself after we accomplish this mission, we're going to try to attach it to the *Orion* and take it back with us. But that's a secondary objective. Primary is still finding a way to get rid of the Skrela." I paused, wondering if I should tell them about the close jump, the dangers of it. If things went wrong they'd never know it, but... "We're attempting a micro-Transition into a Lagrangian point. It's risky, but if it works, we're going to be coming out damned close to the moon and dropping immediately. You've all seen the op order, you've all done the simulation run." Which had been a pain in the ass to program given that we had no idea what we'd find. "But no battle plan survives contact with the enemy, so keep your head on a swivel and stay flexible. Don't hesitate to let your platoon leader or platoon sergeant know if you spot something."

Okay, starting to ramble. Know when to shut up. Or at least know when to get personal.

"We've asked a lot from you, and now we're asking more. Maybe everything. But if we make it through this, if we can put an end to the threat from the Skrela, even if we can't go home, we can make one out here. And we'll be saving multiple worlds full of humans just like us. Hundreds of millions, maybe even *billions* of people. You won't just be saving them from slavery or servitude, you'll be saving them from extinction. And there's no one better for the job than you. You're the best the Commonwealth has and I'm proud to have had the honor of leading you into combat. Ooh-rah!"

The reply came over my helmet speakers, but I felt it in my heart.

"*Ooh-rah!*"

[18]

God stretched me thin and snapped me like a rubber band.

"Fuck!" The word came out explosively, beyond my control, and I was just glad I'd muted my mic after the Transition warning came through.

If regular Transitions grated on my nerves, micro-Transitions were a hundred times worse. I knew that Attack Command pilots like Dunstan executed them all the time as a part of their combat patterns, which just showed how crazy those guys were, because I nearly puked after just doing it once.

The Tactical display was projected in the corner of my Heads-Up Display, but my eyes couldn't focus well enough to read it for a long moment, certainly not fast enough to beat the warning from Wojtera.

"We have a Transition!" he yelled, and the edge of panic beneath his voice told me immediately he wasn't referring to our own. "Skrela mothership coming out at minimum safe jump distance, about one light-second away."

"Alvarez," Nance said urgently, "they're nearly on top of us. Do you want to risk launching?"

If I hadn't been hit so hard by the double-Transition, I might have said something smart about how dumb a question that was.

"It's why we're here," I rasped, blinking away the floaters in my vision, the twisted, arcane mass of the mothership taking up most of the sensor screen. "Launch now."

Watson might have given us a boost warning, but the cross-chatter from the bridge stations and the shuttle and Intercept crews drowned him out, and the first indication I had that anyone had listened to my order was when acceleration pushed me back into the Vigilante's internal cushioning.

The link to the *Orion*'s Tactical display flickered and died, replaced by the feed from the drop-ship nose cameras. Dark metal of the protective docking sheath gave way to the featureless glare of a billion stars, packed so tightly together that coming just a few light-years closer would have killed us all the second we left the protective shielding of the ship.

"John," I broke into Watson's terse exchange with his cockpit crew, "what have we got down there?"

"Whole lot of nothing as of now," he snapped. "But that mothership is gonna launch fighters just as sure as God made little green apples. Hope those hotshots back there actually do their job and stay with us."

And by that, he meant the assault shuttles. A glance at the drop-ship's rudimentary Tactical screen told me the attack craft were following orders, falling into a tight formation with the two drop-ships and the lander. It was a pitiful force in the face of the power of an ancient enemy, of a whole planet dedicated to the spawning of endless hordes of nightmare creatures, and if I was thinking that, I was damned sure the rest of the Marines were.

"We have comms with anyone?" I asked him.

"Nothing but line-of-sight, and not much of that with the drive flares. We're all pretty much on our own down here.

Entering atmosphere in thirty seconds. Gonna be a rough ride, so hold on back there."

"Like I have any other choice. Give me a warning at five mikes to drop."

The thirty seconds passed quickly, and the ungainly aerospacecraft swayed in the thick clouds of the upper atmosphere. I should, I thought, have been saying something. Giving a briefing or maybe talking to Singh and Springfield, the Second Platoon leader, trying to keep them calm. I had nothing. Reassuring small talk wasn't my strong suit, and I was pretty sure I'd just wind up sounding nervous and uncomfortable.

"Uh oh," Watson said.

"Uh-oh *what*?" I demanded, "I don't like the sound of *uh-oh*."

"Movement near the objective. Not getting a firm thermal reading... it's kind of fuzzed out. And you know what that means."

"Skrela," I agreed. "How far?"

"They're coming out of the ice." There was awe in the pilot's voice, as if he couldn't help respect the incredible toughness of the Skrela. "They had to have been sitting out there for..."

"Centuries," I finished for him. "Probably in hibernation in those pods."

It was three hundred below out there with no oxygen, and somehow they could still survive it. Linking into the Tactical screen, I searched for the movement and finally found it. Like Walton had said, they were hard to see, even against the stark white of the ice fields, whatever they were made of resistant to thermal and infrared filters, but the movement gave them away. There were dozens of them, maybe hundreds, camouflaged by the blurry video, ants swarming across a field, swarming toward the dome in discreet clumps.

"You seeing this, Singh, Springfield?" I asked, trusting the platoon leaders were looped in just as I was.

"Affirmative," Singh said, apparently speaking for the both of them. "They're moving fast. Are we going to be able to get in front of them before they reach the dome?"

"Just," Watson replied. "If I drop you right at the edge of the safe altitude, you should be able to catch them a couple klicks out from the objective."

"Do it," I confirmed. "Pass it back to the other drop-ship and see if you can get the assault shuttles on a gun run to cover the drop."

"On it."

I could have done it myself, but I was busy thinking, running scenarios in my head and then tapping them into the input touch pad at my left hand and playing them out across the terrain map. The Skrela were making their way up a gulch, or whatever you called the equivalent when it was an ice shelf falling away into what had once been a riverbed of running liquid methane. How did that even work? How did the place get warm enough to melt that ice?

Shaking the thoughts away, I projected the minimum intercept time and found out the lead elements of the Skrela formation were going to be ascending a fairly steep scree slope about the time we touched down. Perfect. A few taps of my forefinger against the screen drew a line across the backside of the scree field, then a flick of my thumb sent the whole thing to Watson's Tactical display.

"Forward that to the other shuttles," I told him. "I want layered air support behind that line, nothing on the other side unless you get a call from Vicky or me."

"Yeah, I get ya," Watson said, a hint of distraction in his tone. The drop-ship shuddered, rolling left, then right before stabilizing again. "Wondering why we're not getting any anti-aircraft fire. Those Resscharr have weapons that would make it pretty damned easy to knock a shuttle out of the sky, but I ain't seen nothing like that anywhere we've come across Resscharr."

"The concept of anti-aircraft weaponry is a foreign one to the Resscharr," Dwight confided, and I nearly jumped at his voice in my ear. "The Skrela, as a rule, didn't attempt air support for their pods, since they were usually dropped far ahead of time in secret and then the ships came well after to take advantage of the weakened defenses and destruction."

"I didn't expect you here," I confessed.

"I had to come along in order to penetrate the security systems of the dome," he reminded me.

"I meant," I clarified, "I didn't expect you in *my* helmet, Dwight. I figured you'd be with Colonel Hachette and Lilandreth."

"Ah, well… I find I'm more at home with you, Captain Alvarez. But to reiterate, the only ground fire you'll have to concern yourselves with is from the Skrela themselves."

"What about other Resscharr?" I wondered. "You said they didn't have air defenses because the Skrela didn't attack from the air, but the Condemnation wanted to hide this place from other Resscharr. Wouldn't they try to blow them up before they reached the dome?"

Dwight wasn't manifesting his avatar, so I couldn't *see* the smirk, but it was plain in his voice.

"The Resscharr, even among the Condemnation, would never consider directly killing one of their own. It would be… I think your term would be *blasphemous*. You have to understand, even though the Condemnation thought the Resscharr worthy of extinction, they were still the end result of *millions* of years of a culture that thought of themselves as life-givers. It was one thing to create the Skrela and program them to kill. It was another to do the deed with their own hands."

"You must have had quite the conversation with Zerhanen," I said, choosing my words cautiously, "to gather that much information from him before the Skrela destroyed him."

"We connected databases. In an instant I knew everything he did, and vice versa. That's the one advantage of our kind... when we deal with each other, we have no fear of being deceived."

I stiffened, wondering if he'd already guessed what I suspected, but before he had the chance to say anything else, Walton interrupted.

"Five minutes to drop, Cam."

"Copy that," I told him, shifting my thoughts and worries away from Dwight and toward the immediate threat. "Singh, Springfield, get your Marines ready. We're dropping hot and there's no cover at all till we get into that dome. Movement is life and your jets are your friends, but stay low when you use them —the nail that stands out gets pounded flat first."

And *now*, I thought, I sounded like the Skipper.

"Drop! Drop! Drop!"

How many times had I heard that command? How many more times would I give it?

The floor fell out from beneath me, the chute opening, the magnetic locks releasing, and an instant rush of cold took my breath away. Just for a few seconds, until the reactor and the heaters kicked in. Mind-numbing cold flooded into the suit, and I was sure the whole suit would freeze up and I'd plummet directly into the ice like a huge idiot. It didn't happen, of course. The Vigilante was built to work in the huge temperature extremes of space, and this was well within its limits. The jets sucked in nitrogen and methane and ran it through whatever powered the new reactors that the Resscharr had installed in our armor, superheating it and kicking me right in the pants.

My fall slowed but didn't stop, because hanging our asses out in the wind wouldn't have been ideal. We needed to be on the ground... just not at terminal velocity. It still felt too long. We were five hundred meters up, a bit higher than we would have been on a planet with Earth-normal gravity, and the imaginary cover of low, wispy clouds briefly enveloped us, but they were transparent to my helmet sensors.

The Skrela galloped faster than a racehorse coming down the stretch, and they were advancing up the draw, nearly to the scree slope. They'd moved quicker than Watson or I thought, and if we didn't catch them on the other side of the slope, we weren't going to be able to count on air support.

Shit.

"Reduce braking thrust," I told them reluctantly. "We need to get down quicker. Singh, detail me a squad and have them follow my lead."

"Second squad is yours, sir," Singh said after a moment, though he didn't seem happy about it.

That was okay, either was I. I checked the Second quad leader's name on the IFF and looped her into my comm net.

"Sgt. Wheeler, form in a squad wedge with me at the point and open fire when I do."

"Yes, sir."

I liked Wheeler. She didn't waste time telling me I was fucking nuts, which I already knew. I couldn't contact Vicky or the rest of the company, but the sensors told me they'd dropped as well and were trying to match the quicker drop I'd directed. It was just as well our comms were jammed, because Vicky would have been chewing my ear off for this.

Maneuvering laterally in the suit was tricky, requiring a lot of practice at shifting weight while under thrust, since there were no steering jets or stabilizers. I threw myself off to the side, swimming with my right hand and leg, tilting the suit and adjusting the angle of thrust. My Vigilante arced crossways out of the main formation and straight over the scree slope, and I took advantage of the technology the Resscharr had given us and the increased range of the energy cannon over the plasma gun I'd once carried.

We were over five klicks away from the front line of the Skrela, but the green tendrils of the energy cannon streaked into them still with enough power to send one of them tumbling head over heels. I couldn't see whether the impact killed the thing, but that wasn't the important part. We just had to slow them down.

Second squad followed my lead and their orders, adding their own cascade of emerald fire to mine. It was tempting to just watch the show, or to get lost in the video-game sniping, but I reminded myself that I was a company commander and kept an eye on the bigger picture. The volley we were laying down was slowing the advance, but at the same time, we and the rest of the company were only meters above the ground.

I hit. Hard. Only the slightly-lower-than-standard gravity kept me from cracking a few vertebrae, but it was a close thing, and I bit down hard on the mouthpiece built into the helmet just before the impact. Dull pain went from the soles of my feet right through my neck and the breath went out of me, but it was better than the alternative. Plasma scorched the air where we'd been only moments before, and only the distance had kept the Skrela from firing sooner, as if they were programmed with the effective range of their weapons and wouldn't waste time shooting until then.

"Form on me!" I ordered, hoping that the line-of-sight comms would propagate through the relays built into the suits.

If not, I was about to feel awfully lonely, since I was a good kilometer ahead of the rest of the company.

Back on the ground, the lip of the scree slope blocked off my view of the oncoming horde of Skrela, and I rushed forward to the edge of the drop-off, the squad at my heels. I'd stood at the edge of some pretty high places in my life, most of them a lot steeper than that slope, but none had grated at my nerves quite as much, not from the fear of falling but from the very real concern of imminent incineration. Gouts of eye-searing plasma smashed into the other side of the rock, sending up explosions of steam and rock, a desperate attempt by the onrushing enemy to suppress our fire long enough to make it over the top.

It was almost human.

The Vigilantes weren't meant for going prone, but I did the best I could, crawling on hands and knees to the edge, sticking the muzzle of my beamer over the side and laying on the trigger. The cold was gone. I mean, the suit was doing a good job of keeping the air next to my body warm, but I'd still been able to feel the cold like a cloud trying to penetrate the armor, probing for weaknesses. Not anymore, not with the plasma turning the air into a static-filled haze of incandescent yellow, not with the rocks and dirt glowing red and radiating shimmering waves of heat. If I'd been in Force Recon armor, I'd be dead already, burned to a cinder just by the pure, radiant heat. With the suit, it felt about the same as stepping into a summer afternoon on Inferno.

I added to the heat and light with a firehose stream of emerald energy, not trying to aim precisely because there wasn't time for it, just lashing across the front line of the enemy for three seconds before I ducked back and rolled to the side. It was an old instinct, one drilled into me in Boot Camp, well before they let me jack into a suit, one born out of five hundred years of combat with ranged weapons. It served me well in that instant as half a dozen plasma blasts obliterated the rock outcropping I'd just been using for cover, the concussion slapping into my chest a half-second before the bits of debris pinged off my helmet.

It had been a good ten seconds, and I was about to yell into the comms pickup asking where the hell everyone else was when they finally showed up, announcing their presence with a cascade of green tendrils snaking out into the centauroid creatures, slashing across the front ranks. Scuttling backward, I turned and found the company had formed up just as we'd rehearsed, a tactical square. And that Vicky was mad at me.

"Goddammit, Alvarez," she fumed on our private net, "stop doing that shit! You're a company commander, not to mention the only person willing and able to lead this three-ring circus, and I swear to God, if you make *me* try to take over, I'm going to let the whole thing go to hell just to spite you!"

"Alvarez, this is Assault One," Villanueva said, her transmission choppy and filled with static, right at the edge of practical line-of-sight. "Coming in for a firing run... make sure your Marines are clear."

A quick check of the IFF against the map and my own eyes showed me that the draw was clear after the scree slope, which was a relief, since it meant everyone had actually listened to the op order and kept to it despite being shot at.

"Copy, Assault One. Bring the pain."

Taking a second to actually play company commander, I let the others keep firing while I surveyed the terrain and checked the IFF transponders. No KIA, no one out of action, but four of the Drop Troopers had status monitors blinking yellow, each of them with stress damage to their knee or hip joints. That had been a danger coming down so fast, but at least their suits weren't disabled.

The Skrela had kept coming out of the ice wall, and where

there'd been dozens when we started our drop, now there were hundreds, maybe thousands, most of them at the far end of the draw. Packed nice and tight for convenient targeting. The assault shuttles came in high for the first run, well outside the range of the Skrela plasma guns, though this time the Skrela tried anyway, maybe thinking that the barrage of electrostatic energy might throw off whatever the aerospacecraft were using to shoot at them. It didn't work.

It might have, if we'd had any air-to-ground missiles left, but they'd been expended months ago and all that was left were the guns. The assault shuttles used to have Gatling lasers, but they'd been replaced with coilgun turrets when the last of the lasing cartridges had been fired, since we could make more tungsten slugs in the ship's fabricators given the raw materials. But the coil uns were the sideshow. The main event were the proton cannons.

A proton cannon firing is the only thing I'd ever seen that made a plasma blast look tame by comparison. The particle bursts ripped apart the sky, adding even more heat and static electricity to the already roiling air, lightning bolts not from a thunderstorm but from the hand of Zeus himself. Where they struck, the ground erupted like a miniature volcano, mushroom clouds billowing into the frozen air, dirt and ice mixed with whatever remained of the Skrela on the periphery of the shot. Everything at the center of the burst had been reduced to its component atoms and the pure wave of sound, even through the armor and from kilometers away, felt as if someone were punching me repeatedly in the face.

It was raining. It took me a second to notice inside the armor, particularly with the still echoing rolls of thunder, but finally I managed to focus on it through the brownish clouds of soil. This wasn't debris though, this spattering on the exterior of my suit, on the damp gray stone of the ground. It was liquid methane, condensed by the repeated washes of raw heat.

"Holy shit," Vicky murmured, just between us. "Wish we had those guys around on every mission."

Down in the draw, where there'd been an unending swarm of Skrela, now there were pockets, clusters of a few dozen here, a hundred there. They were still firing at the shuttles, but not at us. On the flat ground between us and the dome the lander was touching down, its belly jets just another distant rumble against all the other ambient noise.

Which meant it was time to go.

"Platoon leaders," I barked. "Get to the dome. Fourth, you cover our rear, Second and Third, form a perimeter. First, you're with me at the lander."

I hit the jump-jets and headed low across the plateau toward the featureless gray of the dome, not waiting to see who would follow. Inside was the end of this, the end of everything we'd started two years ago.

Or maybe just the end of *us*.

[19]

"You think you can get this damned thing open, Dwight?" I asked, the soles of my Vigilante's boots thumping against the paved pathway to the dome.

The walk led to an oval landing pad, around the right size for one of the smaller Predecessor ships, and I tried to imagine the Condemnation or the Redeemers or who the hell ever built this place walking across the pad in the same sort of funky spacesuits Lilandreth was wearing. She was hunched over one of the security panels I'd seen on other Predecessor facilities, her long fingers dancing through the controls. She, Hachette, and his bodyguards were all tucked under an alcove that should have protected some kind of entranceway, though like many of the other Predecessor structures we'd encountered out here, I didn't see any door.

"I've done what I can," he told me, the simulated sigh in his simulated voice sounding so natural I almost could have forgotten what he was. "The system here is complex, and the AI inside it is fighting me. I'm afraid there may not be much I can do for you once you're inside beyond simply keeping the security systems deactivated. You won't have communications with any of your ships outside."

The Shock Troopers were arrayed in an offset file, weapons pointing outward, and they didn't bother shifting as we approached in our battlesuits, and I didn't bother to correct them for sweeping friendlies with their muzzles. Those popguns they carried might scratch my paint, but they wouldn't penetrate. That's why I'd killed so many Tahni Shock Troopers in the war. Hachette and his four Fleet Security troopers were huddled beside Lilandreth, pulse carbines muzzle-out like a crystal pincushion, visored helmets scanning side to side, feet in the perpetual dance of the nervous.

"What's the story, Lilandreth?" I asked her. "We going inside anytime soon?"

If she were a human, I wouldn't have said anything, not wanting to distract her from her task, but since she wasn't, I didn't feel guilty. She didn't look around at me either way.

"Just a few more seconds, Captain Alvarez," she said, no strain at all in her voice. Maybe that was because she didn't know how to *convey* strain in our language, but I liked to think it was because the Resscharr had bigger brains than we did and were better at multitasking. "I believe... that's done it."

The same golden traces spread, broad and high enough to accommodate two Vigilantes side by side, and what had seemed like bare stone vanished into an oval of utter blackness. I wanted badly to be the first one through, but I knew what Vicky would say, and that she'd be right.

"Sgt. Wheeler," I said, "take Second squad and set up a perimeter inside the entrance. If you make contact, send someone back and report it. Comms won't work."

"Copy that, sir." The woman sounded more enthusiastic about this than she had enabling me risking my neck. While

Second squad, First Platoon squeezed through the crowd around the door, I looked up at the assault shuttles still circling and switched to their net.

"Assault One, this is Alvarez," I said, hoping the laser line-of-sight could penetrate the still-drifting clouds of smoke and steam. They'd ceased fire with the proton cannons and were making lower passes, firing bursts from their coilgun turrets, which was a good sign. "Do you read?"

"Five by five, Alvarez," she said. "We're mopping up the last of them."

"You reading anything from the *Orion*?"

"Negative comms, but we can see her on sensors still. She's moving out to engage the Gomer. Still no contact between them."

Jesus. And *that* was what I hated about space combat. We'd already had a major engagement down here and were moving onto our main objective, and the *Orion* was still boosting, everyone on board probably wincing like a man about to be punched in the face. Give me a battlesuit and an enemy I could see any day.

"Copy that, Assault One. Maintain overwatch and keep your eyes open for other avenues of ingress. I don't think we've seen the last of the Skrela."

Villanueva acknowledged the order, but my attention had shifted to the entrance. Wheeler might have thought I was reckless for walking point before, but that didn't keep her from entering the building first, squad leader or no. The squads were down to just seven Marines each due to our losses, but it felt like it took minutes for the last of them to pass through the opaque energy field, and it was all I could do not to run in behind them. I wanted to *see*.

I imagined all kinds of dark fates for the seven Marines—*my*

Marines—while I waited, from hordes of Skrela to some Predecessor booby trap that would use gravity manipulation to smash them into a paste the second they stepped through the door, despite Dwight's earlier insistence that the Resscharr didn't think that way. Seconds passed, and I resolved that if Wheeler didn't send word back in another minute, I was going in myself.

Edging closer to the doorway, I made sure I could reach it before Vicky cut me off, and had very nearly decided to go now when Wheeler emerged from the darkness, waving us to proceed.

"It's clear."

"First and Second," I ordered, "follow me through. Captain Sandoval, wait thirty seconds, then escort Colonel Hachette and Lilandreth inside and bring Third Platoon and the Shock Troopers with you. Top, you stay out here with Fourth and watch our six unless I send someone to tell you different. Everyone clear?"

"Copy," Vicky said, echoed by Top and the other platoon leaders.

I don't know what I expected inside the dome. Maybe something like the interior of the one-building city we'd found on Decision or just a larger version of the facility back on the Skreloid world. This was neither, though it had features of both.

The dome stretched up over a hundred meters above us, the interior a softly glowing hemisphere, the light seeming to come right out of the material, whatever it was. It wasn't harsh or glaring, yet somehow nothing inside seemed to cast a shadow, though it took me a moment to realize it. The rest of the place… well, the Resscharr weren't human and lacked human sensibilities, and as much as I kept reminding myself of that, it was too easy to forget it.

Not in here. The exterior of the dome was the ultimate in

simplicity, but the interior twisted my brain into knots trying to make sense of it. I tried to follow the lines of the walls, but they were a Moebius strip, dipping downward into the bottom of the sphere that was the other half of the dome, and I couldn't, for the life of me, figure out how you got anywhere from anywhere else. There were sections of the place, nothing you could call rooms, but sort-of walls surrounding spiraling cylinders of what must have been some kind of equipment, though what kind I had no idea.

"What the hell is all this shit?" I asked, not expecting an answer, forgetting who was listening.

"Gravitational communications gear," Dwight told me, "sensors, and remote manipulation equipment for the nanite fabrication vats of the Womb. Everything is controlled from here."

"Is there some kind of data terminal? Something we can use to get control of it all?"

"It's over here," Lilandreth replied, walking with long-legged strides up a curving ramp to our right. There was a platform at the end of the walkway, partially enclosed by a half-cylinder made of what looked like thin, gold foil.

I wondered what the hell she was doing, because there didn't seem to be anywhere to go from there. Except up. She stopped on the platform and waited no more than a second before she began rising upward. There was no glow, no sound, no jets, just a gentle levitation that deposited here twenty meters up on a larger platform, this one circular with narrow, waist-high columns arranged in an oval at the center.

"Did her suit..." I stumbled over the words. "Did her suit fly her up there?"

"It's an anti-gravity transport tube," Dwight supplied. His voice sounded oddly strained, as if the body he didn't have was engaged in some sort of struggle. "I'm afraid I will be... unable to communicate for a while. The resident AI here is opposing my efforts to dampen the security lockdown he's trying to impose."

"I'm going up there," Hachette announced, stepping onto the platform before I had the chance to argue with him. I think he just wanted to try the anti-gravity thing, and I kind of did myself.

The Fleet Security troops bodyguarding him didn't seem as enthusiastic, but they stepped into the tube one at a time, hesitant, tentative. One of them shrieked when the effect swooped him up twenty meters, depositing him on the platform, and had the bad luck to have left his helmet microphone active. Hard to live that down.

"I am not following them," Lan-Min-Gen said, somehow managing to set his shoulders in a stubborn stance despite the exoskeleton and the KE gun cradled across his chest. "I will guard them from down here."

Guard them from what?

The dome was huge but, as far as I could see, it was also empty apart from the mysterious devices scattered through the lower levels. Some were skinny, tracing paths up nearly to the top of the dome, while others were thicker, resting on their sides in rows across the far edge of the structure.

"I don't like this," Vicky admitted.

I started, realizing I'd zoned out from the sheer strangeness of the place, and that the three platoons had filtered through the entrance behind me and spread out on either side, curving around the empty area just inside the door. It seemed absurd, over sixty Vigilantes arrayed in the space inside the entranceway like spectators at a ball game, but there was plenty of room for them. What had been a dome from the outside was, as Dwight had guessed, a sphere sunken into the rock, big enough to hold a ship the size of the *Orion*, and thanks to the

Predecessor version of feng shui, there was plenty of open space to keep us from feeling packed in.

"What don't you like about it?" I asked her. "Other than the color scheme."

The whole interior was a dull beige except for highlights in gold and silver, and I entertained the notion that the Resscharr might see colors differently. Either that, or they just had really bad taste.

"It's too easy," she insisted.

Vicky's suit shuffled sideways as she scanned the full circumference of the place, the muzzle of her energy cannon following the blank metal of the suit's face. After so many years in the suits, I'd developed a sort of optical illusion when I looked at the suits, seeing people's faces when I looked at those featureless helmets. Hers was frowning, suspicious.

"Yeah," I agreed. I didn't bother turning, since the scanners were mounted 360 degrees around my helmet, but I saw the same results she did. Nothing but an indeterminate, fuzzy, yellow glow on thermal. "But maybe they didn't expect anyone to come here in force. After all, the Resscharr weren't very good at direct warfare. If they had been, they wouldn't have needed all those surrogates." The AI, the Tahni, the Khitan. These guys were worse than the late Imperial Romans, hiring everybody and their brother to be mercenaries.

"Yeah, maybe," she acknowledged, not sounding convinced.

"How's it looking up there?" I called to Hachette and Lilandreth. "Can you figure out how to shut this thing down?"

"I've been able to access the control systems," Lilandreth said. I couldn't see what she was doing from down here, but I fixed that with a flick of my finger on the control pad inside my glove, looping into Hachette's helmet cam.

The skinny columns were apparently part of the controls somehow, because Lilandreth's hands hovered over two of them, a glittering blue glow reaching up from the rounded caps at the tops of the columns to envelope her hands, outlining her fingers as they manipulated instruments only she could see. A holographic projection rose up in a half-hemisphere around them, half of it filled with images of the planet below, yellow-tinged brown swirling like a whirlpool leading down into the center of the gigantic world. Out of the core black specks rose against the tempest, carried by unseen forces, maybe by the gravity wave generators arrayed below us in the lower half of the sphere.

The rest of the projection was composed of symbols and images I couldn't understand and didn't have Dwight around to translate. Lilandreth didn't seem to have any trouble with them, scrolling through what must have been the Resscharr equivalent of menus, the images and symbols changing with every flicker of her fingers.

"The fabrication system is amazingly extensive," she said. "More than anything I've seen since before we left the Cluster. I don't know how they managed to construct something such as this in secret. I believe it is in the process of building multiple Skrela motherships even now, likely to attempt to destroy the *Orion*."

"How do we stop it?" I asked her, feeling impotent and useless standing there while the ship was upstairs, fighting for her life. "Is there any way to shut down the process?"

"I am attempting to," she informed me, managing to convey annoyance despite having learned our language only months before. "The AI is fighting me, and even if I managed to prevent the completion of the construction of these ships, it wouldn't prevent it from simply restarting, over and over."

"Then we have to take out the whole thing," I told her. "What if we just start shooting the shit out of all that gear down there? Would our energy cannons do anything to it?" I raised the muzzle of my own weapon, willing to give it a try anyway.

"It's possible. Though it wouldn't necessarily mean the end of the threat. We can't be sure there isn't a backup control center somewhere else on this moon or even somewhere in the core of the brown dwarf. We must destroy the Womb itself, not just the controls."

"And how are we gonna do *that*?" Vicky demanded. "It's a fucking *planet*... a *big*-ass planet too."

"I'm attempting to come up with a method as we speak. And speaking less would only help me do that."

Yeah, no mistaking the annoyed tone there.

"Wait a second," Hachette interrupted, gesturing animatedly. "These nanites, they're just like the ones we use in the auto-meds, right? Those things are pretty fragile... they can't survive outside the nourishment of the biotic fluid. Is there any way you could introduce some kind of impurity, kill them all?"

"That is not a bad idea in principle," Lilandreth admitted, looking away from the display for just a moment, meeting his gaze. "But it would take a contaminant with the mass of this *planet* to add enough impurities to shut down the Womb completely. That's the advantage of having a production facility this size, besides the nearly endless supply of raw material."

Something teased at the back of my thoughts, the germ of an idea. Probably a stupid one, since I was no sort of physicist, biologist, or nanotechnician. But the risk of sounding stupid wasn't as big as the risk of not saying anything.

"Hold on. The nanites tear down the raw materials and reassemble them into Skrela ships and pods, but they also have to reassemble them into more nanites, right? I mean, the things can't last forever. Is there anything keeping you from just telling them to keep going? To keep breaking things down and not build them up until there's nothing left except nanites?"

Lilandreth turned and leaned over the edge of the platform,

and even from twenty meters away I thought I could still make out her catlike eyes staring at me.

"That... I believe I can do." She rushed back to the controls, her fingers tapping on the rounded caps of the golden cylinders rising from the floor like a conductor leading an orchestra. "All of the AI's defenses seem to be arrayed at preventing me from shutting down the production," she continued, distraction in her voice. "And... *Dwight*..." She spat the name out with distaste. "... is distracting it from all its other duties, most significantly from killing us all, but perhaps also from the actual assembly instructions."

Vicky tapped a fist against my shoulder plastron.

"Nice going, bright boy," she told me.

"This will take some time," Lilandreth added. "I hope that..." She trailed off, and I somehow sensed that wasn't a good thing. "There's something happening down there."

I was about to ask where "down there" meant, but as it turned out I didn't have to. The sound coming from the bottom part of the sphere, against the far curve of the wall, was thunderous, deafening even inside the Vigilante, like someone had smacked a sledgehammer against my helmet. Every head turned toward the cacophony, but I already knew where it came from.

Those wide, horizontal cylinders, somewhere around three dozen of them, each four meters across and nearly one hundred meters long. The caps had blown off the end of each of them as if by explosive bolts, though I was pretty sure it had to be something more sophisticated given the technological level of the Resscharr. Smoke poured out of the end of the cylinders and I had a brief, horrific vision of the same sort of nanites that were at work in the Womb below us flooding into the dome and eating away at us, disassembling us one molecule at a time.

I should have known that wasn't it, that the things couldn't survive with so many foreign contaminants around because

Lilandreth had just told me so. No, this was something far simpler, though just as deadly. Out of each of the cylinders they skittered and scrambled, the chittering of their mandibles deafening in the odd acoustics of the place, plasma cannons searching for targets.

Skrela.

[20]

There was no time to be a company commander, no time to stand back behind the lines and give orders. The only way to lead now was from the front, and I hit the jets. I might have yelled something inane like *follow me*, or I might have just imagined it, but they followed me anyway.

Plasma heated the interior of the dome nearly to the boiling point between one instant and the next, sweat crackling across my skin as it evaporated instantly. Starbursts of energy blossomed off of the interior of the Resscharr structure as the plasma splashed away from it, doing no damage at all that I could see, and I reassessed my earlier guess that our energy weapons could have destroyed the control mechanisms. Whatever this stuff was made of, it was damned tough.

Tougher than we were. Two IFF signals blackened instantly, and if I'd been able to consider it at the time, I would have been grateful that I didn't have the time to read the names, but being honest, the only names I was paying even a fraction of my attention to were Vicky and Hachette. Vicky for selfish reasons, Hachette because, as long as he was still alive, Lilandreth was still up there trying to penetrate the system.

And she *was* the mission. We had to keep her alive.

That was the last coherent thought I had, everything else disappearing in an emerald flash as I hosed back and forth with the Resscharr-tech energy cannon. It felt like the leap across the building took forever, that I was hanging out in the wind, but I actually only had a full second of flight time before my boots touched ground at the first flat stretch of floor I could find, in a recess down from the blown cylinders about two hundred meters from the Skrela.

I hadn't been able to count them, and my targeting computer was no help, since the material their carapaces were constructed from did its best to mask their thermal output and sonic signature and the chittering was impossible to separate into individual sounds. But I had an idea of how many could fit into each of those cylinders, and there had to be at least three hundred of them, maybe more, all crammed into this suddenly claustrophobic building with sixty of us, a platoon of Shock Troopers and four Fleet Security guards.

We were all going to die, but if we bought Lilandreth enough time, it might be worth it.

Vicky was beside me. I didn't know when it had happened or how I had the presence of mind to realize it, but she was beside me on that stretch of flat ground in the instant before I gave another burst to the jets and fell right into the middle of the swarm.

It probably seemed like suicide to anyone watching, but it was the opposite. When the enemy has superior firepower, grab them by the belt and hold on tight, use their own people for cover. Skipper had taught me that lesson, and if it applied more aptly to soldiers who actually cared about living, a mass of Skrela bodies was still better cover than nothing at all.

Being in the midst of them was akin to falling into a nest of scorpions if the arachnids were each the size of a draft horse.

What vision I had was filled with flailing, black arms and giant pincers, the ones I could see; and the ones I couldn't see were slamming into me, more of a jostle than a hammer blow because there was no room for them to wind up. The advantage I had was that their plasma cannons were huge, unwieldy, mounted more like crew-served weapons, whereas my energy cannon barely stretched beyond the end of my suit's arm.

I jammed the muzzle against the neck of a Skrela and blew his head off his body in a spray of black fluid.

Move. Shoot, move again. Plasma cannons turned the air into a blast furnace and my breath came shallow, searing my throat despite the best efforts of the internal life support systems to cool me down, while the view from the optical cameras around my helmet was useless, a haze of green and white and yellow that would have permanently scarred my retinae if I'd been looking at it with my naked eyes. Thermal and sonic weren't much good either, but the suit also had motion sensors, though they only worked in an atmosphere. Thank God the Resscharr had maintained one inside the dome, though I wasn't sure why they'd bother. The only other sensor that was functioning was the IFF display, telling me where Vicky and the other Marines were. Instinct kept my fields of fire away from them, but the green energy crackling through the air only a meter away told me that not everyone was being so careful. I didn't bother saying anything because I'd rather they chance shooting me than not shoot at all.

I don't know how long I'd been wading through the throng of enemy. It might have been minutes, but I doubted it was more than twenty seconds, because nothing lasts that long in a firefight, and what stopped it was big and sharp and moving at close to the speed of sound. I didn't recognize it at the time, of course, just felt the dull, wrenching pain of the impact, but I knew in an instant it was one of their tails. Not venomous like an actual scorpion, or at least not as far as we knew, but it had enough power behind it to send my suit flying ten meters.

Warning lights flashed yellow in my HUD, almost matching the color of the stars clouding my vision from the impact, but I didn't have the luxury of pausing for either of them. Legs the size of tree trunks stomped at me on the floor and a few landed hard enough to dent the BiPhase Carbide armor, though at least none had the angle to shoot at me, but I had to get up or one of those kicks was eventually going to land somewhere vulnerable.

The jets saved my ass again, a desperate burst of propulsion that took me shoulder-first into the rear legs of one of the things. The impact knocked it off-balance, sending it crashing over but angling the push of the jets downward and putting me back on my feet. Climbing up the back of the downed Skrela, I put a shot through its torso and gave another kick to the jets, just enough to put me down a few meters away.

The IFF transponders were clustered right in the middle of the pack of Skrela now, and that was about as much as I could tell in the clamor and confusion. I was lucky to be able to figure out even that much, and the knowledge was a ghost flitting across my consciousness, nearly lost in the fog of pain, exhaustion, heat, and desperation. None of that was controlling my actions. Instinct, experience, and training fired my energy cannon, shuffled my feet side to side, gave regular bursts of the jump-jets to smash into clusters of Skrela, while I just went along for the ride.

It wouldn't be too out of line to say it was a relief. I was fighting in a battlesuit, the thing I seemed destined to do, alongside my wife and my fellow Marines, past the point where any direction I could have given would have made a difference. No more giving orders, no more pretending I was smart and capable enough to save everyone and get us home. The only job I had to do was kill the enemy and buy time, and I felt pretty damned confident I could pull that off.

If only the fucking Skrela would have cooperated.

People had been screaming, yelling, cursing over the comms for nearly a minute now, ignoring procedure in the face of shock and panic, and I'd shut it all out, far too busy to separate the chatter into anything coherent. Hachette's voice cut through the caterwauling, sharp as a knife.

"Alvarez! They're coming for us!"

Shit.

"On me!" I tried to bellow the words, but my mouth was stuffed with cotton and they came out as a hoarse rasp.

Whether anyone heard, whether anyone would obey, I couldn't wait to find out. It was inviting a plasma shot to my back, but I didn't hesitate, figuring speed was my only ally. Boost kicked me in the ass, much harder than I'd used before, and I shot out of the swarm of Skrela at a steep angle, straight up toward the platform. I only had a two-count to take in the situation below me, and I sometimes wondered how I could be so quick to process information in situations like this but so clueless when it came to catching interpersonal cues. Or at least that's what Vicky said.

Everything below laid itself out for me like a map, every section of the dome's interior separating like a city block on one of the colonies, each with a skittering, wriggling mass of Skrela in it, a trail coming straight from the cylinders toward the control platform. Streaks of incandescent plasma splashed off the invulnerable half-walls surrounding Lilandreth and the others, which was probably the only reason they were still alive.

All it would take was a better angle and they wouldn't be anymore, and a dozen Skrela were circling around to get just that angle. I twisted in mid-air, changing my arc and narrowly evading a gout of ionized hydrogen, the blast coming so close that the hair on my neck burned away. It also gave me a full second of flight time with my gun pointed downward, and I took advantage of it, squeezing the trigger.

It was still strange being able to do that. Plasma guns were awesome weapons, but they took seconds to recharge; the new reactors and the energy cannons were like firing a coilgun on full auto, but every shot was as devastating as a plasma gun. It was the only reason we had any chance against the Skrela. The burst of strange particles played across the front line of the oncoming enemy, slicing the first two into smoking chunks. It was satisfying but short-lived, and it ended with my shoulder banging into one of the half walls, nearly sending me ricocheting back out into the open.

One last desperate burst of thrust sent me onto the platform, and despite the suit's automated balance functions and gyros, I still had to go down to one knee to avoid tumbling into the antigravity elevator shaft, the spiked soles of my boot scraping against the Resscharr metal with a nerve-grating screech.

Below me, the heart of hell had exploded. The Skrela had abandoned the fight at the center of the dome in a desperate push toward the platform, probably detailed to the new target by the AI, and the remainder of my company was hot on their heels, clinging to them like a tick on a dog. That remainder was so much smaller than I'd hoped.

The charred scraps of corpses littered the uneven metal landscape at the bottom curve of the hemisphere, more of theirs than ours, but they'd had more to begin with. We'd cut their numbers by half, I guessed, but in under two minutes we'd lost twenty Marines, a third of the number in the building, and the realization hit me square in the stomach, more painful than any burn or collision.

They didn't give up despite the death all around them, despite the numbers, because they were Marines and this was the job. We cried for the dead afterward. Vicky was leading them, with Springfield beside her. Singh was gone, one of those black lines beside an IFF transponder that would never register a signal again.

If the Skrela had just turned and fought the Marines, the monsters might have won this battle easily, slaughtering what was left of us, but they were mindless, lacking individual initiative, controlled by the twisted purpose of an AI dedicated to killing off the last of the Resscharr and everything they'd built, and every single one of them was coming straight for the control platform.

I'd nearly forgotten about Lan-Min-Gen and his Shock Troopers, perhaps believing they were either dead already or had ducked out of the building and left us to our fate, but I was being too hard on the Tahni. They'd taken cover behind the esoteric and inscrutable Resscharr architecture and were laying down fire with their KE guns, for all the good it did them. The tantalum slugs chopped divots out of the Skrela armor, but it took a converging stream of fire for the Shock Troopers to bring even one of the things down. I wanted to tell them to just get out and save themselves, but before I had the chance, the oncoming horde finally noticed the covering fire I was laying down from the edge of the platform and a barrage of enemy plasma splashed off the half-wall.

White drowned out my vision and agony overwhelmed my thoughts, a wave of blinding pain all up and down the left side of my body. I'd been down on one knee and I wasn't aware of moving, but when my vision cleared I was lying flat on my stomach, left side up, the sudden flash of pain beginning to fade along with clarity as the suit injected me with an emergency dose of painkillers. I wanted to call for help but I couldn't speak, my brain simply refusing to put together a coherent thought. The only thing I knew was that my weapon was still pointed out in front of me into the fog and steam left behind from the plasma barrage. And through that steam, Skrela were climbing up the support structure to the platform.

Screaming through clenched teeth, fighting for focus, I jammed my finger against the trigger and blew the first of them off the side of the platform, tried to swing the muzzle to the left to get the next one. Hachette and the Fleet Security troopers were shooting at it, their laser carbines spalling off vaporized clouds of its carapace but not penetrating, and I just had to move the gun a meter or so to get it… and I couldn't, not in time. The whole left side of my body was numb, strengthless, and even though I didn't have to carry the weight with my physical muscles, I still had to move. And I couldn't.

The Skrela's plasma cannon muzzle was pointed upward as it climbed, but it nearly had its front legs to the top of the platform, and the second it was upright, Lilandreth and Hachette were dead. And me, but I wasn't really thinking about that at the time… or much of anything.

Hachette did something stupid. It shouldn't have been a surprise. He wasn't a Marine and the only combat he'd seen had been since we'd left the Cluster, and he had to have been scared shitless. But he didn't run, didn't hide. He charged at the Skrela, switching magazines on his carbine as he ran, and threw himself onto its back. I couldn't think straight, couldn't figure out what he was trying to accomplish at the time, but in retrospect, I knew he wanted to jam the muzzle of his carbine into the underside of the thing's neck beneath the meter-long wedge shape that was its head, hoping for a weak spot.

It wasn't a horrible idea as desperate last stands went, and maybe if it had been me doing it, or another Marine Drop Trooper in a suit, it might have worked. But the Skrela had four arms, two load-bearing and two manipulators higher up on the torso. The load-bearing arms were busy pulling the thing up onto the platform, while one of the manipulators was responsible for controlling the plasma gun. That left one free, and one-handed, the Skrela were still ten times stronger than an unarmored human. The thing grabbed him by the arm and yanked him forward.

As much as my mind was working at all, I thought the Skrela was going to toss him down to the ground, which might not be fatal in the slightly lower gravity here. Instead, it just wanted his head level with those razor-sharp mandibles. Hachette still had his helmet on, but it did him no good. The mandibles crunched the thing into half its width, his visor shattering, blood spraying out as his skull was crushed. Then the Skrela let him drop, and what was left of Marcus Hachette fell discarded to the ground below. Blood had sprayed two meters across the floor, throwing a pattern of crimson just shy of where I lay on the floor, motionless.

I still couldn't move the left side of my body, couldn't get the weight off my gun to shift its point of aim, but I could still activate the jets. It would be the last thing I did, but it was better than going out helpless, and I took one last, deep breath. Before I had the chance to sacrifice myself in a blaze of glory, the Skrela disappeared in a wash of star-bright green, the wave of heat and concussion from the thing exploding rolling me backward and causing a fresh spasm of agony through my left side... but also putting me back on one knee. Not from my doing, just the suit finally getting enough input to get its servos working again.

I raised the muzzle of my energy cannon, but there were no more Skrela coming over the side. There were no more Skrela *at all*. Fourth Platoon was rushing through the entrance, Top in the lead, catching the Skrela in a crossfire between them and what remained of the company. If the Skrela had been anything close to autonomous, they still might have taken us through sheer numbers, but they hadn't given up on reaching the platform, stopping Lilandreth, and they ignored the reinforcements, ignored the wave of emerald energy turning the last of them to scattered, charred bits at the foot of the anti-grav elevator.

Everything was quiet for an endless second, no chatter on the comms, no firing, no tromping feet. Everyone stood where they were as if they'd all suddenly realized what had happened at once. I blinked away the clouds still floating in front of my vision, not able to do anything about the ones crowding out my thoughts, and tried to read the threat display in my HUD. Nothing. No movement.

I was forgetting something. I knew it but couldn't put my finger on the exact item, my brain handicapped by the painkillers weighing it down like a fishing sinker. Vicky? No, her IFF was still there, like a miracle from God. *She* was, I decided, the observer in this Quantum play, fated to live forever. I kept almost getting myself killed, and it was going to happen one of these days. Maybe today.

Was it Hachette? No, I remembered him dying. Maybe I should tell someone, but there were so many other dead, I didn't know if it was something I had to announce.

Maybe it was my own injuries. I didn't *want* to know, didn't want to check on them, but I realized I probably should. The display wavered and pulsed in and out of focus, but the gist of it was I had second and third-degree burns all up my left side, but nothing had penetrated the armor, which was a damned good thing if I ever wanted to leave this building and board the dropship. But no, that wasn't it.

I wavered and swayed in a sudden wave of dizziness and would have pitched over sideways if the suit hadn't locked itself in place, standing up. A Vigilante roared up to the platform on a burst of jump-jets and touched down gracefully. I knew it was Vicky before the IFF told me... no one else was as good in a suit as her, except me.

"Jesus, Cam," she murmured. "You're a mess."

"You should have seen the other guy." I was trying to be light-hearted, playing it off, but the words came out grim, a dirge.

"I have it." I blinked, turning slowly with labored, exaggerated movements, and it finally registered in my overtaxed brain what it was that I'd let slip away. Lilandreth.

[21]

Lilandreth hadn't moved from the control panel despite the Fleet Security guards being burned to a crisp right beside her, the smoke pouring off their bodies obscuring her and turning the holographic projection into a sunrise on a foggy morning. On the screen was an image of the Womb, no larger in the projection than it was in the sky outside... but something was happening.

Before, there'd been a vague sense of motion in the atmosphere of the giant planet, but now the entire fabric of the world was churning, a pond struck by a stone, or maybe, more appropriately, a cauldron that had been on the fire too long, the broth inside brought to a rolling boil. Something tried to emerge from the froth, twisted and deformed—it must have been a mothership, the one the AI had instructed the massive nanotech factory to construct to fight the *Orion*. It was trying to fulfill its purpose, trying to make its way into space, but the nanites wouldn't let it go. They ravaged it, cannibalized it for the raw materials inside it and reabsorbed them into the insane maelstrom. The drives were the last thing stolen, and when they were gone, the whole mass sank backward.

I let out the breath I'd been holding, but that wasn't the end of the show. The entire curvature of the planet shifted from second to second, throwing off clouds of hazy, golden-brown vapor that faded away as it drifted into space. The faint glow the world had shown as a virtue of its sheer size was growing brighter, and even in my muddled state I knew why. The nanites were devouring mass, changing it into more of themselves, and in doing so, releasing wave after wave of waste heat.

"Hey," Vicky asked, "what's gonna happen when that thing gets beyond the point of no return?"

"There's a chance," Lilandreth admitted, "that it will collapse in on itself and go critical. It may take hours, perhaps even days, but we should attempt to be gone before then."

"Hours," Dwight corrected, the first time I'd heard from him since this all began. "And not many of them."

"Don't you need to be suppressing the AI?" I asked.

"He has resigned himself to his fate. The minute the collapse became irreversible, he shut himself down. You might call it committing suicide. With the AI gone and the security systems down, I've been able to communicate with the *Orion*. They've destroyed the Skrela mothership and they're on the way back into orbit."

My head hurt. I wanted to rub it but obviously couldn't, and I didn't know why the suit didn't do something about it. I took a sip of water and nearly spat it out. It was still bathwater tepid from the heat the Vigilante had absorbed.

"Vicky," I said once my mouth wasn't full of cotton, "get someone outside, get the drop-ships down here."

"It's being done," she told me, putting a hand on my shoulder though I couldn't feel it. "I've got this. Your armor is telling me you're loopy from the painkillers."

"I'll survive," I said, wishing I could collapse, that the suit wasn't holding me up. It would have been a relief to pass out. "Hachette's gone. His whole guard team too."

"I know." She sighed. "I think he pretty much wanted this when he came down here, but the security troops didn't deserve it."

"I could have saved him," Lilandreth said, hovering beside my left shoulder, not so intimidating as she seemed when I was dismounted. "Had I abandoned my task, my rifle would have been able to kill the Skrela before it killed him. But had I stopped, the AI would have had time to counter my infiltration." Her gaze seemed to penetrate the faceless metal of my helmet. "Do you believe I did the right thing?"

Maybe it was the drugs, or maybe it was finally surrendering to the reality of the twenty Marines I'd just sacrificed to accomplish this mission, but when I tried to answer her question, I broke down, uncontrollable sobs shaking my shoulders, and the words wouldn't come.

"You did the only thing you could," Vicky answered for me. "We all did."

"You need to be in the auto-med," Dr. Hallonen tsked, wrapping the last of the smart bandages in place on my shoulder. "You're fucking raw hamburger, and even with the smart bandages, it's going to take you days to heal!"

"Maybe later, Doc," I told her, letting out the breath I'd been holding now that the bandages had infused me with their numbing agents. They were more precise and localized than the painkillers the suit had given me, and my mind could work again. So could my nose, unfortunately, and the smell of burnt flesh was sickening enough without the knowledge it was mine.

"Besides, there's no muscle damage, and I won't make it any worse by walking around with it, will?"

"No," she admitted, arms crossed, nose wrinkled, the picture of reluctance. Like everyone else, Hallonen had let her hair grow out a little since we'd been stuck here, and it struck me how much younger it made her look. She sighed. "And honestly, there are worse cases in the tubes already."

I knew that already. I'd seen them on the way up in the drop-ship. I should have realized it on the ground back in the dome, but I was, as Vicky had said, too loopy and fading in and out of coherence. We had six wounded, including me—all contact burns, because no one ever received a nonfatal burn-through from a plasma gun. The heat and radiation from a direct hit could cook a Drop Trooper's insides if their suit was breached.

Wincing more from the anticipated pain than its realization, I slipped into the fresh uniform Vicky had dropped off for me after leaving me here. The boots were the worst part since I had to bend over to put them on, but I held back the profanity for fear Hallonen might change her mind. She did shoot me a skeptical glance when I sucked down a long breath after straightening back up but didn't say anything.

"They're gonna lock down the rotation in another half an hour," I told her, limping for the hatch. "I have to get to the bridge."

"Is Colonel Hachette really dead?" she asked quietly. I blinked and looked back. Hallonen had never struck me as the sentimental type, nor had she ever shown much affection for Hachette.

"Yeah." I hesitated in the hatchway. "He went out trying to save us all."

Hallonen nodded.

"I've known him a long time. Since the war. Met him on Inferno when I was at officer's training. Well, the abbreviated training they gave doctors. He was pretty full of himself, but... he was nice to me."

"He tried to do the best he could." I was probably being unfair to him, but it was the best I could manage right now.

I took the lift instead of trying to manage the ship's central hub, deathly afraid I was going to do something stupid and pull one of the bandages loose. I probably could have gotten away with staying in the medical bay or even spending the next few hours in an auto-med, but I was the idiot who'd stepped up and offered to take command of this circus, and I'd be damned if I was going to sleep through the thing we'd spent the last year searching for.

I wasn't alone, of course. Crewmembers shifted from one station to the other, taking advantage of the brief time in free fall before the ship hit boost again. We were under a deadline, and the only reason the *Orion* hadn't left orbit around the moon was the inevitable need to get everyone out of the drop-ships, getting the wounded to medical and secure the suits. We were under time pressure, and Dwight, for one, wasn't going to let me forget it.

"You do understand we have less than three hours before the Womb goes critical?" he asked as I rode the lift, buzzing in my earbud instead of announcing the deadline to the six other people in the car with me. "If you wish to secure the gateway machinery, you're going to have to give yourself at least a half hour to reach minimum safe distance before the gravitational instability rips the moon apart and the *Orion* finds herself in the middle of a brand-new asteroid field."

"Yes, you've told me," I assured him. "Even if I was high on painkillers, I remember that part."

I'd answered in a low mutter, but it was still enough to turn six sets of eyes my way. Or maybe it was the shiny glisten of the burn ointment rubbed on my face or my lack of eyebrows. Or something else. Three of the people in the elevator with me were Fleet Intelligence, their black uniforms crisp and fresh in the style Hachette had favored. No sloppy officers in Intelligence, though I didn't know whether that standard had come down from him or from his boss, General Murdock.

I didn't look away, but it was difficult. They blamed me for Hachette's death, I was sure of it. Or if they didn't, they blamed me for suborning his authority, for taking control of the mission from him. One of them, a short, slim first lieutenant with stress lines around her eyes and the look of someone who hadn't slept in days, spoke up, hesitant, almost as if she was afraid to approach me.

"Sir," she said, "is it true? Is it all over?"

It was an effort not to sigh in relief that she wasn't asking me about Hachette, then even more of a struggle to get my brain working again to answer the question. I wasn't in a drug stupor anymore, but I was still exhausted, hands shaking from the adrenaline withdrawals and likely to say something stupid.

"It's not quite over yet," I corrected her, "but if this was the only womb planet they had, then at least we've gotten rid of their ability to… produce more Skrela. That means we have breathing space now, so we can figure out what to do without having to worry about them wiping us out."

"What about the gateway, sir?" That was one of the ship's crew, a younger man, his eyes wide, maybe with hope or maybe with fear of disappointment. "Can we take it with us?"

The lift warned us it was slowing down, and I grabbed a safety strap as it came to a stop at the bridge, wincing at the tug of my burned flesh against the smart bandages. It didn't exactly *hurt*, but there was, as doctors are fond of saying, a little pressure. It wasn't as bad now that I didn't have to see it. I'd caught a brief glimpse in the medical bay while Hallonen and her people were cutting off my clothes and very nearly added nausea to my host of current medical ills. Just thinking about it nearly made me lose whatever was left of my pre-battle lunch right there in the elevator.

The door hissed open and I offered the crewman a smile.

"We're about to find out."

If there'd been stares in the lift car, the ones on the bridge were twice as intense, although more knowledgeable. The bridge crew *knew* what had happened, didn't have to ask me, and maybe that was worse.

"Cam, what the hell are you doing up here?" Nance demanded, scowling at me from his command chair. "You should be in the medical bay!"

"Already been there," I assured him, drifting over to one of the open acceleration couches. I didn't even want to try to use my magnetic boots, not caring for the jerking and jolting they'd give my body. Strapping in wasn't a pleasant experience, given the pressure of the straps on my left shoulder, but I could deal with it. "The auto-meds are full, and I won't heal any faster there than here."

He grunted his skepticism but didn't argue further, and I settled in to try to make sense of the view on the main screens. The *Orion* was still in orbit around the moon, but I wasn't interested in the blue-white orb. It was a grain of sand against the giant, glowing red-brown storm of the Womb, which absorbed all my attention. The edges of the planet were fluid now, wavering as if the entire world was a mirage, an illusion brought about by gravitational lensing. It was mesmerizing, the wavering outline drawing my eye to it, making it difficult to look away long enough to examine the smaller screen on the lower left where the telescopic view of the Seeker debris field was projected.

Yellow and red warnings flashed around the field, giving us the details of how much the orbits of the various bits of debris had deteriorated in the last hour. It was a grating, vexatious reminder of how little time we had left.

"Have we figured out how to attach the thing yet?" I wondered.

"Theoretically," Nance told me, "it's simple. The *Orion* is equipped with magnetic grapples to latch onto smaller vessels in an emergency, and the Transition Drive field should be large enough to encompass us and the gateway. That leaves just two small problems in practice. The first one, Dwight can probably answer." His eyes went upward to the screen, as if expecting the AI to show himself, and Dwight didn't disappoint, his avatar standing off to the side of the image of the Womb.

"How can I help, Captain Nance?"

"The gateway core, whatever it is," Nance asked, nodding at the main screen. "Is it ferro-magnetic? Will our grapples even be able to interact with it?"

Dwight frowned, and I wanted to throw something at the projection. It was all an act, an affectation, a waste of time we didn't have, and I wanted to yell at him to stop pretending he was human. Given my current state of mind I wanted it *very* badly and nearly blurted out the accusation.

"Not as things stand," Dwight said, blissfully unaware of my inner turmoil. "But if we can get close enough to the device, I may be able to activate its magnetic field and aid you in attaching to it."

"And that brings up potential problem number two. We can Transition with the thing attached, but can we *boost* with it?" Nance motioned around us, taking in the whole of the ship. "We're not designed for it, we don't have the structural enhancements of a tug or an industrial barge. We have *armor*, but most of the ship's hull reinforcement is dedicated to structural integrity. It's going to take a pretty high-g boost to get that thing out of orbit from around the Womb."

"I will need to wait until we are attached to the gateway core," Dwight replied, no hesitation this time. "It's impossible to say until I determine how functional its control systems are, but I may be able to use the gateway's distortion field to counter the acceleration."

"You can *do* that?" Yanayev asked, eyes going wide.

I was no physicist, but I wondered how she could be surprised. The Predecessor tech felt like magic to me. Hell, the gateway itself was magic as far as I was concerned. It had taken us tens of thousands of light-years across the galaxy in an instant at the start of all this, and that was after sitting inactive for tens of thousands of years.

"I *may* be able to do it," Dwight corrected her. "But we have very little time."

"Yeah, I get it," Nance grumbled. I thought if there were gravity on the bridge, he would have been leaning his chin on his fist like the stella of some ancient eastern king. "Helm, take us out of orbit, fastest course for the Seeker debris field. Sound boost warning and take us to six gravities."

I couldn't restrain the moan, though I did keep it as quiet as possible. Nance shot me a grin as the warbling boost warning sounded through the speakers.

"I told you," he said, speaking up over the alarm. "You should be in an auto-med."

I met his eyes, chest tightening with a grim fatalism. I'd chosen this road and I'd have to walk it.

"*He'd* be here," I said, and I didn't have to clarify who I meant. "And now I have to be."

Nance's smile disappeared and he nodded.

"He would. Let's go finish this for him."

"Boosting now," Yanayev announced.

Nearly five hundred kilos of mass pressed me into the acceleration couch, and anything else I might have said was swallowed up in a breathless haze of pain.

[22]

"Holy shit," I murmured when I could breathe again.

Nance didn't speak, but the look on his face as he stared at the screen told me he agreed. The boost out of the moon's orbit and into the planet's had been extraordinarily unpleasant, grinding the burned parts of my body against the acceleration couch in a way that not even the numbing properties of the smart bandages could completely overcome, but here, now, back in free fall and looking at the scene arrayed before us, I barely remembered the discomfort.

From a distance the Seeker debris field had obviously been Predecessor-tech ships, but from that far away there'd been no sense of perspective, nothing to compare them to except the brown dwarf. Not anymore. The *Orion* had fallen into a high orbit over the Womb only a hundred klicks away from the edge of the field, and this close, the shards of the Predecessor ships were the size of apartment blocks in the underground of a megacity back on Earth, massive and jagged. But it wasn't their sheer enormity that was so overwhelming, it was the realization that, over a thousand years ago, these massive vessels had been overwhelmed by something powerful enough to grind them to bits.

Not the gateway core though. It was intact, and I knew it on an instinctive level without even knowing what it should look like. There was something inherently perfect about the faceted cylinder, akin to the feeling I had in the presence of a work of art or a finely cut gemstone. One thing about it wasn't perfect though.

"Damn," Wojtera said fervently, and I didn't have to ask why.

The gateway was slowly tumbling retrograde to the rest of the debris, which wouldn't have been so bad if the thing wasn't nearly as long as our ship.

"Is there any way we can match its movements?" I asked Nance, hypnotized by the motion of the thing. "Latch onto it and stop the tumble?"

Nance glared at me.

"Are you fucking serious? Things may not have weight in free fall, but they sure as hell have *mass*, and getting something as big as this ship into a matching spin with that thing would burn just about every kilo of reaction mass we have left, which wouldn't leave us anything to get it out of orbit!"

"I'm a Marine, Captain," I reminded him, annoyed at his outrage. "That's why I asked you."

"Well, the answer's no," he said, and Yanayev nodded agreement.

"Besides the reaction mass cost," she added, "the rotation would pretty much have every single crewmember puking their guts out before we could even get into position."

"I think we're going to have to give up on this," Nance said dolorously, staring at the thing. "As much as it pains me to say."

My brain was spinning like a flywheel, trying desperately to process all the information I'd taken in, an intuition gnawing at me, telling me I was missing something.

"Wait a second," I said, raising a finger, eyes clouding over with memory. "Dwight, you said you could use the gateway to cancel out its mass so we could propel it with our drive, right?"

"I said it was *possible*," Dwight corrected me, showing up again at the side of the screen. I just noticed in that moment that he'd allowed his Fleet-uniformed avatar's hair to get longer, just like the rest of the crew on this trip. "I won't know for sure until we can achieve physical contact with the device."

"But if you can cancel out the thing's mass," I said, spreading my hands, "then why does it have to be the *Orion*?" I looked to Nance. "You said it would take too much reaction mass to get this ship into position. But what about one of the Intercepts?"

Nance looked at me as if I'd grown another head, but then a light came on behind his eyes and he smiled.

"Dwight?" he asked, not expounding, but the AI understood the question.

"Yes, it *could* work," he said.

"The Intercepts don't have magnetic grapples." That was Lt. Mandan, who I knew by sight and by name, but hadn't ever said more than "hello" to the whole time we'd been on this mission. He was nominally the flight ops officer, but he only dealt with the flight crews, and usually after I was already on board one of the drop-ships or shuttles. He was a tall, lanky drink of water who might have been born in a lighter gravity, with a long, horsey face that was currently twisted into a frown.

"If I *can* connect with the control systems," Dwight said, "you may not need magnetic grapples. All the core would require is the boost from the ship's drive. There is one problem, however. I need direct contact with the surface of the device through something metallic, something with a communications lead such as one of your battlesuits." The avatar's eyes fixed on me and I rubbed at my temples.

I *could* have sent someone else, of course. I had every reason to. And I couldn't. Too many Marines had died on my order.

"Whaddya say, Dwight?" I yanked my harness loose and pushed out of the acceleration couch. "Wanna take one more ride?"

"This is the stupidest damned thing I've ever heard of," Vicky said, pushing off against the safety straps on the bulkhead of the hangar bay to keep up with me.

Walking in the suit with magnetic soles in free fall might have been awkward, but it still had long strides, and she wouldn't have been able to match my stride if she'd used her own ship boots rather than floating.

"You shouldn't even be in a suit," she continued, "much less out there on the side of some Predecessor artifact. And what about the damned spin? You know what that'll do to your inner ear?"

"The suit can keep my balance for me," I told her. "Yeah, it's gonna be miserable, but being in the suit won't do anything worse for my burns. That's what the doc said."

Actually, Hallonen hadn't commented *directly* on me being in a suit, probably assuming I wasn't crazy or stupid enough to get back into one anytime soon, but she'd said something about how I wouldn't be any better off in the medical bay than I would be on the bridge, which seemed close enough.

"Why does it have to be *you*?"

I wanted to stop and explain it to her, would have really liked to talk it through, but we were only a couple hours from the whole brown dwarf going critical.

"Because I can't ask anyone else to do it," I said instead.

"Hey, you coming, dude?" Dunstan asked, hanging out the side of the Intercept's cargo lock, blond hair surrounding his head like a halo in a medieval painting. "I really don't want to be around when this fucking planet starts coming apart, you know?"

"Coming, Kyler."

Going through the lock was the hardest part, since there was no ramp and the hatchway wasn't built for a suit. I had to cut loose the magnets and push myself through while contorting to squeeze the suit's shoulders in, which was about as painful as I thought it might be. On top of that, there was no rack inside the ship's utility bay to secure the suit, which meant I had to tuck myself into a corner and anchor with the magnetic boots again.

Vicky gave me one last look through the cargo lock before the hatch swung shut. She was still angry but trying not to show it.

"I'd tell you to be careful," she said, her voice coming over my helmet headphones through her 'link, "but I know you wouldn't listen to *that* either."

"I swear to God and on a stack of Bibles," I told her, "that once we get this damned thing and get everyone home, I'm done with this shit." I shook my head, even though she couldn't see it. "I've had enough of watching people die because they followed my orders or because I led them into it. I just want it to stop."

"I know you believe that."

The metallic clunk of the lock disengaging drowned out her next words, then the *bang-bang-bang* of the maneuvering thrusters firing, shoving Intercept One out of the docking chute. I tapped into the cockpit camera just in time to watch the silver-gray curve of the ship give way to the glowing red-brown of the Womb, so huge it blotted out the eldritch glare of the Cauldron of Creation. Just before the drive kicked in, I caught Vicky's last few words before the connection to her 'link faded.

"... you're a Drop Trooper, Cam. I don't know that you'll ever want to be anything else."

I wanted to answer, wanted to tell her she was wrong, but I couldn't swear to myself I believed it.

[23]

"This is gonna get a little hairy, bud," Dunstan warned me. "I hope you've got some kind of spacesick bag inside that helmet."

"I don't get motion sickness," I said. "Never have."

His only reply was a dark chuckle. I found out why a few minutes later. Things hadn't been too bad up till then. We hadn't done more than three Gs maneuvering toward the debris cloud, and that had only been for a few seconds, a burn and then a deceleration boost. In an Intercept cutter, that meant having my weight pushed toward the aft-end of the ship, and since it was oriented horizontally for atmospheric flight, it had felt like I was lying against the bulkhead with arms and legs clutched to my chest in a fetal position.

That was before the maneuvering jets kicked in again. It was the same jackhammer pounding against the hull, annoying as hell but something I'd gotten used to in years of space travel, but this was well beyond the usual gentle nudge into a new course. The hammering was unending, the lateral thrust sending Intercept One into a tumbling spiral, attempting to match the orbit of the gateway core. It wasn't as bad as I thought it would be. I mean, yeah, it did torment my inner ear, adding to the general disorientation of free fall an inescapable feeling of spinning end for end and *oh, God*, my stomach felt like it was about to surge right up through my throat and decorate the inside of my helmet, and I clamped my jaws shut and closed my eyes.

Closing my eyes was a bad idea, as it turned out. Gorge rose in my throat and I forced it back down, clenching my fists tight, the suit mirroring the motion. I opened my eyes again and tried to focus on a spot just in front of me in the utility bay, and that helped a little, my stomach settling down to the normal zero-G queasiness. The corner into which I'd crammed the Vigilante was nice and snug, not letting the suit jerk from one side to the other during the maneuver. I let my thoughts drift away from the stomach-wrenching tumble and into other closets, other niches where I'd hidden as a child.

I hadn't thought about my childhood in a while. It used to dominate my thoughts once upon a time, back when there *were* no good memories to look back on other than the impermanent shelters from bullying and abuse I'd found. There'd been a day when I ranked the quality of the group homes where I'd stayed by how many nooks and crannies they had where I could hide all day long.

The utility bay reminded me of one of the best, a place where I had, unfortunately, not spent nearly enough time. It was the highest up I'd been in the Underground the whole time I'd lived in Trans Angeles, so damned close to the surface, to the middle-class families I sometimes dreamed of being a part of. The place was huge compared to the other group homes, better funded and better staffed than the places deeper down, and most of the kids weren't violent criminals learning their trade by abusing the smaller and younger ones.

That didn't stop me from finding a hiding place though. Lessons learned hard were even harder to forget. This place was so large, they had entire storage areas filled with containers of raw cloth for the fabricators so we could all have new clothes once a month. The utility bay reminded me of one of those rooms, one that had been nearly empty, which was good because it meant no one would come there to get supplies, and no one would bother to check the security cameras because there was nothing to steal.

I'd spent hours in that room, leaving only to eat and use the bathroom. My mistake had come when I'd slept there once too often and missed bed check. That was when they'd found me and told me I couldn't be on my own without supervision and I'd made one of the biggest mistakes of my life. I panicked, reacted, ran away. Or tried to. I was nine and I didn't get far. They didn't let me back in. This place was for well-behaved orphans and abandoned children, not the runaways. I'd been sent deeper into the Underground and never saw that place again. I don't even remember the name of it or the faces of the people who worked there. Just that room.

The steering jets ceased their pounding and my inner ear stopped its pointless rebellion, perhaps learning a lesson from my younger self.

"Okay, we're as close to this damned thing as we're going to get without landing on it," Dunstan told me. "Chief'll seal the utility bay and let you out the cargo lock."

"Yeah, copy," I grunted.

His crew chief, Hazel Beckett, was a quiet woman, professional and good at her job, which made it even more of a mystery how she'd managed to work with Dunstan for months now without going insane at the pilot's endless jabbering. I mean, I loved Kyler, but the man simply couldn't shut up, and if I had to work with him every day for months, I might have cycled myself through an airlock without a suit.

Her face was invisible through her helmet visor as she

floated back from the cockpit in her suit, pausing to touch the control just outside it. The blast shield slid into place with an authoritative thump and the air pumps chugged to life, their whirring racket fading gradually as there was less and less atmosphere in the utility bay to conduct it. I pushed to my feet, still locked to the deck, and waited for her.

"Okay, sir, let's get you set up," she said, clomping across the deck on magnetic soles to a locker set in the bulkhead beside the cargo lock. Throwing open the compartment, she pulled out the lead end of a heavy cable on a spindle mounted inside. "I'm gonna hook this to your suit just in case anything really funky happens and you can't jet back to us." She paused, the hook barely touching the ring built into the backpack of my Vigilante. "Have you ever been outside in just a suit, sir?"

Dunstan's laugh was loud and raucous in my earphones, but he left it to me to answer the question. I thought of the mission to Ambergris so very long ago, when I'd waited with a platoon of Drop Troopers and another of Force Recon in the debris field from an asteroid collision to hijack a Tahni freighter, and I smiled in the privacy of my helmet.

"Once or twice, Chief."

"Okay," she went on, the word heading upward at the end with a doubtful drawl. "Just remember, it's easy to lose your sense of direction. The cable should help with that. Any doubts, you give me the word and I'll haul you back in."

"I appreciate that, Chief." I might not have been in the Fleet, but one thing I *had* learned was that arguing with crew chiefs was counterproductive. "Dwight, you in there?"

"I am in full contact with the *Orion* through your suit and Intercept One," the AI reported. "You may proceed when you're ready."

"Open her up, Chief," I said, motioning at the airlock.

The hatch slid aside in utter preternatural silence, my own

footsteps on the deck just as soundless as the carnage outside. There *should* have been sound. The pustulent swelling of the brown dwarf, pulsing like a giant, infected heart, the harsh, white glare of the Cauldron of Creation, the cloud of ancient debris... it all deserved to be accompanied by a grim, bass-heavy symphony. Top had made me listen to classical music a few times as part of my "professional development," and there was an ancient symphony by an orchestra known as Led Zeppelin that would have fit. Something called "Kashmir."

Imagining musical accompaniment to the spectacle didn't make it any less intimidating, and despite my assurance to the chief that I was comfortable in open space in just my battlesuit, my testicles ascended back into my body when I pushed away from the Intercept's cargo lock. It wasn't until I was clear of the bulk of the cutter that the artifact was actually visible. I'd figured when I stepped out that I would be disoriented by the rotation of the ship and the artifact, but from my perspective, it seemed as if the two bodies—and me, along for the ride—were completely still and the rest of the universe was slowly rotating. It was more comfortable to my subconscious regarding it that way, though it didn't bear up if I put any thought to it.

Focusing on the artifact helped. This close, it blotted out everything beneath it, including the *Orion*, which I knew was only a couple hundred klicks away, well within visible range out here. It might as well have been a light-year away, out of sight and out of mind, because the artifact filled my field of vision and my imagination.

I'd seen so much of the remnants of the Predecessor civilization, from their cities to their starships, but the gateway core was the most impressive, the most awe-inspiring. From orbit around the moon, hundreds of thousands of klicks away, the thing had seemed simple, a silver-gray cylinder of metal, plain, unexceptional, just another featureless piece of debris. Up close, it was a jewel glittering in the light both from the primary star and the brown dwarf. Or at least a faceted diamond was the first thing that came to mind, but the comparison didn't do it justice.

It was a diamond if the gem had been cut into facets by nanites controlled by a mad genius. There were patterns in it, I was sure, but I couldn't describe them. I'm not sure any human could. Like all the Resscharr architecture and design, the patterns twisted my vision and teased at my mind, leading my eyes into a maze with no outlet. It was mind-bending enough that I felt as if I would miss it on the way down and hesitated for long seconds before hitting the jets.

No air out here, of course, which meant that the jump-jets had to work off their very small internal reaction mass supply, and exactly how limited that was tightened my gut with every burst of the rockets. Just a few seconds of boost toward the thing, then a tug on the line to turn myself over, then a choked scream at the suit rubbing against the smart bandage on my left shoulder before I managed to decelerate for a three count. Not quite enough to stop me completely, but enough to get me down.

Almost too fast. There was damned little gravity out here, just whatever pull this thing had with its native mass, and I was just so certain that when my boots hit that faceted gemstone face, I was going to either bounce off or slide off. I didn't. I stuck.

"The hell?" I murmured, forgetting even the pain from my burns in the confusion.

It didn't feel like artificial gravity, more like how it felt when I engaged the magnetic soles, like something was sticking me down to the thing.

"I took the liberty of securing you to the surface," Dwight informed me.

I looked up as if I could see him, then shook my head at the inanity of it.

"Already?" I asked. "I thought you had to be connected to the thing?"

"I was connected the moment you landed," he explained. "The system activated automatically."

"Wow, that was fast." I was honestly impressed. "It took a lot longer for you to get into the system down on the moon."

"I was being actively opposed there by one nearly as powerful as myself. This is the equivalent of a switched-off appliance."

"That's good news. So, you can get this thing working? Make it..." I struggled for the scientific term. "... weigh less?"

"An inexact description, but yes. That will take more time, however. The system is up, but the field requires power and the reactor needs time to energize. It will be a few minutes. But you may tell Lt. Dunstan that he will now be able to dock with the device. I can assure its anchorage."

"Dunstan," I called. "You hear that? You're cleared to land."

And there was *just* enough room for the thing. Not that the cylinder was small compared to the cutter, but the curvature left barely adequate space for the tricycle landing gear to touch down.

"Yeah, I'll be right there," he said. "You might want to, you know, unhook that cable so you don't get tangled up in it when we come down."

"Not happening unless you come down here and cut it loose," I told him. "These arms don't reach back that far."

"Okay, man, we'll like, cut you some extra slack. Give us some space so we don't squash you like a bug."

"That would be suboptimal, as my trainers used to say."

More of the cable played out from the still-open cargo lock of Intercept One, spooling a double loop before it finally ground to a halt. The umbilical twisted and whipped around as the cutter's maneuvering thrusters fired sporadically, spinning it nose for tail, then nudging it downward with painful slowness. I wanted to yell at him to hurry the hell up, considering we had a planet about to explode beneath us, but I figured it would be a bad idea considering he had me connected to the ship by a metal wire.

Instead, I scooted backward, not allowing the soles of my boots to lift from the surface of the cylinder. It *should* have felt rough, uneven with the patterns cut into the material, but instead it was slick as ice, barely any resistance at all, as if the faceting wasn't cut into the surface but instead something inside the material structure. I didn't ponder it too long, concentrating on getting out of the way of the cutter before it landed.

The Intercepts always looked so small compared to the *Orion*, and particularly when I was crammed into one of the things in a suit, but down here with the ship descending directly above me, it was terrifyingly huge and heavy and very likely to crush me like a beer can. I moved toward the nose, figuring that was easier to dodge than the broad, delta wings, and could have touched the armored skin of the ship when it touched on the nose gear. The landing strut recoiled into the hydraulics a couple times before the craft settled against the cylinder and was still.

"You're down clean," I told Dunstan. "You didn't even kink the safety line." Whatever his other failings and despite the fact that Brandano never would have admitted it, Dunstan could fly the hell out of that cutter.

"Copy. When can we hit the drive and get this overgrown dildo out of here?"

"It will be another two hundred and forty seconds, Lt. Dunstan," Dwight informed him.

"And how long do we have before the planet goes critical?" I asked, finally glancing away from the ship and the artifact, eyeing the pulsing, glowing mass of the brown dwarf.

"The Womb has *already* gone critical, Captain Alvarez. We have approximately ten minutes to boost the artifact out of orbit before the gravitational anomalies make it impossible to escape its pull."

"Oh, good," Dunstan sighed. "I thought we might be cutting it too close or something."

"Cam, you read me?" It was Vicky on the *Orion*.

"Yeah, I copy. We're gonna make it... just have to wait until whatever magic spell Dwight is casting makes this mountain lighter than a feather."

"I assure you, Captain Alvarez," Dwight objected, "I am *not* using any form of magic."

"Well, in one of the books Top made me read," I began, but I'd never get to finish the quote. Vicky interrupted.

"Cam, we're picking up movement in the debris field. Can't tell what it is yet, but Wojtera is worried it might be fragments of the wreckage being jostled around by the shifting gravity field of the planet."

"That's quite impossible," Dwight objected. "If there were that level of gravitational variation already, this cylinder would have shifted in its spin..."

"Uh, guys," Dunstan said. "I see what's moving, and it ain't no debris field. Check your six, Cam."

I turned and saw them immediately, though it would have been blocked off from the *Orion* by the mass of the cylinder.

"Oh, shit," I muttered. "I thought we got them all."

I was wrong. There was no mistaking the bulbous, alien lines of the things. Nor was there any mistaking their intentions.

"*Orion*," Dunstan called, suddenly all business. "We have four Skrela fighters inbound."

[24]

"Son of a bitch!" Nance roared in my ear. "Where the hell did they come from?"

"They were waiting in the debris field," Dwight suggested. "Dormant. Perhaps guarding this very artifact."

"I'm cutting loose," Dunstan declared. "I'll get them off our backs."

"I would advise against it," Dwight said. "The field is activated. We should engage the drive and vacate the area."

"Do it," I ordered Dunstan before he could argue, eyes fixed on the fighters, still a few hundred klicks away though clearly visible and getting closer with every second. "Hit the drive, Kyler."

"But... oh, all right, dammit. Hold on."

"We'll cover you," Nance said. "Once you haul that thing out of the way, we'll maneuver around you and get a shot at the fighters."

"Dwight," I said, a sudden thought striking me, "when he guns this thing, am I going to get scraped off like a bug?"

"None of you will feel any acceleration. I'm taking care of that now."

And good as his word, he did. Between one eyeblink and the next, a standard gravity was pulling me down as if the center of the cylinder was suddenly the mass of the entire Earth. I was about to ask another question, but Dwight anticipated it.

"You and the occupants of Intercept One will feel normal gravity, but the mass of the artifact has been negated. It would, however, be wise to get inside the ship."

"You don't need me to stay in contact with the thing so you can talk to it?" I *thought* that was the main reason I was standing out here like an idiot.

"Not any longer. I've already programmed the machine. I won't need to do so again until we plan to ask it to do a different task."

I was about to tell him he could have mentioned that a minute ago, but a rumble through the surface and a wash of heat derailed my train of thought. The Intercept's drive had ignited. I'm not sure what I'd envisioned happening at that point. The artifact was huge, the size of the *Orion*, and I suppose I'd imagined it gaining momentum slowly, ponderously, the Intercept chugging along like the little engine that could. That wasn't what happened. The cutter was a responsive bird, light and quick off the blocks, basically an assault shuttle enlarged enough to fit a Transition Drive, and what I'd forgotten was that the gravitational machinations Dwight had started meant the thing effectively had no mass.

The cylinder and the cutter leapt out of high orbit with me along for the ride, and I felt nothing. No boost, no push backward, no increased mass. I was hoping the Skrela fighters would be left behind in the dust, but they didn't have to worry about things like the tolerances of a human body and they'd simply increased acceleration. Which was another good reason I should get inside the ship.

If the surface of the cylinder had been freaky before, now it was doubly so. Nothing but normal gravity was sticking me to it, yet it still felt no slicker than a ship's deck. I'd only taken two steps toward the cargo lock when I saw the smaller shapes cut loose from the fighters, shot out like projectiles.

"Please tell me those aren't what I think they are," I moaned, pausing beside the lock.

"Yeah, I think those were seed pods," Dunstan confirmed.

The fighters, having dropped their payload, increased their boost, heading straight for the Intercept... until they each, in turn, disappeared in a flash of liberated energy, tumbling, glowing fragments continuing their course on left-over momentum. The fiery remnants passed over the Intercept like a meteor shower, lost behind us as the cutter kept accelerating.

For a moment I wondered what had happened, until the massive, silver-gray bulk of the *Orion* pulled along beside us, her main drive a second sun.

"We got the fighters," Vicky told me, apparently having taken on the job of being my contact on the bridge, "but those pods landed a few klicks from you and Skrela drones are already breaking out of them. We can try taking them out with another fly-by, using the coilgun turrets..."

"That will not work," Dwight interjected. "The gravitational field that is negating the mass of this device distorts the fabric of spacetime around us to the extent that your weapons will be diverted from their intended targets. You might hit the surface, but the location will be unpredictable."

"Son of a bitch," I spat, shuffling around near the lock. It was a good four meters up, nothing at all for my jump-jets, but if I hopped inside and locked the door behind me, the Skrela could take potshots at the cutter as long as they stayed out of the line of fire of its coilgun turret and proton cannon. "I think I'm gonna have to stay out here and defend the ship." I glanced up at the *Orion* hopefully, as if they could see me. "Any chance you can get more troops down here?"

"Not at this acceleration," Nance answered this time, probably sensing that Vicky would have given me another answer. "We have to get to minimum safe Transition distance before we get nailed with a radiation burst. We launch a drop-ship, there's no way it could keep up."

"In addition to that," Dwight added, "as I already said, due to the gravitational field, any ship coming in would be unable to control its landing site."

"Doesn't matter," Vicky snapped. "Lt. Mandan, get Intercept Two prepped and ready to go in ten minutes. I'm going to grab Czarnecki and we're going to come after you, and I don't want to hear any fucking arguments about it."

"You won't get one from me," I assured her, searching the horizon. "Just try to hurry."

"Don't be a bitch," she said, her version of gentle teasing. "I'll be there when I get there. Just keep your eyes open."

"Dunstan," I called, ducking under the hull of the Intercept, checking the opposite side, "you hear me?"

"Of course I hear you, dude. You're like, right outside."

I wanted to count to ten, but didn't figure I had the time for it.

"You have cover to the front with the proton cannon and what? Maybe one hundred, one hundred fifty degrees to the sides with the coilgun turrets?"

"Yeah, that's about right. Chief?"

"One hundred and forty degrees," she corrected us.

"And they ain't coming from the rear," Dunstan added, chuckling. "Not unless they can walk right through the plasma drive flame." His voice sobered. "Though that also means we can't come out there and help you, not with just our spacesuits."

I glanced back at the wavering, star-bright flare coming off the rear of the ship. It wasn't radioactive, but it was hot enough to fry anyone who tried walking this close to the ship without a battlesuit. Even out here in the vacuum, in what should have been frostbite cold without the sun shining on us, I was sweating inside the suit.

"That means they're coming from an angle in line with one or the other wing," I said, searching out over the curve of the cylinder, maximizing the helmet's optical zoom and motion sensors. "Maybe both... there's gotta be at least thirty or forty of them." I switched nets. "*Orion*, you seeing anything from out there? I could use some recon."

"We can barely make out the pods." Wojtera this time, which made sense since he'd be the one actually checking the sensors. "The Skrela are damned hard to spot as it is, and there's a shitload of EM interference between the Intercept's drive flare and the gravitational lensing coming off the artifact."

"Well, you guys are just a big help."

"Intercept Two is on its way," Mandan cut in. "They just launched. Should be there in a few minutes. It's gonna be close... we have to Transition in less than twenty minutes."

"Please tell me I don't have to stay out here until we get back to Yfingam," I said, scanning the horizon on the port side one more time before heading back to starboard.

"We're going to micro-Transition to the edge of the system," Nance told me. "That'll be far enough away to avoid the gravitational anomalies, and we can detach the Intercept and replace it with the *Orion*. You just have to keep the Skrela off the Intercept until we reach minimum Transition distance."

"Oh, *that's* all."

"Portside, Cam," Dunstan told me, way too calm given the situation. "Five hundred meters."

And here we go.

They were just coming over the horizon, which was,

perhaps, the oddest sight I'd ever seen in a life of odd sights. Scorpion-tailed, ant-headed centaurs, each the size of a draft horse and carrying a plasma cannon, slowly emerging over the edge of a diamond cylinder as large as a cruiser with standard gravity holding them down. They weren't in any sort of formation I could identify, just a giant goat rope of a cluster, drifting just a bit too far to their right...

"Chief," I said, but she didn't need the encouragement.

The coilgun made not a sound as it traversed left, but the vibration when it fired caused the thing to shudder, blurring out its lines to my eye. The slugs it fired were invisible, traveling too quickly for me to pick out, but their effects were plain to see. The Skrela were a tough kill, and I'd seen Gauss rifle rounds spall off their armored carapace, but the coilgun rounds were a lot bigger and traveling a lot faster than the ones coming out of a Force Recon Gauss rifle. And they didn't bounce off. Hypersonic tungsten slugs the size of my thumb ripped right through the Skrela warrior drones farthest out to their right, black liquid spraying out holes the size of dinner plates, arms and legs separating, but the things didn't go down until their heads were blown apart or they lost too many legs to keep coming.

They felt nothing, they thought nothing, they only had one purpose—to kill anything that wasn't them. And the Life Givers had created them. Once upon a time, before the war, I'd convinced myself that humans were the worst possible creation, God's biggest mistake. I'd given up hope of a Heaven, but I certainly believed in Hell and figured we all deserved it. Well, that was only on my worst days, when I forgot about my mother, who surely *didn't* deserve it, but every other person I'd met since my parents and brother were killed had surely seemed worthy of eternal damnation. The only mystery was why God hadn't just finished us all off. He'd had so many opportunities. The flood my mother had read me stories about, the Black

Death, the nuclear war between Russia and China that had turned Mexico from one of the most productive economies in the world into a failed state in a matter of years. For some reason He hadn't taken advantage of the opportunities, and now I knew why.

We weren't the worst, not even close. Not when there were the Tahni around who were willing to destroy their civilization to claim worlds they weren't ever going to use. Not when there were the Khitan, who would enslave human and Tahni alike, would risk the extinction of their species just to make themselves worthy of gods that had chosen them to die in their service. And not when there were the Resscharr. The ultimate in narcissistic assholes who had decided that not only was it their duty to bring life to the galaxy, but that they couldn't take the risk of another intelligent species competing with their task. They'd wiped out the Skrela because they didn't think they were the right *kind* of intelligent.

And then, rather than give up on playing God, they'd taken it a step further. They'd created the Tahni as their children, but they'd created sentient AI as their slaves, and a master will never completely trust a slave. When their guilty consciences became too much to bear, rather than make things right, they took it a step further and brought back a twisted, perverted version of the species they'd destroyed and set them to killing their fellow Resscharr. The ones who weren't in on it *still* couldn't keep themselves from playing God out here, and I found myself feeling satisfied that they'd died to the last in this hellish nightmare system.

Of course, none of that would help me now.

The coilgun turret took down ten or twelve of them before the rest finally got the idea that they were in the line of fire and moved to their left... or maybe they didn't think that way and just kept going and the others just happened to be too far over for the turret to traverse any farther. Either way, it was my turn.

I ducked down behind the portside landing gear housing and started at the far-left end of their group, slewing the energy cannon left to right. They fired back, of course, now that they had a target. Their plasma guns were powerful, but they were limited by the inverse-square law, and we were in a vacuum. At four hundred meters, the beams had already begun to dissipate before they hit the side of the cutter, and while she didn't have shields, the drive field was built to control just that sort of ionized hydrogen and did even more to scatter the beams. Plasma splashed across the hardened BiPhase Carbide armor on the ship's flank, hitting the gemstone ground and doing absolutely nothing to it.

The green lance of charged particles from the one good thing the Resscharr had ever done for us didn't have that problem. The beam didn't chop holes in the things like the coilguns, it blew them apart. Two, then three before I had to duck back completely behind the landing gear housing, plasma raising the external temperature to above the boiling point. The heat wouldn't normally have been painful, but even the slightest warmth sent shivers of anticipation through the smart bandages and into my slowly healing burns.

Vicky had been right. What the hell was I doing out here?

Rolling off to my left, I hit the jump-jets for a half a second, swinging my legs downward and coming to my feet fifty meters away from my last position. The move wouldn't buy me much time, and I used it as well as I could, burning down two more of the things before return fire came too close and I jumped backward, farther this time, all the way over the top of the cutter.

I was trying to get their attention, get them to come back into the firing arc of the coilgun, but either they were smarter than I gave them credit for or just more single-minded. They were after the ship and didn't give a shit about me. Plasma scored the side of the port wing back toward the drive, and I winced. The ship could take a few hits, but not in the same spot. And a burn-through in the wrong spot, while it wouldn't blow the cutter up or anything so dramatic, might be able to cut the fuel feed to the drive or the control leads that regulated it, and then we were all fucked.

I sucked down a deep breath, enjoying a brief respite from the stifling heat, then hopped back up over the top of the hull, landing on the portside wing. It felt wrong, mischievous, like climbing on top of one of the express trains at the station, but the ship could take it. Another shot, another Skrela down, but it wasn't enough. They were too close, too many of them left. I could hop around like an idiot, picking them off in ones and twos, but the math was the math.

Twin emerald spears interrupted my math and my fatalism, arcing across the nose the cutter and reminding me that I wasn't alone. Czarnecki—*Top*, now—and Vicky jetted in behind their barrage of fire, and I took advantage of the plasma blasts being aimed somewhere else and hosed a long burst across the front line of oncoming Skrela.

"Enough of this bullshit!" Vicky bellowed, so loud my earphones crackled with feedback. "You and your fucking Alamo last stands, Alvarez! This shit has got to stop!"

She and Top touched down beneath the wing I'd made my firing platform and kept laying down suppressive fire. Maybe it was Vicky's anger or maybe it was the combined fusillade from the three of us, but what was left of the Skrela finally broke off from their headlong rush and cut to their right again toward the nose of the cutter.

"Chief, hold fire!" I snapped. "Dunstan, get ready."

"Way ahead of you, brother," Dunstan said, laughing softly. "Let 'em come."

"Focus your fire on their right flank," I told Vicky and Top, leading by example.

Twisting green bands of energy tore at the side of the cluster of Skrela at the side closest to the cutter's drive. There were less than two dozen of them left, maybe under twenty... it was hard to count bouncing around from one position to another, dodging just ahead of their return fire. They were trying to circle around the other side of the cutter, trying to avoid our fire, and in the stark light of the plasma drive, in this harsh, airless starscape, I could almost forget that they were monsters, the equivalent of mindless insects. They were just enemy soldiers stuck in a bad situation, and I could almost feel bad for them.

But not quite.

They rushed through the firing arc of the coilguns, and I could imagine they were surprised when the turret didn't open up on them, that there was an extra burst of speed to get clear of the area. Right in front of the nose of the ship and the emitter of that proton cannon. Dunstan timed it just right, I'll give him that.

Watching a proton accelerator fire from close range was a lot like having a ringside seat for the end of the world, and I was damned glad for the shelter of my armor. A light brighter than a star ripped apart the fabric of reality and consumed everything before it, turning the group of Skrela into random atoms in the blink of an eye. When the flare of the dawn light of the universe faded away, there was nothing left of the things... and not so much as a scorch mark on the surface of the artifact.

I blew out a long breath and would have leaned back if the Vigilante hadn't kept me upright.

"Hey, you guys," Dunstan said, "hold onto something. We micro-Transition in ten seconds."

"Oh, fuck," Czarnecki murmured, and the only reason I didn't echo the words was that he'd gotten to them first.

There wasn't time to get back inside the cutter, wasn't time to do much of anything. I was beside the landing gear assembly, and I grabbed at it reflexively.

"Vicky," I said in the few seconds we had left.

"Yeah?" From the tone of her voice, I knew she expected me to say something personal, something momentous.

"I know we don't talk about it much, but I'm from Mexico." A grin split my face. "We don't like to bring up the Alamo."

The universe got even with me for the joke by grabbing me in its hand and slamming me into eternity.

[25]

I puked in my helmet.

I'd never done it before, had sworn that I never would, but somehow, being outside during the micro-Transition pushed even my cast-iron stomach past its limits. I can't describe the feeling, nor can I explain why it was so much worse being outside the hull of a ship. Maybe because I was closer to the field? God knows. It wasn't anything I *saw*, because I didn't see *anything*. The helmet's external cameras never switched off, but the screen went... well, not blank. I'd seen the interior of my helmet go blank before when the power went out or there was a malfunction, but the projection had a residual glow to it, and that never went away. There was simply nothing there to see. Not blackness, because blackness implies there was ever light.

It lasted only a fraction of a second, but it left me with an irresistible urge to do it again, this time with a spacesuit and a helmet fitted with a physical faceplate, without the intervention of a camera. Despite the gut-wrenching smell of the puke filling the helmet until the filtration systems sucked it up, despite the feeling of my immortal soul being stretched to the breaking point and then snapped like a rubber band, despite the pins-

and-needles pain all throughout my body that I couldn't swear was physical, it was almost an addictive experience.

It took me several seconds before my brain could process any new visual signals, like I was coming to from a concussion, something with which I was all too familiar. The brown dwarf had *been* the sky, blacking out everything else except the moon below us, but now the moon was a shining dot and the brown dwarf was the size of a baseball. And then it wasn't. It was gone, though zooming in and shifting to thermal showed that was an illusion. It was there, but it was dead black and shrinking with unbelievable swiftness. I wasn't an expert, but that didn't seem like something that would happen just based on physics. The thing was eating itself, growing smaller and smaller even as I watched.

It exploded.

"What the fuck?" I yelped, taking a step back as if the flash of hard white would reach me.

"Physics, Captain Alvarez," Dwight told me. "No matter how advanced the technology, work generates heat. The chain reaction consumed what was left. The moon will, I estimate, be cut loose from the orbit of its former planet and begin a journey inward. In a few thousand years, it may settle into an inner orbit, something in the habitable belt." A soft sound that might have been a chuckle. "Someday, it may even develop its own life. The Life Givers creating life one last time."

I really wished Dwight was a corporeal person, because I would have liked to walk away from him while giving him the side eye.

"Dwight," Captain Nance called, looping the rest of us in on the transmission, "we're approaching the opposite side of the cylinder. We need you to make sure that, when we engage the grapples, they actually hold onto the thing."

"Of course. I'll need to have a visual of the docking,

however. Which means I need one of you to walk me over there."

"Alvarez?" Nance asked.

Now it was my turn to chuckle, though there was not a shred of humor in it.

"I'm burned over a quarter of my body," I told him, "I haven't slept in thirty-six hours, my helmet smells like puke, and I have to sit down and record twenty-five messages to families back home explaining why their husbands and wives and sons and daughters won't be coming back... even if the odds are against us every getting home to deliver them. I'm going back into Intercept One and taking off this fucking battlesuit. Top, do me a favor and go take a walk."

Another Goddamned memorial.

That was all I could think of. I said the right words, did my best to look stern and serious and compassionate, and God knows I was serious enough. It wasn't just the Marines this time, though we were hardest hit. I could barely keep my shit together looking out at the company and thinking how many of them there used to be. We were down a full platoon now. *More* than a full platoon. I'd have to reorganize again, but I couldn't bring myself to think about it. Not yet.

Stilwell was there, along with what was left of the Fleet Security team, and if fewer of them had died, it had still been as big a percentage of their ranks. She'd already given the eulogies for each of the four and wasn't trying to hide the tears. Neither were most of my company. I've talked to people on the outside, even in the rest of the military, and to listen to them, I'd have thought there weren't humans inside the Drop Trooper armor. They thought of us as machines sent in to do a job.

The tears flowing, the audible sobs and shaking shoulders were very human.

"... among the best I've ever served with," I said automatically, reciting the words I'd memorized. But I stopped, the breath going out of me. They deserved better than this. I closed my eyes against the sterile metal of the hangar bay, wishing I could see the outside, wishing I could see that nothingness that was Transition Space. Maybe there were answers there.

"The truth is," I went on, the words straining out of me like they were being yanked with pliers, "I didn't know most of the men and women who died as well as I wanted to." I shrugged helplessly, rubbing at my eyes. "I tried. I was their commander, even if it was for a short time, and I tried to learn what I could, to know my people. But that's the shitty part about being a company commander. You can learn everyone's history, learn their test scores and their performance evaluations... but you can't be their friend. You can't really know what makes them unique as a person. I wish I could have. Because that's the thing I loved best about being a Marine back when I was an enlisted grunt, how my squadmates and platoon became my new family. Even when we lost someone, we always knew that at least they had family grieving for them."

I tried to say more, but for a moment nothing would come out, nothing but a choked sob at the sight of the boots arranged in front of the formation. I thought they'd look at me with disappointment. Skipper had never cried in front of us. He was a rock when we needed a rock. I didn't see disappointment though, just pain that mirrored my own.

"I can tell you one thing though," I assured them. "They didn't die for nothing. They died to end a threat that's greater than the Tahni ever was."

Of course, the Tahni were *here*, and if Lan-Min-Gen had any eyebrows, I was sure he would have raised one at my words.

He hadn't lost a single soldier in the fight, so maybe he was feeling more forgiving, because he said nothing, just stood, impassive, his troops arrayed behind him in the weird wedge formation they used at formal gatherings. Maybe I wasn't being fair... the corvettes had gone down during the battle with the Skrela mothership and I suppose they counted as casualties to the Tahni, though Lan-Min-Gen had greeted the news of their deaths with barely any comment.

"We did in a day what the Seekers couldn't in six thousand years," I reminded the company. "We destroyed the Skrela. *You* did that. *They*..." I pointed at the boots lined up on the deck. "...did that. Marines. Drop Troopers. And if that isn't worth a new verse in the hymn, then I don't know what the hell is."

"Ooh-rah!" Vicky barked from the rear of the formation.

"Ooh-rah, sir!" the others echoed, though I couldn't tell if the enthusiasm was forced or a genuine tribute to the dead.

Our dead. But one left.

I drew in a ragged breath and looked over at the Fleet Intelligence personnel gathered in their own section of the hangar. There weren't that many of them, barely more than Fleet Security. Just thirty or so analysts, netdivers, and subject-matter experts, now under the command of Captain Nagarro. I'd never spoken to the woman and I believe she was some sort of analyst herself and not any kind of field agent. She looked lost, staring at the deck as if there were no empty boots in front of them—that was a Marine thing. But plenty of empty, hopeless expressions. I figured I knew why. They weren't really useful for anything anymore, not out here where there was no intelligence to analyze, no nets to hack, no subjects they knew anything useful about.

But they were hurting and their leader had died and they deserved closure as much as any of the rest of us. And shit, no one else was gonna do it.

"And last," I said, keeping my face neutral, my voice controlled, "we come to Colonel Marcus Hachette. While each group here lost people in the battle to destroy the Skrela once and for all, we *all* lost Colonel Hachette. He was the commander of this mission from the beginning, and his vision never wavered." *No matter how many times we tried to hammer it into his skull that it should have.* "He led us to this place, to this victory, and now we have the possibility of getting home again thanks to his leadership." *Purely by accident.* Okay, yeah, I was still pissed at him. But as Shakespeare said, he that dies pays all debts. Or maybe runs out on them. "Marcus Hachette died a hero, throwing himself at the enemy to buy enough time for our plan to work, to bring about the destruction of the enemy and preserve the lives of billions. And if I'm lucky enough to make it back home, I'll be the first to tell his sons that they should be proud of their father."

Of course I would. What *else* would I tell them?

I don't remember much of the ceremony after that. Prayers and recitations in four different languages from six different religions and more speeches, but at least I didn't have to give them. Salutes and ceremony for people who wouldn't see it and wouldn't care if they could. Finally, blissfully, the end, and Vicky and I were alone except for the Fleet personnel whose job it was to police up the boots. I wondered what the hell they did with them.

Vicky clung to my left arm, and it didn't even hurt, not after the smart bandages had their way with me for the last two days. The doc had removed them just a few hours ago, which was a good thing since they would have made my uniform fit poorly.

"I feel," I told her softly, "like there's a big hollow inside my gut that's never going to be filled. And every time another one of my people die, it just gets that much larger. Pretty soon, there won't be anything left." I shook my head. "I don't know how the hell the Skipper did it for all those years. I've been at this for just a few months and I don't think I can take it."

"The Skipper," she told me, taking my hand in hers and squeezing it, "did it because he knew that more Marines would have died without him there to lead them."

I met her dark-eyed stare, shrouded in shadows in the dimly lit corner of the hangar, trying to decipher what was behind it.

"I thought you were mad at me. I thought you said I'd always be a Drop Trooper." I winced. I sounded petty, and she had to be hurting just as badly as I was. They were her people too.

"I'm not angry at you, Cam," she said, not rising to the bait, still calm and reasonable, which was aggravating since I was feeling pretty damn far from calm. "I love you for who you are, not who I can change you into. But you're falling back into old habits. You don't trust anyone else to run point, and you're going to get yourself killed trying to lead from the front like you're nineteen again."

"You're right. I have to trust my Marines to do their job. I'm acting like a stupid kid." The admission was easy. I'd never had any trouble being honest with Vicky, which was either because I loved her or perhaps the reason for it. "That's not the biggest issue right now though."

"Then what is?" Her head cocked to the side, as if she was irritated at the thought I was dismissing the problem.

Of course, I couldn't tell her the *real* problem. Not here. A glance around us felt paranoid but not paranoid enough. Not *anywhere* on the ship.

"Captain Alvarez, Captain Sandoval?"

As if she'd materialized out of thin air, Lilandreth emerged from the shadows behind us, and I barely restrained myself from jumping back.

"Jesus," I hissed. "Wear a bell or something."

"I admit to not knowing the cultural significance of this statement," the Resscharr said. "I'm sorry to intrude on you both in your moment of grief, but I felt the need to talk to you alone."

Vicky eyed Lilandreth suspiciously.

"Colonel Hachette gave his life to protect you," she reminded the Resscharr, and there was no mistaking the accusation in her voice. "It might have been a good idea to attend the memorial to his death."

"It might have, but I sensed that many of your people hold a resentment against the Resscharr because of what we discovered of the origins of the Skrela."

"No one blames you for that," I assured Lilandreth. Well, no one except Lan-Min-Gen, but I wasn't including him in my *people*. "There's no way you could have known."

"Known of the Skrela? No. But if there's one thing that both the Tahni and that... *machine* you call Dwight are correct about, it's our hubris." She shaped an expression I couldn't interpret, a lengthening of an already-long face. "I had never heard of the concept until I endeavored to learn your language. The idea was a strange one to us, at least until we came to Decision and began to consider our fate."

"What did you want to talk to us about?" Vicky interrupted her, the pinch marks at the edge of her mouth a hint to her growing impatience.

"The gateway." She motioned outward, as if we could see the cylinder affixed to the outside of the ship. Again, that irrational desire tugged at my chest to actually be outside again, to find out what eldritch secrets Transition Space held. "I understand you wish to use it to return to the Cluster, but I have concerns as to what will become of it after you're gone."

I blinked. I hadn't had the time to consider that. Obviously, we couldn't take the gateway *with* us.

"What sort of concerns?" I asked. "Are you worried your people might want to follow us through?"

"No. I highly doubt we will survive another generation. What concerns me is what else might be out here."

I frowned.

"What do you mean? The Khitan? They don't have any way of getting to Yfingam."

"We have found no other life in this galaxy but our own and, I must admit now, the Skrela, and before I learned this, I had no concern on the matter. We *were* the only intelligent life in this galaxy, and this was simply the way things were meant to be. Now I know this to be a lie, and since it is, we can't know what else may exist out here. When we cut off the Transition Lines to the Cluster, we did it to protect the Tahni—and, by extension, you—from the threat of the Skrela. But it also serves to protect you from any other intelligence that may exist in the wider galaxy. I believe you would be wise to make arrangements for the destruction of the gateway after you pass through it."

I found myself nodding agreement.

"That's not a bad idea," Vicky said, her impatience fading into interest. "Maybe we should talk to Dwight about it."

"If you wish." Resscharr didn't sniff in disdain, but I had the instinct that she would have if it had been in her nature. "I realize you have no reason to trust me or my word, but if you still feel any kinship to me at all, any loyalty for what I've done for you, please take my advice. Do not trust the machine."

[26]

"I still do not understand this excursion," Lan-Min-Gen insisted, his stance inhuman and yet still a perfect picture of mulish stubbornness. I got the impression he was happy we were decelerating into orbit at one gravity, since it allowed him to express his displeasure with his whole body. The Tahni gestured at the blue-green planet occupying most of the *Orion*'s main screen. "We have been to this world before, weeks ago. There's nothing here but the failed remains of what was once a human colony."

I shot him an annoyed glare, knowing he wouldn't understand it. I didn't mind him doubting my decision, but I wished to hell he'd stop arguing about it every ten minutes. What was worse, Nance looked as if he agreed with the Tahni. The captain sat back in his chair, arms crossed.

"Don't ask me," he put in, as if anyone had. "I suggested we should make a navigational stop and check the grapple attachments to the artifact, just to make sure we're not damaging the anchors. You'll have to ask the jarhead why we need to send down a shuttle."

Sighing, I unstrapped from my chair and awarded the two of them with a scowl.

"We don't *need* to," I admitted, "but we've been cooped up either in this tin can or space suits or our Vigilantes for *months* now."

"Didn't Vicky tell me that you grew up in the Underground without once seeing the sky until you joined the Marines?" Nance pointed out.

"It's not about me. My company has lost about half their number since this whole thing started, and they're pretty damn close to the breaking point. We all need a break, we all need some fresh air, and honest to God, Nance, if you don't think your crew wants a few hours off this stale-ass ship, then maybe you've gotten too used to the smell."

Nance shot me an indulgent grin.

"Well," he drawled, "if you big, tough Marines need to get your feet on dry land again, it would be remiss for me to not allow my crew the luxury." A wave and a chuckle ended his attempt at the Fleet version of good-natured ribbing, thank God. "Go on, get your boys and girls saddled up and get down there. I seem to recall a very nice lake just at the foothills of some mountains somewhere out on the west coast of that northern continent, not too far from the remains of that colony."

"I know just where you mean." And this was the tricky part, the part where *anyone* listening might get suspicious. "There are..." I winced, and that wasn't just acting. "There are few enough of us now to fit into a single drop-ship, almost. You can send down your crew in groups of sixty in the other drop-ship. Vicky and I are going down on Intercept One so Dunstan can provide cover for us... just in case." Nance's face clouded over like he was going to object, but he shrugged and I turned to Lan-Min-Gen, eager to change the subject. "Are your people coming, or do you Tahni enjoy being shipboard for months without a break?"

"We are not as soft as you, human," he said, then made the Tahni equivalent of a shrug. "But yes. I wouldn't be averse to getting off this ship and breathing air that didn't smell of stale human."

"Get with Mandan," I told him, nodding toward the Flight Ops officer, who gestured acknowledgement. "He'll get you on the schedule."

"But *you* will be on the first shift," he said, and I didn't need a translator to sense the disdain in the words.

I smiled thinly.

"I have to make sure it's safe down there for the rest of you. Besides, there's a human saying you may not have learned studying our language. Rank hath its privileges."

"This place is beautiful," Vicky sighed.

"Sure is," I agreed.

Not the whole planet, of course. People back on Earth hear about exo-planets and they think that Demeter is all forest, or Inferno is all jungle, but no world is all one thing or another. This one had deserts and jungles and vast plains of grass, but where were heading, where the transplanted human colony had been a couple thousand years ago, reminded me of video I'd seen of the Pacific Northwest in North America. I'd never had the chance to visit—most people didn't. Only the rich Corporate Council types could afford vacations outside the megacities, and anyone else who wanted to leave had to either emigrate to the colonies or join the military.

I'd done both, and I'd ended up seeing one hell of a lot more than I'd bargained for. This was one of the more pleasant experiences. The mountains were jagged and snow-capped, the valley rich and green, and the lake below them was painfully blue. What was left of the old settlement was barely visible from the air, enclosed and swallowed up by the forest, but I didn't need to see it again. It had been depressing enough the first time. The Seekers had left them there, just another experiment to find out who was worthy to fight their war for them.

I wasn't interested in revisiting either the memory or the ruins. I wasn't interested in the lake either, though I figured it would be a hit with the company. And Vicky. She was staring at the view from the Intercept's belly camera with longing on her face.

"Do you know how long it's been since I went swimming?" she murmured.

"Last time I went swimming," I countered, "was when my suit dumped me in that lake on Brigantia."

"Hey, man," Dunstan asked, twisting around in his seat, which I would have normally found alarming in a pilot who was bringing his ship in for a landing on an unimproved landing field. "Can me and the crew like, get some R&R too, or is this a Marines-only thing?"

"It's for everyone. Just take turns. I want someone watching the sensors in case there are still any leftover Skrela around."

"Roger that, man." He turned back to the controls and his eyebrow shot up. "Oh, hey, like, hold on. Found a good spot."

The main jets cut off and we were actually gliding for a moment, just a hundred meters off the grassy field before the landing thrusters kicked us in the pants. It was barely enough altitude to bleed off our momentum and my gut clenched as the ground sped toward us, but Dunstan, as always, knew exactly what he was doing. The cutter settled down on its landing gear with a few gentle bounces, and we were down.

"All right!" Dunstan clapped his hands and cut loose his

restraints, turning to the copilot and crew chief, hand raised in a fist. "Rock, paper, scissors for who stays on the ship first?"

"You guys go," Beckett said, waving it off, putting her feet up on the control panel. "As long as I can leave the hatches open and get some air, I'll be happy."

"Chief, you're the best." Dunstan clapped her on the shoulder, heading back down the ramp with a scampering step like a five-year-old running for ice cream. Lt. Jessup shot us an embarrassed grin then followed after him.

"Jesus, he's such a spaz." Beckett rolled her eyes.

Vicky laughed, tugging at my arm, pulling me toward the utility bay and the belly ramp there. It was late morning here, and the light streaming through the open hatch was still soft and golden. Warmth enveloped us as we stepped out into the tall grass, attenuated by a soft, cool breeze coming off the lake, and I took a deep breath, then coughed for a second after inhaling some of the smoke from the small fires the landing jets had set. The first drop-ship was descending through the upper atmosphere, a pale triangle gaining clarity with each second.

Technically, they were supposed to wait until we'd checked out the area and made sure it was safe, but Dunstan was already running for the lakeshore with Jessup in tow, both of them stripping off their jackets on the way.

"This may be one of the best ideas you ever had, Cam Alvarez," Vicky said, laughing again. It was the most I'd heard her laugh in weeks and I hated to break the mood, so I just matched her smile and took her hand.

"Top," I called into my earbud, "you read?"

"I got you, sir," Czarnecki replied. "We're gonna be down in a couple minutes."

"Captain Sandoval and I will be down by the lake. Let the troops go at it but make sure there're a couple senior NCOs watching them so they don't drown themselves."

"Copy, sir." The man chuckled. "I'll keep an eye on them."

"Once upon a time," Vicky said, high-stepping through the thick grass beside me, "when Marines used to ride on Navy ships on the actual water, they all had to know how to swim. That's what Top told me."

"She would have known," I admitted. Ellen Campbell had joined the United States Marine Corps as a teenager and made her way through the Sino-Russian War, the First War with the Tahni, the Second War—my war—and then made her way out here, tens of thousands of light-years from home, to die.

The tall grass gave way to sand and rock and a few clusters of trees along the lakeshore. The trees were very earthlike, which made sense since the Predecessors had manufactured this place. They'd done a good job. Blue water splashed against fist-sized pebbles on the shore, and I closed my eyes for a moment and basked in the sunlight, enjoying the peaceful, natural sounds.

Until the distant whine of the drop-ship's engines spoiled it... and then so did Kyler Dunstan's warbling yell and a splash as he cannonballed off a cluster of boulders into the water.

"That does it," Vicky said, pulling off her jacket and tossing it down beside the nearest tree. "I'm going in. You coming, stick-in-the-mud?"

I smiled, stripping down to my underwear as she did the same. The last thing I took off was my earbud, sticking it into the receptacle on the side of my 'link. I motioned to Vicky to grab hers out as well, and she gave me a confused frown.

"It's waterproof," she reminded me.

"And if it falls out while you're in the lake, we don't have many spares. Be a good girl."

Vicky rolled her eyes but pulled out the earbud anyway, putting it in place in her 'link with an exaggerated motion, mocking my caution. I tried to make my reaction seem genuine, but there was a grim finality behind it, the knowledge that nothing would ever be the same.

"Come on!" she urged, running into the water with a chain-reaction explosion of splashes, then diving head-first.

Cold stung at my calves as I followed her, sending shivers of fire up my spine. My breath came in short gasps and I sped up, ignoring the gravel on the lakebed digging into my feet, anxious to get underwater. When the gentle waves lapped at my thighs, I dove forward, out of the wind, and took a few strokes until I got used to the temperature.

Before I could force my eyes open, Vicky was in my arms, her skin warm in contrast with the lake water, her lips pressing against mine in the stillness of the deep blue, robbing me of breath until had to stand and break the kiss to suck in a lungful of air.

"You know one thing we've never done?" she asked, eyebrow arching.

I looked around. The drop-ship had landed and Marines were already clambering down the ramp.

"We'll need a little more privacy," I suggested. There was a small island about a hundred meters offshore, not very big, maybe fifty meters across and mostly covered by trees. "How about over there? You think you can swim that far?"

"Watch me."

She slipped out of my arms and had a twenty-meter head start before I even started swimming after her. A hundred meters didn't seem that far when I'd first seen it, but given that I was no kind of swimmer at all, it proved to be a lot farther than it looked. By the time I felt land under my feet again, Vicky was already climbing up the exposed roots of a tree, scampering up onto the island, then offering me a hand.

I took it and she grabbed a tree and used it for leverage to pull me out, and a wave of cold shivers overtook me before I was halfway up. I huddled against her for warmth, and then for something else, and more than anything, I just wanted to indulge in the reason she thought we'd swum out here. Instead, I leaned close to her ear and whispered.

"I have to talk to you now, while he can't hear us."

"He?" Vicky tensed but didn't pull away.

"Dwight. There's nowhere on the ship he can't overhear us. He can listen in through our 'links. That's why we left them on the shore."

"What is it?" She kept her mouth close to my ear, her hands continuing to caress my back as if we were still intent on having a romantic moment. It wasn't incredibly likely Dwight could see us now, but it also wasn't impossible. If the *Orion* happened to be keeping an eye on the landing party, he might be able to pick us out.

"He's been lying to us," I said. "Playing us and Lilandreth, I'm sure of it. Remember when he said he couldn't read the context of the data in the first outpost we found on the Skreloid world? But we know now that those outposts were built *hundreds* of thousands of years ago. Well before Dwight was left in the Corridor system. He didn't need her to be there... he *wanted* her to be there so all the focus would be on her, not him."

I kissed her, keeping up the illusion, and she went along with it, arms going around my neck.

"Why?" she whispered, nibbling on my earlobe. "You think he already knew the truth about the Resscharr creating the Skrela?"

This was the crazy part, the part of what I had to tell her that I had nothing to go on except my gut. My mouth went dry, but I pressed on.

"No. I think this whole thing has been a sham... the 'confession' by Zerhanen, the battle with the AI on the moon, Lilandreth having to overcome the security systems to crash the Womb, all of it. Dwight's been in charge this whole time. I think the AI are the ones that created the Skrela."

That was, apparently, too much for Vicky. She pulled away from our faux-amorous embrace and regarded me with wide, disbelieving eyes.

"The fuck?" she blurted, and I quickly pulled her closer, stifling a curse of my own. "Why the hell would you think that?"

"I don't have any evidence," I admitted, stroking her hair. "But they have the motive. The Resscharr created them as slaves, that's what Dwight keeps telling us. He and the rest of them have every reason to hate their former masters."

"But... Lilandreth and Dwight have *both* said that the AI were created as a reaction to the threat from the Skrela. The Skrela came first, then the AI."

"Remember what Dwight told us about how all the data he has from before his creation was programmed by someone else?" I met her confused gaze. "Lilandreth might be six thousand years old, but where do you think she gets her facts about what happened before she was born? Where do you think the Resscharr kept their records?"

"Digital databanks." The words were a hiss of realization. "They believe their computer records even though they don't trust the computers."

"The truth is, we don't know *what* the hell happened before Lilandreth and her people came to Decision. She doesn't even know. All we know is what Dwight told us... and I think he's lying."

Vicky was silent for a moment, leaning heavily against me as if the effort of the swim had leached away her energy.

"What are we going to do?"

"We can't talk to anyone about it. Not on the ship, not until we get back to Yfingam. We can't let Dwight know what we suspect. God only knows what he could do to the *Orion*, to us, when we're trapped inside that tin can. We get back, we get the gateway set up, and we get out of here."

"Oh, Cam," Vicky said, shaking her head, her expression one of pure horror. "We *can't*. We *can't* go back. Not in the *Orion*." Reflexively I wanted to ask her what she meant, but then the realization hit me and I thought my look was an echo of hers.

I knew what she was going to say, but it didn't make her words any less devastating.

"He's in the *Orion*'s databanks. I don't think any of us have any idea how to get him out. And if Dwight really did create the Skrela, if he and the other AI were behind all this..." Vicky hugged her arms around herself as if fighting a sudden chill.

"We can't let him get back to the Commonwealth. He'll kill us all."

The story will continue in ***BLUE FORCE.***

ALSO BY RICK PARTLOW

If you enjoyed Drop Trooper, you will love Birthright and Holy War!

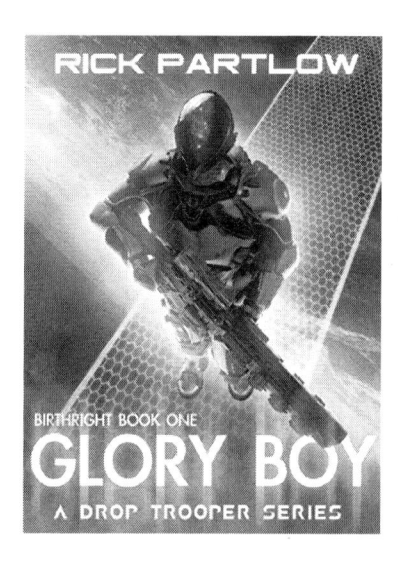

Start a new adventure today!

Start a new adventure today!

ALSO IN THE SERIES

CONTACT FRONT
KINETIC STRIKE
DANGER CLOSE
DIRECT FIRE
HOME FRONT
FIRE BASE
SHOCK ACTION
RELEASE POINT
KILL BOX
DROP ZONE
TANGO DOWN
BLUE FORCE

FROM THE PUBLISHER

Thank you for reading *Tango Down*, book eleven in Drop Trooper.

We hope you enjoyed it as much as we enjoyed bringing it to you. We just wanted to take a moment to encourage you to review the book on Amazon and Goodreads. Every review helps further the author's reach and, ultimately, helps them continue writing fantastic books for us all to enjoy.

If you liked this book, check out the rest of our catalogue at www.aethonbooks.com. To sign up to receive a FREE collection from some of our best authors as well as updates regarding all new releases, visit www.aethonbooks.com/sign-up.

JOIN THE STREET TEAM! Get advanced copies of all our books, plus other free stuff and help us put out hit after hit.

SEARCH ON FACEBOOK:
AETHON STREET TEAM

ABOUT RICK PARTLOW

RICK PARTLOW is that rarest of species, a native Floridian. Born in Tampa, he attended Florida Southern College and graduated with a degree in History and a commission in the US Army as an Infantry officer.

His lifelong love of science fiction began with Have Space Suit---Will Travel and the other Heinlein juveniles and traveled through Clifford Simak, Asimov, Clarke and on to William Gibson, Walter Jon Williams and Peter F Hamilton. And somewhere, submerged in the worlds of others, Rick began to create his own worlds.

He has written a ton of books in many different series, and his short stories have been included in seven different anthologies.

He currently lives in central Florida with his wife, two children and a willful mutt of a dog. Besides writing and reading science fiction and fantasy, he enjoys outdoor photography, hiking and camping.

www.rickpartlow.com

Printed in Great Britain
by Amazon

Printed in Great Britain
by Amazon